A NEW TRADITION?

She stood on the opposite side of the wooden tub, her gaze alighting on his chest, then tracing the rivulet of black hair that flowed down his flat belly.

"Come," he said, staring at her through half-lidded eyes.

"Ridiculous," she breathed. "You are but a stranger to me."

Wading to the other side, he reached for her. As her arms unfolded, he took her hand and pulled her toward him so that she was leaning over the edge of the tub. "Join me."

"No." She reared back.

He found her other hand, grasped her fingers and pulled her toward him again. She rocked back on her heels, but hers was a slight figure compared to his, and he easily held her captive.

"Stevyn, no! I—I am fully clothed!"

"Then disrobe," he said, grinning. "Please. Indulge me. I am a guest in your castle. Is it not the local custom for the lady of the house to assist her guest in bathing?"

"Aye, but the custom does not include hopping into the tub naked with the guest."

"Then we shall begin a new tradition."

SUPER ROMANCE

Other *Leisure* books by Cindy Harris:
THE MAIDEN BRIDE

A Man of Steel

Cindy Harris

LEISURE BOOKS NEW YORK CITY

This book is for Swank

A LEISURE BOOK®

December 2000

Published by

Dorchester Publishing Co., Inc.
276 Fifth Avenue
New York, NY 10001

Cover Art by John Ennis.
www.ennisart.com

ISBN 0-8439-4807-8

Printed in the United States of America.

Visit us on the web at www.dorchesterpub.com.

A Man of Steel

Chapter One

Wickinghamshire, northern England, 1346

Life as she knew it was about to end.

Camilla Rosedown lifted her face to the cool autumn breeze, inhaling the briny scent of the coastal waters just a mile or so to the east. Everywhere she looked, the beauty of the Northumbrian landscape pressed in on her. But, for once, she took no comfort in the familiarity of her surroundings or the security of her position. Her future husband was on his way to Wickinghamshire, and the freedom she'd enjoyed as chatelaine of the sheriff's castle would soon be replaced by the drudgery of married life, the conjugal boredom of the bedroom and the life-jeopardizing uncertainties of childbirth.

That's what Camilla had to look forward to . . . if she was lucky.

Whirling slowly, she surveyed the scenery that

was her world. To the west, the Cheviot hillside scalloped the clouds, then spilled out toward the Scottish border in a lap of black peat and gorse. Behind her were rolling meadows dotted with fluffy sheep and that ferocious breed of white cattle distinct to Northumbria. And to the north, floating in a haze of vapor, was Wickingham Castle, its lime-washed stone towers and parapets as stark against the sky as a Celtic cross planted on a lonely grave.

She considered her options. She could run away.

But, she had already experienced poverty and homelessness once in her life, and she did not relish the thought of it again.

She could marry Risby, the sheriff's son, whom she'd never laid eyes on, and pretend she was happy.

Or . . .

Or, nothing. Those were her options.

She waded through clumps of gorse and knee-high stands of scrubby yellow grass, a sense of unease overtaking her.

Which was hardly surprising, given that this was the very location where she'd been caught poaching by Godric, sheriff of Wickinghamshire, some five years earlier. Even the rustle of the heather, the happy panting of her faithful dog Bramble, and the cry of her prized falcon Atalanta, which always filled her with happiness, failed to mitigate her nervousness.

Risby would soon be home, and she would have to marry him even if he smelled like a billy goat and had a wart on his nose longer than his middle finger.

Clad in a roughly woven tunic and leather boots, her long blond hair tucked beneath a woolen cap, Camilla drew to a halt. Thoughts of Risby flew from her mind. Bramble had frozen before a low ledge of tangled brush. His pointed tail quivered, his nose twitched and his right paw folded up beneath his chest.

Silence thickened the tension. Camilla's gaze swept heavenward, and her heart leapt as Atalanta began her descent. A rustle of wings and feathers sounded in the thatch. Then, the inevitable explosion of plump, plumed game birds blackened the sky like splattered ink. Atalanta snagged her prey. Bramble erupted in a fit of barks and yelps.

Camilla gave a sharp, two-fingered whistle, drawing her falcon's attention. "Ho!" she cried as Atalanta gracefully arced, banked, then glided on the breeze toward Camilla's upraised arm.

Deftly, Camilla took the lifeless grouse from her falcon's beak and slipped it into the leather bag slung low around her hips. Atalanta was a young hunter, barely three months old and weighing little more than a loaf of hard bread. But, the bird's instincts were keen, and she was fast showing the potential to be one of Camilla's finest hunters. Already, Atalanta had learned to fly free without a *creance,* or leather leash, returning to Camilla's fist immediately after a kill.

"That's enough for one day, Atalanta. Bramble looks as if he could use a rest, too." Talking to her birds and animals was as natural to Camilla as talking to humans. Perhaps more so. She was quite certain Bramble understood every word she said. And that was more than she could say for Godric, her guardian and future father-in-law.

"Come on, Bramble, time to go home." She

smiled wistfully as the hound turned and loped back toward her.

A horse's hooves sounded on the old Roman road bordering the open field. Perhaps it was one of Godric's men, scouring the Crown's properties for poachers. Camilla's pulse quickened a bit at the thought, even though she'd been awarded special rights to hunt these grounds. Now that she was under the protection of the sheriff himself, affianced to his son Risby, no less, she shared in the sheriff's privilege of hunting these fields.

Still, the memory of how she'd come to Godric's attention in the first place haunted her, reminding her of his power over her and her obligation to him. She might be honorary chatelaine of Wickingham Castle, but if she didn't marry his son Risby, her privileges would be forfeit. And life as she knew it would cease to exist.

Her anxiety transferred immediately to the falcon on her fist. Atalanta made a skittish hop, and Camilla caught the leather jesses tied around her ankle just before the bird flew away.

The rider rounded a sharp bend in the road, coming into view with all the subtlety of an invading army. A huge warhorse materialized, followed by a big shaggy wolfhound. And astride the horse was a stranger, a tall and broad-shouldered man, very definitely not a native of Wickinghamshire, for Camilla would have remembered if she'd ever seen this man before.

He was also very definitely not Risby, Godric's son, for he would have with him a full retinue of liege men, soldiers, pages and retainers. With a tiny pang of guilt, Camilla breathed a sigh of relief. She simply wasn't ready to face her soon-to-be husband. She wasn't ready to look her pitiful future straight in the eyes and say, "I do."

He lifted his hand in greeting. Not a woman who warmed quickly to strangers, especially men, Camilla nodded brusquely. Approximately fifty feet from the rider, she wasn't fearful of his superior size and obvious strength. Her short dagger was strapped to her belt, and Bramble would be ferocious if her safety was threatened.

Her dog's treasonous behavior, then, could not have been more shocking to her. Two more strides and Bramble would have been at Camilla's side. Instead, he suddenly jerked to his right and headed toward the road, toward the horse and rider. Toward the big shaggy wolfhound that was twice his size.

"Merde!" The rider's oath carried on the breeze. Drawing his mount to an abrupt halt, he slid from his saddle and made a grab for the thick leather collar cuffing the wolfhound's neck.

But, his actions were too little and too late. While the destrier rolled its eyes, snorting and pawing the ground, the wolfhound leapt into action, racing toward Bramble with such speed that it appeared the two dogs would collide.

"Bramble, stop! Come back!" Camilla watched in horror as her dog raced toward the wolfhound. If the two beasts set to fighting, Bramble would be torn to shreds. Thoughtlessly, she took off after him, mindless of the dangers of interfering in a dogfight—and mindless of the falcon perched on her fist.

What happened next would later be a blur in Camilla's memory. Events clashed so quickly. Atalanta lifted from her arm with a great flapping of wings. His jesses slipped through Camilla's fingers as she ran toward the dogs.

At the same time, the man whose unfettered animal had caused this ruckus plunged into the field. "Daisy, heel!" he yelled in a deep, booming voice. But, his dog ignored him and skid to a halt just as Bramble pounced on her.

The dogs, teeth bared, hair rippling with tension, whirled and ducked and nipped at each other's tails and haunches. Camilla approached warily, slowing her gait. Dagger drawn, she said venomously to the stranger, "If your dog harms a hair on my dog's head, I will slit its throat."

A much larger dagger, in fact, a gleaming short sword, slid with a rasp from the stranger's leather belt. "If that bag of fleas you call a dog so much as nips at Daisy's flesh, I will carve him to pieces."

Camilla drew in a quick breath. How dare this impudent stranger threaten Bramble! Her blood boiled with fear and anger . . . and something else she wasn't prepared to surrender to. Bramble was as dear to her as any human being, perhaps more so, and she would risk life and limb to see that he wasn't ripped to pieces by this overgrown brute of a man, or his beastly dog. The fact that he was a *handsome* brute only stirred her passions more violently, and boosted her defensive instincts.

A yelp from Bramble stirred her maternal instincts, as well. Blood squirted from the hound's ear and his tail tucked between his legs. Hunkered down, Bramble took a defensive, somewhat submissive position, while Daisy, hardly a name fit for such an aggressive hellhound, snarled and growled and shook her great shaggy head.

Against her better judgment, Camilla reached for Bramble's collar. The stranger yelled something that Camilla took as a warning, but, ignoring him, she grabbed Bramble's nape and started to drag him to safety.

As she did, the wolfhound leapt at her.

Acting on reflex, Camilla raised her dagger to ward off the attack. With Bramble struggling against her hold, she fended off the other dog's advance as best she could, managing only to nick her front paw before she landed on the ground with a thud.

"How dare you—" Now the stranger entered the fray, yanking his own dog back by the scruff of the neck. But, Daisy, bucking like a rabid beast, managed to escape her master's grasp. The man grabbed for her again, but before he had a secure hold, Daisy made another foray at Camilla.

This time, she was ready, dagger held tightly in her left hand, Bramble squirming against the hold she had on him with her right one. As Daisy sailed through the air, Camilla eyed the dog's great hairy chest and prepared to plunge her dagger in it.

But her weapon never found its mark. Instead, a great wall of human flesh and muscle flung itself at Camilla, slamming into her like a battering ram. Her breath was knocked from her lungs; the earth pummeled her like a rug beater. Pain shot through her bones like hot pokers as Camilla found herself on her back, a strange dizzying sensation overtaking her.

The last thing she remembered about that moment was the sight of Atalanta soaring above her and the odious stranger's face, his incongruously *handsome* face, staring down at her with an expression of mingled consternation and amusement. As her stomach roiled and everything went black, it occurred to Camilla that she hated this man whose dog had pounced on Bramble. *Hated* him.

Stevyn lunged, inserting his body between Daisy's and the mad young man who threatened to plunge a knife into the dog's chest. What sort of fool would dare pull a dagger on such a fine specimen as his Daisy? Diving between knife and dog, he managed to knock the wolfhound out of the air and to the ground, where she landed in a heap, dazed.

At the same time, he tackled the paperscull who would have killed his dog. The top of the knave's dagger scraped his knuckles, but Stevyn's superior strength and size stunned the boy. With surprising ease, he grabbed the lad's wrist and fell on top of him, startled at the slender framework of the boy's body beneath his own weight.

The knife fell from the boy's fingers into a thick patch of grass, while the falcon who'd been spooked by the fracas flew overhead, and the two dogs who'd nearly ripped each other's throats out now began a ritual of circling, growling and sniffing.

"Daisy, your timing is insufferable." Not one to confide in humans, Stevyn had long ago developed the habit of chatting with Daisy.

The dog, whose condition had manifested itself on the road a day or two earlier, ignored him. Stevyn shook his head. Up till now, Daisy's condition hadn't been a major cause for concern. Absent any creature upon which the dog could direct her wanton impulses, her female cycle was but a mild distraction. With a male dog sniffing at her heels, however, Daisy appeared in the full bloom of her season, and, as such, was totally oblivious to her master's commands. Painfully aware that he should have been more vigilant of his faithful companion as he neared Wickingham Castle, Stevyn felt a pang of guilt.

"I'd say it was *your* timing, sirrah, that was a bit importunate."

The boy's velvety voice sent a strange tingle up Stevyn's spine, distracting him from his ruminations about Daisy. "What did you say?" he asked, looking more closely at his captive.

"Well, aren't you going to release me?"

"In due course." Stevyn barely managed to shift his weight in time to avoid being gored in his private parts by the boy's knee. "Why, you insolent little—"

Something not quite anger, but sharper than annoyance, surged through Stevyn's veins. This puny ruffian would have killed Daisy, and now he dared to provoke Stevyn's anger by attempting to knee him in the groin! Spitefully, Stevyn suddenly pressed his weight harder atop the writhing little rascal.

The little rascal, however, was wily, and amazingly strong for his size. If Stevyn hadn't outweighed him so heavily, the lad might have wriggled and kicked his way to freedom.

With a mild oath, Stevyn grasped the struggling falconer's shoulders, pinning his absurdly thin bones to the ground.

"Get off me, I said!" He must have been all of thirteen years, because the lad's voice hadn't even deepened yet.

Stevyn lifted his head to get a closer look.

And the lad's chin was as smooth and hairless as polished marble.

Shifting to his side, Stevyn peered more closely. A strange, somewhat perverse thought came to his mind as he studied the boy.

His captive—obviously uncomfortable beneath Stevyn's penetrating stare—renewed his struggle.

"Whoa. . . . Just a minute, young man," Stevyn said, surprised by the liquid depth of his own voice. It was a tone he normally reserved for Daisy, usually when the dog jerked fitfully in her sleep. Rescued from the jaws of a steel lynx trap, the dog suffered from nightmares nearly as often as Stevyn did.

But, what sort of young man was this, Stevyn thought, boldly running his hand down the length of his prisoner's body. What sort of boy had jutting hips and long, thrashing legs . . . a suspiciously soft and mounded chest . . . and a perfume of soap and heather?

What sort of man, indeed. Stevyn's body suddenly reacted. Rearing back, his hands still cuffed around the *boy's* wrists, he studied the heart-shaped face, the cornflower-blue eyes, the delicately shaped lips.

"God's teeth!" A streak of shock jolted his senses. But, Stevyn didn't dare release her, not yet. In fact, the discovery that he had pinned a woman beneath his body created a strange sensation that flooded his chest and warmed his blood. It had been, well, several days, since he'd had a woman, and this one was surprisingly well shaped.

And strong.

"You're a . . . a woman!"

Her gaze rolled heavenward. Then, she gave a little snort of derision and said, "Your powers of observation are astounding. I suppose you didn't see me and my dog as you rounded the bend, either!"

"Too late, I'm afraid."

"Well, that saber-toothed monster of yours damn near killed Bramble!" Her hips bucked beneath his. "Not to mention what she might have done to me if you hadn't knocked us both to the ground. Now, get off me!"

"When I'm damned ready."

The fact she didn't spit at him spoke volumes for her breeding. Instead, she fought valiantly against the hold he had on her. But, Stevyn weighed nearly twice what she did and there was no way she could escape him.

The soft curves of her body, pressed against his, had sparked his arousal. Now her flashing eyes and her defiant expression intensified his interest. This was no squeamish girl, no fearful greenie. This was a spirited woman who wasn't afraid to pique the anger of a man who could have killed her with one blow to her face, a man who could take her as easily as he could take a breath, a stranger whose motives and morals were total unknowns.

"If you don't release me, you'll be sorry," she said in a low hiss. "You don't know who I am."

"Threats mean nothing to me." Even to him, his voice sounded strange, menacingly quiet, heavy with desire.

Suddenly, she stilled beneath him. Her gaze, wary and amazingly blue, bore into him.

"You'd better get off me before Bramble chews your lousy mutt to ribbons."

Stevyn glanced at the dogs, circling and sniffing. "I seriously doubt that will happen. Daisy's a saucy wench, but I've only seen her in this condition once, and I don't recall that anyone got hurt."

Her head turned, then, and when she realized what the dogs were doing, her cheeks darkened. Looking back at Stevyn, she said, "Your mutt's too big for Bramble. They'll never mate."

"Opposites attract, gel. Haven't you ever heard that?" Releasing his grip on one of her shoulders, Stevyn pulled the woolen cap off her head.

Blond hair tumbled to the girl's shoulders like a flaxen waterfall.

While a freed arm reached out, and a balled fist caught him on his jaw.

"Christ on a raft!" Stevyn easily caught her wrist and pinned it to the earth again. "Are you crazy, woman? Do you normally go around picking fights with men twice your size?"

"Only those who throw themselves on top of me," she replied. "What do you intend to do to me? Rape me? Well, if that is your goal, then be warned that Bramble will tear anyone from limb to limb who dares raise his voice to me. Much less harms a hair on my head! Bramble, come boy! Come here!"

Stevyn couldn't resist a chuckle. "Dear girl, in the state he is in at the moment, Bramble wouldn't raise his leg for you if you were on fire. I would think a woman who was so experienced with animals would understand that. I'm afraid you are completely at my mercy."

Her eyes widened slightly when Stevyn lowered his head and nuzzled her neck.

"Poor Bramble. . . . I believe I know quite how he feels," Stevyn whispered, moving on top of the woman, pressing his arousal into her soft belly. He should have felt guilty about what he was doing, he supposed, but he had so much more to feel guilty about. And, the woman beneath him aroused him so . . . and, of course, it had been so long . . . *three days, at least*.

Her body was totally motionless. But, when she spoke, her words were breathy and rushed. "You don't want to do this. . . . I promise you you'll regret it. . . . You don't know who I am—" Stevyn sensed the quickening of her heart, her fear, and her excitement.

"If I repulse you, say so, and I will release you." But, Stevyn saw the flicker of fire in her eyes.

"You do not repulse me, sir. But, I am engage—"

He had his answer. Covering her mouth with his, Stevyn kissed her, molding her slightly parted lips to his, staring down into her glistening eyes.

He pulled her hands above her head, truly capturing her beneath him. She squirmed and tried to move her head to the side, but her movements served only to expose her long slender neck. When Stevyn kissed her there, she closed her eyes and shivered.

"You like it," he murmured. "Don't fight me."

"Don't flatter yourself," she returned groggily. "I don't like it so much. I just want to know what it feels like to be kissed by a stranger."

But, her body betrayed her. She did like it, *very much*. It wasn't difficult to wedge himself between her legs, and in her woven britches, she was free to draw her knees up around his hips. He kissed her neck and her face and her lips, tasting her fragrant skin, licking her soft, warm flesh, moving atop her with an urgency he couldn't suppress.

His need for her seemed suddenly as overwhelming as Daisy's urge to mate. She was a stranger, some faint voice in the back of his head called out. He knew nothing of her, nothing of whom she'd been with before him, nothing of her character. Not even if she was married.

All of which should have been enough to restrain Stevyn's urges. And perhaps it would have been, years ago. But, that was before he fell from grace, before he'd ruined his life and abandoned any hope he'd ever had of living a normal, decent life.

Stevyn's body craved a woman, and the one beneath him was growing more irresistible by the second.

Camilla couldn't believe what she was doing. Had she lost her mind? If Godric or his bailiff, or any of the sheriff's men, spied her in the middle of a field, flat on her back with a man who was not Risby atop her, she would be tossed out of Wickinghamshire in a flash!

Where was Bramble when she needed him? Why didn't Atalanta swoop down and sink her talons into this vile brigand's neck? Why didn't someone rescue her from this urge that had overtaken her?

But her dog and her falcon were taken up with their own interests, and offering little in the way of help. And Godric's men were nowhere in sight. The realization that she was all alone, free to do as she wished with this dangerous stranger who knew nothing about her, hit Camilla like a ton of mortar.

He was twice her size and he was as strong as Samson. Yet the weight of his body felt good, and the superiority of his physical strength, while intimidating, stole her breath away. She met his gaze and recognized a glimmer of surprise there, too, as if he were equally shocked by the emotions that swirled around them. And somehow she knew that she needn't fear him raping her; he was as swept up as she in the wild eroticism of the moment. Yet, she saw the kindness in his gaze and knew that if she asked him to stop, he would.

Which was a good thing. At least someone was in control of his emotions. After all, it was Camilla's breathing that broke the silence between them. When she felt him loosen his grip on her shoulders, she wrapped her arms around his broad, muscular back, pulling him down to her, lifting her hips to his.

He reared back again, and stared down at her. "Aren't you afraid that I will take advantage of you, lady?"

"I am afraid that you won't, sir." Her voice was low and throaty.

He answered her by tenderly brushing his fingers through her hair, then touching her cheek, then lowering his head to kiss her.

His lips were warm and firm, his mouth perfectly shaped to fit hers. Camilla heard a kittenish moan, and, before she realized the sound had escaped her own throat, she was answered by a deep rumbling groan that seemed wrenched from the stranger's soul. His need startled and aroused her. It had been so many years since she'd held a man in her arms, since she'd felt desirable . . . since she'd experienced this kind of raw physical urge.

And just a few moments earlier, she had thought her life was ending.

Instinctively, Camilla arched her back and pressed her breasts to his body. A sense of unreality washed over her, wiping away her fear, absorbing her sense of decency. Hungrily, she deepened their kiss, gasping at the warm salty taste of the stranger's mouth. She'd had a man before—once—but she didn't remember Gavin McGavin tasting this good, or feeling this good. She didn't remember craving a man's touch, or feeling the need to melt into him like she did with the stranger.

The animal urges that had overtaken Bramble and Daisy seemed a contagion, a hot, feverish contagion that Camilla couldn't resist. Her fingertips dug into the stranger's back; her legs wrapped around his hips. She clung to him, moving beneath him, pulling him onto her so that she could feel the hard length of his arousal. His harsh breathing chafed her skin and drew goose pimples to her flesh. She shuddered in his embrace, and he tightened his hold around her.

"Mon Dieu," the man whispered. Burying his head in the crook of her neck, he groaned and ground his arousal hard against her body.

Fire spread through her limbs as he moved rhythmically on top of her, his weight bearing down, his breathing increasingly labored. Though she hadn't been with a man for years, Camilla recognized that the stranger was close to release and when he stiffened in her arms, crying out with a strangled *"Dear God,"* she murmured, "Sweet Jesus," without knowing precisely why, and she held him even tighter, kissing the side of his face and smoothing his tousled hair.

He stilled in her arms, his chest heaving, the warmth from his body seeping into hers. For a long moment, Camilla held him, rubbing her hand along his back, her breath mingling with his, her lips pressed to his temple.

"Hardly what I would consider a satisfying experience for you," the man muttered wryly.

Camilla sighed. As her sanity slowly returned, a nervous laugh bubbled from her throat. No, the stranger was right. She supposed it was funny, in a way. For years, she'd tamped down her physical needs, pretending she didn't want a man, convincing herself that lovemaking was an overrated drudgery that only imprisoned a woman's heart and, when pregnancy resulted, assaulted her body.

Yet, in a flash, in a wild impulsive moment, on an otherwise perfectly normal afternoon, she'd tossed her repressions aside and followed her wildest instincts.

Only to find herself frustrated and breathless, pinned beneath a man who'd taken his satisfaction in the blink of an eye, leaving her body aching for more. More of him. More of this ruthlessly handsome stranger.

"You find the situation amusing, do you?" With a groan of exhaustion—or was it satiated lust?—he rolled off her. Lying on his side in the tall grass, he propped his head on his hand and stared at her. Stared at her with such intensity that a prickly heat suffused Camilla's face.

"I'm afraid I do." A burst of laughter convulsed her. "Here I was, desperate for you to ravish me. Then, when I all but gave you permission, you hadn't even the decency to diddle me properly! See if I submit to the next rogue who throws himself on me in the middle of nowhere! I believe, sir, that I have learned a very important lesson here."

His lips quirked, and his cheeks darkened.

"You humble me, ma'am. I had not realized I was ravishing such an experienced woman. Had I known, I would have been more careful to see to your pleasure before taking my own. Perhaps you will allow me a second chance?"

She whooped, covering her mouth with her hand, barely managing to speak through her laughter. "Oh, my, you are a randy fellow, aren't you? Or a simple braggart? Are you suggesting another go at it, sir? Want to give it another try?"

But, her teasing brought to his features a look of mild irritation. "What sort of young woman dresses as a boy and wanders around alone, without escort or chaperone? You're putting yourself at risk, you know. There are bandits prowling all over these parts. I wouldn't have raped you, but there are many men who would have. And claimed it was your fault, for putting yourself in harm's way."

Sobered by his words, Camilla regretted that she'd mocked him. "I am sorry, sir. I am not the sort of woman who routinely puts myself at risk, not in the way you are suggesting. Indeed, my garb should tell you that I am not flaunting my feminine wares."

"Aye." His eyes scanned the length of her body. "Hardly an alluring costume."

"I should have forced you to leave me be."

"You couldn't have. I'm stronger than you."

She considered his words, studied his eyes and swiftly appraised him. "You would have released me, had I demanded it."

After a long moment, he asked, "Who are you?"

But, Camilla was already on her feet, brushing grass and dirt from the seat of her pants, scanning the horizon for signs of Atalanta. Sanity had returned to her in a trice, and suddenly she didn't know what had got into her. Perhaps it was a physical stirring, much like Bramble's, a natural impulse that had hit her at the wrong moment.

In the wrong place.

In the presence of the wrong man.

"Ho!" She called the bird's name, then gave a shrug of bemusement as she watched Bramble and Daisy, still circling each other warily, still whimpering and growling in their respective states of anguish.

The stranger rose to his full height, also. Wordlessly, he strode toward the dogs, and with a swift sureness that surprised both beasts, swept Daisy up in his arms. As meek as a sheep, she laid her head on his shoulder and breathed a great sigh.

"Had enough for one day, eh, old girl?" he said sympathetically.

"You'd best stay away from these parts," Camilla warned him as he stalked toward the road. She felt a twinge of emptiness as he continued away from her, never turning to glance over his shoulder, never halting to respond to her warning.

Mounted on his destrier, his giant dog straddled across the saddle like a rack of venison, the stranger looked at the sky. Darkness was quickly falling. The air was turning chill. The stranger's face was carved in stone, his eyes as cold and gray as slate. He nudged his impatient horse forward, then drew him up short and gazed down at Camilla.

Her heart leapt in her throat as the stranger's black gaze bore into her. She wanted more of him, she admitted to herself. She would have agreed to a second round of lovemaking had the stranger seriously endeavored to pleasure her some more. Because no matter how brief their encounter, how lightning-quick the stranger's passion had flared and consumed him, the stirrings he'd awakened in Camilla's body were far from being doused. And once she was married to Risby, those feelings might never be kindled again.

Risby. The very sound of his name crawled across her skin like a fuzzy worm. But, Camilla shook off her trepidation. Or, she tried to. It did no good to worry about something she couldn't change. She was engaged to be married to Godric's son, and there was no getting out of it.

Why, then, had she thrown herself at this handsome stranger passing through the countryside? Why had she chosen this particular man, one she would never seen again, to exorcize all the pent-up emotions that threatened to possess her?

Staring at him brought the answers to her. His broad shoulders and slender hips attracted her. His kisses, rough, tender and warm, excited her. His kind, half-amused expression intrigued her.

And he was not Risby, Godric's son.

"Will you be all right?" he asked her.

She would have liked to ask him what he was smiling about, but there was no point. He was going to ride off into the sunset and she would never see him again.

She hoped.

She nodded, unable to speak above the lump in her throat. But, as he galloped off, a tear slid down Camilla's cheek. She lifted her arm and Atalanta dutifully returned to her fist. Tail tucked between his legs, Bramble also returned, albeit somewhat sheepishly.

"So you've had enough, too, is that it, Bramble?" She rubbed the dog behind his ears, and sighed. "You're all alike, aren't you. Love a woman, then leave her without looking back."

But, when the dog looked up at her, his eyes were round and unhappy. If Camilla hadn't known better, she would have thought her sad old hound had fallen in love with an impossibly incompatible wench.

Chapter Two

She heard the din of the evening meal as she completed her toilette. Godric would be waiting for her, she knew, eager to hear tell of her day, anxious to share his news that his son Risby would soon be arriving at the castle.

She already knew the news. It had been the cause of her earlier attack of panic. Bertha, Camilla's personal maid, had overheard the scullery wenches whispering about the return of the prodigal son. It seemed that Risby's imminent return had created quite a stir among the womenfolk of the castle.

Why the suspense, Camilla didn't comprehend, and Bertha, who'd lived in Wickingham Castle less time than she, was unable to ferret out the reason. The mysterious gossiping, however, gave both women pause to wonder: What sort of man was this Risby, about whom the serving wenches spoke in hushed tones, their eyes round in anticipation?

"Do you think he is handsome?" In her comfortable solar, Camilla sat on a low stool while Bertha brushed the tangles and burrs from her long golden mane.

A middle-aged woman with thick hips and a quick wit, Bertha met Camilla's gaze in the polished glass. "Can't shed much light on that one, my lady. All's I know is that Hilda's daughter like to fainted when she heard Risby was returning. Hilda said it was the heat from the rotisserie what bowled her over, but I seen it with me own eyes. The lass was kneadin' bread one minute and lookin' strong as an ancient oak. Then Risby's name was mentioned and she turned as white as a sapling birch."

A thread of distrust rippled up Camilla's spine. Instinctively, she glanced over at Bramble, curled up on the hearth. But, after today's excitement, the dog was oblivious to her edginess. "Perhaps the girl is infatuated with Risby. After all, I have been told that Risby was a high-spirited lad when he left here to fight in France. Godric says his son is handsome, and by all rights he should be. Although, knowing my luck, he will look like a toad."

"Um." Bertha frowned at the tangles in Camilla's thick hair. "If he takes after his father, he'll be handsome enough."

"He might have flirted with Hilda's daughter," Camilla continued. "Perhaps she deluded herself into thinking the sheriff's scion would marry her."

"If she thought that, she's an idiot as well as a mute."

"Mute?"

"Ain't never uttered a word, not as long as I've been around."

"If she's pretty, maybe Risby didn't mind that she couldn't speak."

Bertha gave a little snort of derision. "Hilda's daughter? Paired off with the son of Godric, the sheriff of Wickinghamshire? Merde! I'd have a better chance of marrying the king of England."

Camilla chuckled. Godric had told her only good things about his son Risby, and though she suspected a mild exaggeration in the accolades that were heaped on the man who was to be her husband, she had no reason to believe that he was anything other than handsome, strong and brave. "Oh, Bertha. I just hope he is kind."

The maid behind her smiled. "Well, I hope he favors a lady what has burrs and tangles in her hair. Because I've done all the brushing me poor arms can stand—"

"You have done an excellent job. Now, hurry, and let me go below stairs, Bertha. For Godric has told me there is to be a great feast tonight."

Camilla fidgeted while Bertha coiled the braided locks in two buns above her ears. Then, she stood and smoothed the front of her burgundy-colored surcoat. Beneath the overdress, she wore a tunic, simply made, but cut from the finest imported lawn. Since she'd been a guest of Godric's, not a farthing had been spared in outfitting her in the finest clothes. Adjusting the delicate pearl caplet that fringed her head, she gave her maid a shaky smile.

"Perhaps he has come tonight. Perhaps that is why the sheriff is throwing such a lavish banquet."

Bertha gave Camilla a frank head-to-toe appraisal. "If the boy is returning tonight, 'twill be a surprise for all in the castle. Fer I've heard nothing of an entourage approaching from the south. Risby would have sent a messenger up ahead to warn of his arrival."

"Wouldn't it be like Godric to keep the news of Risby's arrival a secret? The sheriff does have a wicked sense of humor."

"Well, if it is a surprise you want, my lady, then I hope you get a good one."

Camilla squeezed her maid's hands, grateful to have a confidante. It seemed the other womenfolk in the castle nurtured secrets that would never be revealed. They tended to fall silent when Camilla entered a room, and, when she left, they whispered behind their hands like jealous girls.

Risby's return would change all that.

Camilla patted her yellow hound on the head, smiling as he snored and jerked in his sleep. Then, she descended the stone staircase that led to the Great Hall of the castle.

Carefully, lest she trip over her fashionable fashionable pointy-toed shoes, she stepped into the bustling hall. As always, she took a deep breath as she scanned the crowded room. Though Godric had spared her life that day in the royal fields five years ago, then taken her into his home and eventually arranged for her to be engaged to Risby, she still felt a certain unease in the company of the sheriff and his liege men. Especially when the lot of them was drinking.

A great roar of male laughter erupted as Camilla strode past the rough trestle tables where the sheriff's retainers sat. The punch line of a crude joke drifted to her ears and brought a wave of heat to her neck. Suppressing her jitters, Camilla lifted her chin a notch and made her way to the raised table at the end of the room.

"Good evening, my lady." Godric stood. Though he was not the sort of man who ever lost control of himself, an overindulgence in ale or wine made him inordinately attentive toward Camilla. And his attentions, while cloaked in fatherly language, sometimes made her uncomfortable.

Which, in turn, made her feel like an ungrateful tabby. "You spoil me, Godric." Camilla sat on his left side. "Sit down, please. There is not a man in this hall who rises from a chair when a lady enters. None but you, that is."

The wooden chair creaked as Godric lowered his great weight into it. Tall and broad-shouldered, he wore a thick beard shot through with silver, and gazed out from piercing blue eyes beneath shaggy black brows. Widowed since Risby's birth, he was a handsome man, reputedly lusty and extremely virile for his age. According to castle rumor, Godric shared his bed with at least one woman, sometimes two or three, each night.

"Perhaps the men will learn from my example." The sheriff's gaze shot to the benches below where one man picked his teeth, then cleaned his ear, with a wishbone. "On the other hand, perhaps not."

With a chuckle, Camilla lifted the jeweled mazer in front of her. Godric's cellar contained only the best wines and meads, and since she'd come to Wickinghamshire, she'd acquired an appreciation for them, along with a sophisticated palate.

"May I ask, sir, what is the occasion for this festivity?" Camilla's mouth watered as serving wenches appeared with trenchers of roasted nightingale, peacock and pheasant.

"We are expecting a guest, lady. Indeed, I am told he arrived late this afternoon, but he has sequestered himself in a tiny chamber near the south tower. Tired from his journey, I suppose."

"And who is this esteemed visitor to have warranted such a fuss?" Camilla's pulse quickened, for she expected Godric to announce Risby's return. Inexplicably, a thread of apprehension mingled with her excitement. What if Risby wasn't the man his father described to her? What if she didn't like him? Worse, what if he didn't care for her?

"His name is Sir Stevyn Strongbow, King's Justice, sent from Londontown to dispense justice among the heathen. What do you think, Frederick? Can one of the king's fancy men teach me what he's learned from a book about how to keep peace in this godforsaken wilderness?"

The sheriff's bailiff, seated on his right, laughed heartily. As did several of the other men who overheard Godric's comment. Of course, when a man was lord and master of the greatest castle in the shire, as well as the chief law enforcement official of the surrounding countries, his jokes, whether clever or dull, never failed to elicit a jolly response. And the idea of any man coming from Londontown to straighten out Godric's people was laughable, indeed.

Camilla smiled tightly. "The king's justice? What happened to Sir Alfred?"

Before Godric could answer, his gaze shot to the opposite end of the Great Hall. Following the sheriff's stare, Camilla was shocked to see the stranger she'd nearly made love to earlier that afternoon.

"Merde," she whispered, crossing herself.

Godric gave her a sharp look. "What did you say?"

Swallowing hard, she shook her head. "I am feeling a bit faint, that is all. Mayhaps the wine was too strong for me tonight."

But, Camilla knew it wasn't the wine that brought a flush of heat to her face. It was the man crossing the room, striding the length of the hall like a slinky black panther, that made her blood boil.

Awash in a wave of queasy dread, Camilla watched the stranger pace the floor. Heads turned as Godric's men surveyed the newcomer. Even men as crude and unmannered as they recognized the elegant bearing of a proud, handsome man when he passed among them.

And, mon Dieu, was he handsome. Leather boots fit snug to his thickly muscled calves, while coarsely woven hose hugged the sculpted lines of his thighs. As he walked, his shoulders and hips moved gracefully, in a gait that was full of dignity and raw, masculine power.

Releasing a breath, Camilla stole a glance at Godric. She was amused to see his jaw tense and his eyes narrow as the stranger approached. But, when the newcomer stood before their table, Godric's features smoothed instantly into a warm, welcoming smile.

Standing, the sheriff reached across the table to clasp the newcomer's hand. "Sir Stevyn Strongbow. We meet at last. Damme, but I thought you were never going to descend from that stuffy room!"

"Good evening, Godric. I apologize for my

rudeness in not appearing earlier. But, I have had much reading to do. And half a dozen letters to write. I'm afraid my work is often consuming, to the point where my manners are remiss."

"I would like to introduce you to Camilla, the lady of the castle," Godric said, turning toward her with a wide, avuncular smile.

Sir Stevyn looked her square in the eye. If he'd seen her from across the hall, he didn't show it. If he recognized her as the girl in the fields, his expression revealed nothing. Nothing that Godric or any of the other men could have detected, that is. But, to Camilla, his amusement was clear. The nod of his head, the slight wrinkling at the corners of his eyes and the wry quirking of his lips as he said her name revealed his enjoyment of the situation.

"Camilla." His deep, honeyed voice lit a fire in Camilla's belly. To Godric, the stranger said, "You have a beautiful daughter, sheriff."

Then, his gaze returned to her and lingered for a beat, the span of a heartbeat really, but long enough for Camilla to experience a rising sense of panic. Who was this Sir Stevyn Strongbow with whom she had been cavorting in the open fields today? What would happen to her if Godric discovered her indiscretion?

"She is not my daughter," Godric replied. "Not yet, anyway. She is engaged to marry Risby, my son. But, since I have no wife or daughters of my own, and since the girl is so dear to me, she is the castle's unofficial chatelaine. Isn't that right, Camilla?"

"You are too kind, Godric," Camilla murmured, tearing her gaze from Stevyn's. Though it was torturous to look at him, she soon realized that it was even more painful not to.

"Sit, sir!" Godric commanded as a young page pushed a wooden chair toward Stevyn.

When the men were settled on opposite sides of the table, more food was brought from the kitchens. Roasted fowl, stewed root vegetables, steamed oysters, candied nuts and puddings graced the table. It was a feast fit for a king, meant to impress this Sir Stevyn Strongbow, whoever he was, Camilla reckoned, but her stomach would allow her to eat hardly more than a bite.

Sir Stevyn ate heartily, but with manners that few men at Wickingham Castle had ever aspired to. As she watched him, Camilla grew more intrigued. A handsome man, to be sure, with his thick brown hair and prominent nose. Perhaps his chin wasn't strong enough, she mused. And, perhaps his arms weren't as thickly muscled as Godric's. But, his eyes were heavily fringed with sooty lashes, and his gaze, whenever and wherever it lit on her, conveyed a warmth. His voice was like a ribbon of honey, rich, thick and seductive. Sir Stevyn might be a stranger to Wickingham, but the heat his presence created in Camilla's body was a tad too familiar for her own comfort.

"Tell me, Sir Stevyn, what do you expect to do while in Wickingham?" Godric leaned back in his chair while a young serving girl refilled his trencher with braised squab and roasted partridge. When the girl moved away, she brushed her body against the sheriff's shoulder and he repaid her with a firm slap on her bottom.

Stevyn's expression registered an instant of surprise before his smile returned. *So,* Camilla thought, *the young justice is as practiced in hiding his thoughts as Godric*. They were like two sly foxes sniffing each other, two powerful male animals appraising each other's prowess. Greatly entertained, she sipped her wine and watched. And listened.

"It is assize term, is it not?" Stevyn said. "I have come at the king's instructions, to conduct an investigation and to conduct trials for the criminals you have in your gaol."

"I was expecting Sir Alfred," Godric remarked. "For years, it has been Sir Alfred who tried cases involving offenses against the Crown in this shire."

"Alfred is dead." Stevyn's gaze never left the sheriff's as he spoke. "Murdered. Butchered in his bed, to be more specific."

Godric leaned forward, forearms framing his trencher, fingertips chafing. "Who did this dastardly deed?"

"Who indeed?" Stevyn leaned back to study the sheriff. " 'Tis a mystery, sure enough."

"Have the London authorities any suspects?"

"Alfred was a justice of the king's court. There are hundreds of suspects. One has only to look at the cases he has decided in the past year and see the scores of people who would have considered him their enemy. Each time a justice decides a case, he makes one enemy."

"And one friend," Camilla said, drawing Stevyn's heated stare. And Godric's startled attention. "Have you any reason to believe that Alfred was murdered by a dissatisfied litigant?"

"My future daughter-in-law has a right brazen tongue," the sheriff said. "Pay her no mind."

But, Stevyn's gaze remained fixed upon her. Turning in his chair, he appraised her, reminding her silently of their interlude in the grass, taunting her with the memory of her own passion.

"A brazen tongue, perhaps," he said at last. "But, the girl has a quick mind. In law, it is more important to ask the right question than it is to know the correct answers."

Godric's stern look reminded her of Risby and her promise to marry the sheriff's son when he returned from France. It was a sobering reminder, one that created as much heated panic in Camilla's bosom as did Stevyn's gaze. But, for entirely different reasons.

"I liked Sir Alfred." She lifted her chin. "His visits to Wickinghamshire were occasions of great festivity, Sir Stevyn. I am saddened to hear of his death."

"Festivity?" Stevyn leaned forward, his elbows propped on the table.

Godric cleared his throat. "We are an isolated people. When Alfred came, he brought gossip from London and news from the continent. In return, we laid out a bountiful table for the man."

"As you have done for me."

"As we would do for any of the king's men," Godric replied. "We show no favoritism to the justices who preside over our district."

"And I trust that Sir Alfred showed no favoritism to anyone in Wickinghamshire."

"One hand washes another," Godric suggested.

"Not in my line of work," Stevyn returned coolly.

Godric's smile vanished, and his spine straightened.

Nibbling on a slice of bread, Camilla watched as the two men parried with each other. Tension enveloped them. Was Godric aware of her attraction to the stranger? Had someone spied them in the fields that afternoon, and reported her impulsive indiscretion to the sheriff?

Surely, if Godric knew what she'd done, he'd already have tossed her out of Wickingham Castle on her head. Her position in the castle was tenuous as it was. A former thief, arrested for poaching, then offered clemency in exchange for her agreement to marry the sheriff's son? Why, the very thought of it was fantastic! But, to think the sheriff would countenance her near-rutting in an open field with a passing stranger was even more absurd.

The bread she swallowed suddenly felt like a rock lodged in her throat. How foolish she'd been to let this handsome king's justice paw all over her! In one reckless moment, she'd jeopardized her entire future. She could have lost everything. She could have been tossed into gaol to serve out the sentence she'd earned. She could have been hung from a gibbet, if that was Godric's fancy. After all, it was his word that was law in this shire. The king might be ruler over England, but the king was a long way from Wickinghamshire.

A fact that Sir Stevyn Strongbow seemed to be unaware of, Camilla noted.

"I am glad to hear that Alfred was well received in Wickinghamshire," the new justice said. "I hope my actions do not dim the respect your people have for the king's justice system."

"Let us hope not," Godric murmured. His voice took on a new strength as he leaned forward. "Tell me, then, sir, what cases do you expect to hear this term?"

"The king has given me a special commission." Stevyn fell silent until the serving girl had filled his wine glass and sauntered off. He cut his eyes in Camilla's direction, hesitating as if unsure whether she could be trusted to hear what he was about to say. Then, apparently having decided she could be, he said, "The king has taken a harsh view of this recent outbreak of illegal relic selling."

Godric's brows shot up. "Relic selling?"

"It is said that the abbot of Wickinghamshire has made himself a fortune selling fraudulent relics," Stevyn added.

Camilla couldn't resist interjecting, "But, relic selling is not illegal. Barnabas the abbot sells many relics. The money is used to support the church, to support its many charitable endeavors. 'Tis a good thing—"

"Hush, gel!" Godric's rebuke lacked the note of indulgence she'd heard in his earlier admonishment. Yet, when he addressed Stevyn, his expression was one of only mild bemusement. "The woman talks too much, but she tells the truth. Relic selling is not illegal. Unless the king has recently made it so."

"Relic selling is not illegal if the seller is truthful about what he sells, and the buyer does not pay an outrageous sum of money for a forgery. It has been the king's observation, however, and mine, too, that if all the splinters of Christ's cross that have been sold over the last few years were added together, there would be enough wood to make a forest."

Godric threw back his head and let go a loud bark of laughter. "That is most amusing, sir. But, tell me, how do you intend to prove whether any particular relic sold is a forgery? Can you say with certainty that a splinter came from this or that tree? Can you know beyond any doubt that the splinter did *not* come from Christ's crucifix?"

Camilla fidgeted. Relic selling provided substantial revenue for the unwed mother's sanctuary and nursery she and Barnabas operated. It was a place where young women in trouble came to have their babies, a place of refuge and hope for women who had no other place to go. If this new justice planned to make relic selling illegal, the place known as Barnabas's Sanctuary would cease to exist.

At length, Stevyn said, "When a peasant gives his life savings in exchange for a scrap of dirty linen that the Church calls a piece of Christ's shroud, that is a crime. Unless of course the Church can prove the linen is part of the shroud of Jesus. 'Tis of no moment that the crime is committed by the Church, or by a so-called man of God. The deed remains a punishable offense, the perpetrator a mountebank. And if I uncover evidence of criminal activity in Wickinghamshire, I shall prosecute whoever is responsible."

Godric's face darkened, and his shaggy brows knit together. "You are talking about prosecuting Barnabas the abbot. You will find great resistance to such an endeavor, sir. Barnabas is a venerated figure in this shire, much loved by his parishioners, especially by the womenfolk."

Stevyn's gaze shot to Camilla. "Is that so? And why precisely is Barnabas so beloved among the womenfolk of Wickinghamshire?"

She swallowed hard, acutely aware of Godric's growing agitation. "Barnabas is a benevolent man. He has made it his life's work to help unmarried women who are in trouble." Her voice faded as heat fanned over her shoulders and face. Even talking of unplanned pregnancies in polite company was considered rude. And however accustomed she was to dealing with young unwed mothers, Camilla found it embarrassing to discuss the matter with a stranger.

But, he was hardly a stranger if he had lain atop her and smothered her with kisses.

"Continue," Godric said harshly.

Stevyn shot the sheriff a look of irritation. Then, he turned in his chair and scrutinized Camilla in a way no man had ever done.

It seemed there were only the two of them in the room. Camilla felt that same liquid heat spread over her body, the same burning sensation that had consumed her earlier that afternoon. Sir Stevyn's voice, when he drawled, "Go on, I'd like to hear more," filled her with an uneasy awareness—awareness of the man's powerful magnetism, his honeyed charm and the dreadfully antagonistic effect his arrogant attitude was having on Godric.

Somehow she forced herself to meet the justice's gaze. "If a young woman finds herself with child, and has no place to go, she can find food and shelter at Barnabas's Sanctuary. She can stay there, no questions asked, for as long as she needs to. She can have her baby there, too, with a proper midwife, hot water and clean linens. And, after the baby is born, she can stay as long as she likes, until she finds decent work or her family allows her to return home."

Stevyn rubbed his chin. "A worthy cause, this sanctuary. Am I to assume you have a hand in running the place, my lady?"

"Yes." That was an understatement. "For the last four and a half years, I have worked side by side with Barnabas the abbot. Were it not for the sanctuary—"

"Yes?" Stevyn nodded. His eyes, black and earnest, penetrated Camilla, drawing her out, warming her, seducing her. "If it were not for the sanctuary, what?"

She tilted toward him, her fingers gripping the edge of the trestle table, her heart thudding erratically. Yes, there was something in this man's demeanor that made her want to tell him more, made her want to confess everything, made her want to abandon the carefully constructed defenses she'd built around herself.

But, Godric's voice catapulted her back to reality. "If it were not for the sanctuary, you would be but an idle girl, roaming this great castle with nothing to do but herd the servants and practice your needlework. Isn't that right, Camilla?"

"Aye." If it were not for the sanctuary, she might be dead. When the sheriff had arrested her, Camilla was pregnant and newly widowed. Even now, the pain of the stillbirth, and the kindness Barnabas had showed her, remained fresh in her mind.

Godric turned to Stevyn. "You see, sir, you are wasting your time. There is no illegal relic selling going on in Wickinghamshire. The amount of money the Church takes in from the business of relic selling is minuscule. You'll find no peasants who have given their life savings for a scrap of dirty cloth. And, besides, whatever relics Barnabas sells are authentic."

"If Barnabas can prove to my satisfaction that his relics are authentic, then he shall be safe from prosecution."

"Barnabas has proved to *my* satisfaction that his relics are real," the sheriff growled. "And I am the primary law officer in this territory."

"Perhaps." Stevyn, a slight smirk on his face, slowly rose. "But 'tis King Edward who makes the laws you must enforce, Godric. I trust you have not forgotten that."

The sheriff rose, too, so abruptly in fact, that his chair scraped roughly along the stone floor. "You will find no one in this shire who will utter a single word of condemnation against Barnabas. No one!"

"He is a good man," Camilla felt obliged to add, though her stomach roiled when Godric lifted a hand to silence her.

For a long moment, the two men stared at each other. Then, silently, Stevyn turned to Camilla and dipped his head. "Good night, Lady Camilla. Tell the good abbot I shall be looking for him in the morn. If he is as saintly as the sheriff says, he has nothing to worry about."

"You are a foolish man," Godric said in a low, menacing tone, his fists clenched at his sides. "This is my shire, and these are my people, and I will not countenance some young upstart from Londontown coming into my castle and commencing some idiotic investigation—"

"Are you threatening me?" Stevyn's tone was quiet, unruffled, and his expression, to Camilla's amazement, continued to hold a hint of amusement. Had the man no fear at all?

Exhaling harshly, Godric took his seat. He quaffed his ale and banged the tankard on the table. Then, without looking at Stevyn, he dismissed him with a wave of his hand. "Sleep well, sir. You must do what the king has sent you to do. And I must do my job as well."

Stevyn nodded. Then, he met Camilla's gaze, holding it for an instant longer than necessary, scorching her with his black quixotic stare. When the king's justice turned and walked the length of the room, Camilla released the breath she'd been holding.

Drained, she lacked the energy even to finish her meal, much less perform her duties as dinner companion to Godric. The man was drinking heavily now that Stevyn had departed the room, and his mood was darkening with each tankard of beer he downed. A cloud was descending over Wickingham Castle, and Camilla had the ominous feeling that life as she knew it would never be the same.

Standing, she offered the sheriff a weak smile. "If you will excuse me, Godric, I would like to retire to my solar."

But, her future father-in-law, rather than dismissing her from the dinner table, grabbed her wrist and bade her resume her seat. "I have a few things to discuss with you, Camilla."

Her knees wobbled as she lowered herself into her chair.

Inhaling his beer, Godric studied her with glittering eyes. There was an air of wicked intent about him that made Camilla's skin crawl.

"Surely, you are as disgusted by Sir Stevyn's accusations as I am."

She nodded. "Barnabas's Sanctuary for Unwed Mothers is my life's work. If this stranger's investigation causes the shelter to shut down, there will be many bastard babes born without roofs over their heads. And many pregnant girls left homeless."

" 'Twould be a crying shame." The sheriff paused, staring at Camilla as if he were measuring her mettle. "There is something you can do to help these young unwed wenches."

"I will do anything."

Godric chuckled. "That is what I thought you would say."

After a moment, Camilla leaned forward. "What is your plan, sir?"

"Seduce him," the sheriff replied, all mirth removed from his voice, all glitter gone from his eyes. "Seduce the son of a bitch, and persuade him to leave Wickingham Castle. I give you leave to do what you must, gel, short of bedding the man, of course. Your future, as well as the future of every unwed mother in this shire, is at stake. 'Tis perhaps the most important thing I will ever ask you to do. Other than marry my son Risby, that is."

Camilla gasped. In the background, the din of Godric's men-at-arms faded to a dull buzz. Overhead, the thick oaken rafters seemed to sway, and the intricately woven tapestries gracing the stone walls rippled like pennants in a gentle breeze. She couldn't have possibly heard what she thought she heard. Had her future father-in-law, the man who spared her life five years ago, when she herself was desperate and homeless, truly asked her to seduce Sir Stevyn Strongbow?

"Short of bedding the man," she repeated dully. Well, she'd already done everything short of bedding the man. But, she couldn't explain to Godric how dangerous his suggestion was. "What if he tries to . . . He is a powerful man. . . . What if he gets the wrong notion . . . ?"

"Of course, he will get the wrong notion." It had been years since Godric had spoken to her in such a tone, as if she were a child, as if she had no will of her own and was totally dependent on his whim and mercy. "You must gain his confidence, get close to him, earn his trust. 'Tis obvious he is a man of integrity. He will not lightly tell his secrets to a woman, even a woman he lusts for."

"So I am to ply his secrets from him, is that it?" The thought sent shivers up Camilla's spine.

"You are to remain close to the man. Befriend him. Lead him to believe you are eager to share his bed. Bat your eyes at him, smile that alluring little smile of yours. Find out all Sir Stevyn knows about Barnabas, then report back to me. I want to know everyone he talks to and every scrap of information he plans to use against the good abbot. You don't want to see your friend Barnabas hanging from a gibbet, do you?"

A shudder wracked Camilla's shoulders as the horrible image flashed in her mind. "But, it is wrong to mislead a man."

"As a general rule, 'tis wrong to kill a man. But, when a soldier kills his enemy on the field of battle, no one condemns his soul to hell, do they?"

Puzzled by the sheriff's convoluted logic, Camilla said nothing.

Godric leaned closer to her, touching her arm, speaking in a low, conspiratorial tone. "Consider this a holy war, Camilla. The king has sent this man to shut down your sanctuary for homeless unwed mothers. And this Sir Stevyn, with his self-righteous airs and arrogant manners, would do just that! What does he care for the pregnant wenches who will die without your assistance? What does he care about those poor, unfortunate women, Camilla?"

"Nothing," she whispered. The sheriff was right. Nothing was more important to her than helping those unwed mothers. Nothing! And if it was Sir Stevyn who threatened to destroy her life's work, then woe to him.

"You do not have to swyve the man," Godric said, sighing. "I am not asking my daughter to prostitute herself. But, Risby will be proud of you when he learns what you have done, you can count on that. And you will prove your loyalty to me by doing this. You are loyal to me, aren't you, Camilla?"

A wave of unease washed over her. "Of course," she managed.

"Good, then. Go and find the man. Instruct the servants to draw him a bath. Offer to wash his back. 'Tis polite for the lady of the house to assist an esteemed visitor with his bath. 'Tis the custom in these parts."

It might be the custom, Camilla thought, but it was a passing strange thing for a woman to wash a man's back without becoming overly intimate with him. She wondered how often esteemed visitors wound up in their hostess's bed.

"I'm not asking you to sleep with him." Godric's repetition had an odd ring to it. It seemed the more he assured Camilla that was not part of his plan, the more her mind dwelled on the possibility. "I'm only asking you to spy on him."

Suddenly, the plan sounded dirty, dirtier than if Godric *had* suggested she bed the man. Promiscuity, after all, was a sin of the flesh, and one that, at least according to Barnabas, Camilla tended to view too leniently. Betrayal was a crime of the heart, however, and an offense she viewed as the most deadly sin of all.

" 'Twill be a thoroughly disgusting chore," she whispered, as she propped her elbows on the table and held her head in her hands.

"Aye," Godric replied tightly. Clearly, he didn't

relish the idea of his son's fiancée cavorting with this strange, handsome young king's justice. "But, it is a chore that must be done if Barnabas's Sanctuary is to be protected. And the man has eyes for you, that is abundantly clear. You are the only one for the job."

A sliver of excitement slid through Camilla's body. So, Godric *had* observed the tension between her and Stevyn. She hadn't been imagining things. But why did her heart spasm so to think Stevyn was attracted to her? She was engaged to Risby. She was foolish to be flattered by Sir Stevyn's rude attentions.

Yet, Godric's suggestion did excite her.

"I can do it," she said, swallowing hard and forcing herself to meet Godric's stare. "Sir Stevyn is a man, that is all. He has been traveling without companionship for nearly a sennight and his hunger for conversation, a hot bath and female company will be sharp."

Godric took another long swallow of ale. "Then, I suggest you visit him soon. Before he finds a willing leman to slake his thirst for, ah, conversation. Before he loses interest in the sheriff's future daughter-in-law. *Before it is too late to save Barnabas's Sanctuary*."

Chapter Three

"Tired, old girl?" In the guest chamber where Stevyn had decamped, he sat before an oaken table strewn with papers. At his feet, Daisy lay on her side, apparently exhausted from the day's events. At the sound of her master's voice, the dog lifted her head. A weary huff escaped her, and her tail thumped the floor. Even as Stevyn reached down to rub her snout, her eyelids flickered shut again.

"Dreaming of Bramble? Well, go back to sleep, you wanton hussy." Behind him, serving women hauled in buckets of hot water, filling the big wooden tub that sat in the corner. Standing, Steven massaged his throbbing temples. How could he work, distracted as he was by the commotion those noisy wenches made?

Or was it something else that distracted him?

When the tub was filled to the rim with steaming water, and he and Daisy were alone behind the closed door of the luxuriously appointed guest chamber, Stevyn peeled off his clothes. His temples weren't the only parts of his body that throbbed. Stark naked, he stood beside the bath. Restless and edgy, he stared at the wisps of steam rising from the water. Bramble wasn't the only male in Wickingham Castle hungry for a woman.

Damn that Lady Camilla, he thought, for putting such disturbing thoughts into his head. He had work to do, and no time to spend mooning over a woman. A woman who, even if he did have time to dally with her, was engaged to marry the sheriff's son.

Testing the water with his fingertips, Stevyn winced. This certainly wasn't the first time he had been attracted to an unavailable woman, and God knew it wasn't the first time an engaged or married woman showed interest in him. Never mind that Godric had made a point of telling him Camilla was the unofficial chatelaine of Wickingham Castle. The lady's cheeks had darkened each time Stevyn looked at her; her lashes had fluttered like a nervous girl's each time he spoke to her.

If she was in love with the absentee Risby, then Stevyn was a jackal's uncle. She felt the tension between them as clearly as he did. And, with a little encouragement, Stevyn guessed, she might even be willing to act on her attraction.

Deep in his thoughts, Stevyn heard Daisy's low growl before he became aware of a gentle rapping on his door. Thinking that a serving wench had returned with soap, or a stack of fresh linens, he called out for her to enter.

But, Camilla's round eyes, peering around the

heavy plank door, sent a jolt of surprise through his loins.

Their gazes locked. Camilla, seemingly frozen in shock, gaped. Her cheeks pinkened, even as the trajectory of her stare dropped to the level of Stevyn's hips. A soft gasp escaped her lips, but her eyes remained riveted to his body.

"You are letting in a draft," he said hoarsely. "Come in, or go out, but whatever you do, close the door before my bath water gets cold."

"What about that nasty beast beneath your desk?"

He turned and looked at Daisy. The animal opened her eyes and lifted her brows, but made no further move. "That hound is so out of sorts at the present, she wouldn't move to defend me if an army of Mongols streamed over that doorstep. Her encounter with Bramble left her unable to eat her dinner, much less bare her teeth at you. Don't worry; she isn't going to budge from that spot."

Nibbling her lower lip, Camilla hesitated. Then, she slipped into his chamber, and closed the door, pressing her back to it as if she were afraid it might fall down. "I brought you a sachet of herbs and dried flowers," she stammered. "I thought you might like them for your bath."

Stevyn's lips twisted. He watched Camilla's gaze flicker from his torso to his thickening arousal to the unimpressed Daisy. The lady's nervousness amused him. But, his body's reaction to her didn't. He was a guest in Wickingham Castle, an unwelcome guest whose purpose apparently offended the sensibilities of his host, the sheriff. Seducing the sheriff's future daughter-in-law could hardly be deemed prudent. It might even get him killed. But, his body didn't share the wisdom of his conscious mind. And as Camilla's stare grew bolder, his physical response to her grew.

"Bring your herbs to me." Stevyn stood tall beside the tub, his arousal fully straining for release, his body aching for the touch of a woman. Inviting the sheriff's future daughter-in-law to approach him was reckless, a direct contradiction of his vow not to let a woman interfere with his work. But, at the present moment, Stevyn's lust was so distracting, he couldn't concentrate on the papers strewn on his desk if his life depended on it. Perhaps what he needed was a physical release that would leave him clearheaded and alert. A diversion.

After all, he *was* a man.

She closed the distance between them as if she were walking on glass. Stevyn's curiosity deepened. Camilla had shown an impulsive, independent streak earlier in the hunting fields. At dinner, she'd proved herself well-spoken and confident. But, now, in the face of Stevyn's obvious arousal, she was shy. Her contradictions made him wonder what she was really about.

Whatever she was about, she was Risby's fiancée. For that reason alone, Stevyn should banish her from his room. But, even as his lips formed the words, "Go away," his desire quashed them. Instead, he smiled as he watched Camilla's eyes rove the length of his body. Her own curiosity was evident, and it stoked his arousal. The mixture of uncertainty and desire so clearly seen in her expression endeared her to him. Telling her to go suddenly seemed the very height of rudeness.

She stood on the opposite side of the wooden

tub. Her voice was barely a whisper. "Have you no shame, Sir Stevyn?"

"Do you see anything that I should be ashamed of, my lady?"

Her gaze lit on his chest, then traced the rivulet of black hair that flowed down his flat belly. "My guess is that you are right proud of your manhood."

He chuckled. "It has served me well. And I've had few complaints from the ladies who were kind enough to share my bed."

"Have there been *many* ladies who shared your bed?"

"Ah, but that is none of your business, is it? Any more than the number of bed partners you have had is my business."

"Most men are proud of the number of women they have conquered."

"I am not most men. I do not view women as potential conquests." Stevyn stepped into the tub and lowered himself into the hot water. Leaning his head back, he draped his arms along the wooden rim. "Would you care to join me?"

She studied him for a moment, then wordlessly untied her little sachet bag and sprinkled the contents into the bath. Delicate lavender and piquant rosemary mingled, their perfume wafting off the surface of the steaming water.

Beads of perspiration trickled down Stevyn's neck, draining him slowly of the tension that so often accompanied a hard day's work. "Come." He stared at her through half-lidded eyes. "Join me."

"Ridiculous," she breathed. "You are but a stranger to me. Do you often find women you have just met willing to bathe with you?"

"No. Nor do I often meet women who are willing to lie beneath me in an open hunting field before they even know my name. But, today has been an unusually lucky day. I am hoping my good fortune continues."

"You are an impudent rascal," she replied, without a hint of genuine disapprobation.

"And you, dear lady, are far too concerned with what is proper and what is not."

"Women who do not behave *properly* often suffer unpleasant consequences."

"Given the context of what you and Barnabas do, I suppose you are referring to the consequence of an unwanted pregnancy. Trust me, woman, I have no intentions of getting you with child. The last thing I need in my life is a squalling brat and a demanding wife."

"Well, then, you should not invite women to share your bath with you."

"If you refuse to join me, then will you scrub my back?"

A reluctant smile tugged at the corner of her mouth. Then, Camilla pressed her lips firmly together, trying, Stevyn supposed, to appear unamused. "I thought you a serious man, Sir Stevyn. Yet you are as mischievous as a little boy."

"I am quite serious about my work." He sluiced some hot water on his face, and ran his wet hands through his hair. The knots in his shoulders had eased while the warmth of the bath seeped through his skin, relaxing him. "I am not so serious about myself."

"I am serious about my work, too, Sir Stevyn. As is Barnabas. The people of Wickinghamshire will not stand idly by while you destroy the sanctuary. Barnabas's refuge is one of the finest examples of Christian charity in northern England."

Stevyn kept his thoughts to himself. But, he wondered if Camilla truly believed Barnabas's relic-selling industry was strictly a charitable operation. Was she so naive that she could participate in an illegal trade without realizing it? Or was *he* so cynical that he couldn't conceive of an enterprise born of charity rather than greed? Perhaps Barnabas was as guileless as a babe. Perhaps Camilla's indignation was justified. Perhaps Stevyn's own cynicism had caused him to prejudge and condemn the actions of a perfectly innocent man.

"If you do not believe me, sir," Camilla said, arms folded across her chest, "you should come to Barnabas's Sanctuary. Meet some of the women who are there. Let them tell you what they know of Barnabas. I believe you will think twice before you accuse Barnabas of any wrongdoing."

"I have an open mind," he replied, pushing off from the side of the tub and standing. Wading to the other side, he reached for her. As her arms unfolded, he took her hand and pulled her toward him so that she was leaning over the edge of the tub. "Come. Join me."

"No." She reared back.

He found her other hand, grasped her fingers and pulled her toward him again. She rocked back on her heels, but hers was a slight figure compared to his, and he easily held her captive at the side of the tub.

"Stevyn, no! I-I am fully clothed!"

"Then disrobe," he said, grinning. "Please. Indulge me. I am a guest in your castle. Is it not the local custom for the lady of the house to assist her guest in bathing?"

"Aye, but the custom does not include hopping into the tub naked with the guest."

"Then we shall begin a new tradition." He placed his hands on her slender hips.

She murmured, "No," but her weight swayed toward him. She arched her back, as if to retreat, but the movement only pressed her lower body against his, creating a friction between them that heightened their intimacy.

"This is not wise," she said on a sigh.

Stevyn knew it wasn't. But, he drew her tightly against his body anyway. Though the rim of the tub separated them, Stevyn felt Camilla's soft breasts crushed against his chest, and through her linen tunic and surcoat, the flat hardness of her belly pressing against his aching arousal.

Cuffing her wrists, he lifted her arms to his neck. Camilla held his gaze with a slightly stunned expression, but, after the briefest of hesitations, her arms wound around his neck and she clung to him as he ran his hands down her hips. Bunching the linen in his fingers, he drew up the hem of her tunic until his fingers felt the bare, hot flesh of her thighs. Then, he slipped his hands beneath her clothes, measuring her waist, cupping her bottom, pressing her body to him as tightly as he could.

"Mon Dieu," she whispered.

He covered her lips with his own, hungry for the taste of her. And Camilla was every bit as sweet as Stevyn remembered, every bit as luscious and ripe as he'd imagined at least twenty times in the few short hours since he'd met her in the open fields outside the walls of Wickingham Castle. God, but he wanted her. Needed her. Reining in his own desire, Stevyn fought the urge to step over the rim of the tub, rip off her clothes and ravish her.

But, it was *her* passion, welling up like an underground spring, that brought him to his senses. Her need, her arousal, indeed, her lack of control, forced Stevyn to control himself. If he couldn't, he knew he might very well wind up with a squalling brat to worry about.

And besides, he had long ago learned to enjoy the exquisite pleasure of giving pleasure to a woman. Among a very small number of London women, Stevyn's stamina and self-control were legendary. One of the Queen's ladies-in-waiting had spread it round the palace that Sir Stevyn Strongbow could make love for hours without losing his strength or his vigor. The rumor, when it was repeated to him by the king, had brought a wave of embarrassed heat to Stevyn's cheeks. But, it was true. Stevyn's greatest pleasure in lovemaking came from making his partner happy, driving her to the brink of madness, taking his own release when she was sated. Except for this afternoon, he thought ruefully. This afternoon Camilla had affected him like no other, driving him to act like a bumbling boy. Not tonight though; tonight he was determined to satisfy Camilla.

Camilla's pleasure, however, would hardly require an enormous deal of coaxing. Indeed, the woman seemed on the verge of collapsing in his arms. A mixture of amusement and sympathy swept over Stevyn as he supported the trembling lady in his embrace. Her head fell back, and a tiny moan escaped her lips. Her thighs parted, and Stevyn's hand slipped between her legs.

She gasped just as his fingers brushed the coarse hair. "No," she managed to whisper, but this time Stevyn was quite certain her protestations were empty.

Her breath, harsh and ragged, raised goose bumps on his skin. Camilla said his name, over and over, as if it were her anchor to reality. As the steam rose from the bath, the tension in the tiny chamber thickened and Stevyn's arousal, hard, thick and aching, grew unbearably painful. But, when Camilla's knees buckled, and he caught her in his arms, it was her satisfaction he was focused on, not his own. The sight of her, overcome with desire, fueled his need.

Lifting her over the side of the tub, Stevyn held Camilla's gaze, nodding in response to her faintly bewildered look. As her body slid into the water, he pulled her tunic over her head and tossed it to the floor. Unhurried, he kissed her lips, ran his tongue down her slender throat, nibbled her bare shoulders. Stevyn Strongbow was not a selfish lover. He would take his time in pleasuring this woman, no matter that in dallying with the sheriff's future daughter-in-law, he was flirting with death.

They submerged themselves shoulder deep in the herb-scented bath, Stevyn with his back pressed against the rim of the tub, Camilla facing him with her legs wrapped around his waist.

Though Stevyn would have liked so dearly to plunge himself inside her, he tamped down the urge to do so. Positioning her on his lap, painfully aware of the warmth that straddled his arousal, he gazed hungrily at her lovely full breasts, glistening with warm water and perspiration.

"Sir," she whispered, leaning forward to press her nipple to his lips.

The movement brought Stevyn to the edge of his desire. Gently, he clasped Camilla's breast, kneading the soft globe with his fingers, sucking greedily from her. Something primal burst within him, robbing him of his control. For an instant, Stevyn knew nothing except the sensation of sucking and nibbling and licking Camilla's breast. His entire body throbbed with desire. He couldn't get enough of her, couldn't tear his lips from the breast she offered him, couldn't cease sucking her hard little nipple. He needed her, every inch of her, every drop of her. His urge to consume spiraled toward a powerful eruption.

He felt her fingers grappling the hair at his nape, felt her breathing quicken and her legs wrap tightly around his waist. Stevyn heard the deep guttural sounds of his own arousal and the shallow pants of Camilla's answering desire. Greedily, he tasted first one breast, then the other.

As Camilla's hands cradled his head, her body rocked rhythmically against his. Her lips pressed hotly against his brow, his temple, the top of his head. He ached for release, ached to be consumed by her, swallowed up by her. If Stevyn could have crawled into Camilla at that moment, he would have.

Her strangled voice, her breathy whisper at his ear, brought him back to reality. "Oh, Stevyn . . . I cannot hold back. . . ."

Struggling to delay his own release, Stevyn met the woman's gaze. Her eyes flickered as she tried to meet his stare, but Camilla was past the point of no return and it was her desire, now, not her mind, that controlled her. Obligingly, Stevyn slid his hands beneath the water, and found the tiny nub of flesh between her legs.

The heat that slicked his fingertips excited him to near frenzy. He wanted desperately to sheathe himself inside her. But, Stevyn's fear of producing a child was nearly as strong as his fear of being found naked with the sheriff's future daughter-in-law. Whether leg-shackled by a woman, or disemboweled by Godric, it was all the same: A lifetime of punishment was too steep a price to pay for a moment of pleasure.

Camilla's excitement made her bold. She bounced on Stevyn's lap, splashing water over the side of the tub. Her fingers wrapped around his hard shaft, and she moved her hand up and down the length of it, stroking him to a blinding plateau of pleasure-pain.

Groaning, Stevyn quickened the movement of his finger inside her. His knowledge of women's bodies served him well, and as he angled his finger toward Camilla's belly button, she squirmed with unabashed delight, crying out, and bucking against the heel of his hand.

The pace of her desire accelerated, galloping wildly toward fulfillment. Sensing that she was on the brink of release, Stevyn plunged his finger deeper inside her, touching her the way he now knew she liked to be touched.

Her cry was one of shock and relief and unmitigated pleasure. Camilla clutched Stevyn's shoulders, buried her face in the crook of his neck, and—giving a low moan that made the heaviness in Stevyn's groin nearly unbearable—shuddered against his embrace.

Behind him, Daisy whined and slapped her tail against the floor. *Poor beast,* Stevyn thought. But he knew how she felt. Unrequited lust was a painful thing.

His fingers slipped gently from Camilla's body, and for a long while afterward, Stevyn held her. When at last her shivering ceased and her breathing returned to normal, Stevyn stroked her hair and kissed the top of her head. His own body remained molten with desire, but control had returned to him, and, in a strange sense, he found a great degree of satisfaction in Camilla's release.

Sighing, she slid off his lap and dipped her shoulders beneath the water. From the opposite side of the tub, she stared at him, her expression a girlish mixture of embarrassment and flirtation. "I did not intend—"

Stevyn interjected as her voice faded. "I did not intend it, either."

"I suppose after this afternoon, you felt the need to prove yourself."

"To redeem myself, perhaps." He chuckled, but when he saw the look of gravity on her face, his smile faded. "I do not regret what we have done."

"Men never do." Camilla turned her head.

"Are you crying?" A woman's physical release was often accompanied by an emotional burst of tears, Stevyn knew that. But, this appeared to be more than a simple explosion of pent-up feelings. As he watched her and waited for her answer, the silence between them grew more complicated.

Stevyn hated it when women cried; he knew Camilla's pain required a response, but he didn't know what to do to make her feel better. How could he, when he had no idea what had caused her upset? Would she push him away if he moved toward her? Uncertain of the correct reaction he sat immobilized.

"Are you angry with me for pulling you into the tub?" he asked, at length.

When she shook her head, strands of blond

hair fell loose from the plaited buns above her ears. Suddenly, Camilla looked more a little girl than the sexy woman Stevyn had held in his arms a moment earlier.

"You didn't force me," she whispered.

He pushed off from the side of the tub, and glided toward her. She shivered when he dashed a tear from her face with his fingertips. Was she recoiling from him? Did she regret the intimacy they'd shared?

"Then tell me why you are crying." His voice was harsher than he intended, but Camilla's reaction to their shared passion was inexplicable. She was hardly a green girl, and he hadn't taken advantage of her. She'd come willingly into the tub and she'd come willingly into his embrace. And, unless he was sorely mistaken, she'd taken pleasure from their lovemaking. Stevyn thought she would have even welcomed him into her body, and, were he not so obsessive about preventing an unwanted pregnancy, he would have gladly put her out of her misery.

Had he misjudged her so? Had he inflicted pain upon this woman, instead of pleasure? Was he such a cad that he had misinterpreted her acquiescence as desire, when in fact she was repulsed by him?

With a harsh sigh, he retreated and stared at her from the opposite side of the tub. "If you do not wish to tell me why you are crying, there is very little I can do to put this situation to rights."

Her chin quivered and her lashes fluttered on tear-stained cheeks. Slowly, she turned her head and met his gaze. In a watery voice, she answered, "You know that I am engaged to be married to Risby, Godric's son. Yet, you trifle with my emotions."

Inwardly, Stevyn cringed. This was just the sort of conversation he sought to avoid. He supposed she would next want to discuss their *relationship*. Well, they had no relationship. And they *would* have no relationship. Because Stevyn didn't want one. Not now. Not in the future. Never again.

"Apparently, my lady, I made a mistake by allowing you into my chamber. But it was you who invited yourself into my room after you saw I was preparing for a bath. You could have departed. No one forced you to cross that floor."

Her eyes flashed. "Are you suggesting that it was I who seduced you, sir?"

"I am suggesting that you are a woman of passion, a woman whose physical needs were as strong and as urgent as mine were tonight. You wanted something from me, and I gave it to you. There is no shame in that. For either one of us. I will not be chastised for having touched you, my lady. I don't know what your motivation is for placing the blame on me—"

"Placing the blame on you?" Camilla's eyes were dry, but round and full of disbelief. She half rose from the water, but realizing her nakedness, quickly submerged herself again, so that the water's surface nearly met her chin. "If you are not to blame, then who is? Sir, if you think to brand me a wanton, then I suggest you reconsider your remark. This is Godric's castle, after all, and I am to be his daughter. If I tell him you took advantage of me, whom do you think he will believe?"

Her suggestion angered Stevyn. "Is that a threat? Do you feel such remorse at your actions that you would turn and accuse me of molesting you?"

"I feel no remorse. I have nothing to be ashamed of. I came here to offer you herbs for your bath. 'Twas an innocent gesture . . . and you . . . you seduced me!"

With a harsh burst of laughter, Stevyn stood. As he stepped over the side, water sloshed violently from the tub. He grabbed a coarse linen towel and, wrapping it around his waist, turned to look at Camilla. She stood also, turning her body from him as if to hide her nudity.

"Here. Cover yourself." He tossed her a towel.

With her back to him, she quickly rubbed her skin dry, then threw on her clothes. He lay on the four-poster bed while she wordlessly slipped on her leather shoes and adjusted her girdle. The tense quiet in the chamber was as prickly as a thornbush, and Stevyn found himself eager for Camilla's departure. She was a typical conniving woman, he tried to tell himself, hungry for a man's touch, but unwilling to admit she wanted it. He'd be lucky if she didn't whine to Godric that he'd tried to rape her. He'd be lucky if his head was still connected to his shoulders by tomorrow's morn.

At the foot of the bed, she stood and stared at him. Her perfectly shaped lips were downturned, the bottom one puffed out in a girlish pout. If he weren't so angry with her, he'd have wanted to kiss that luscious little mouth.

She propped her hands on her hips. "I could have you thrown in the dungeon, you know. Just one word from me, and Godric would gladly do it."

"No trial?" Stevyn chuckled without mirth. Camilla's suggestion was surely a perversion of justice, but he had no doubt that she told the truth. There was, of course, no justice in England's legal system, indeed, no justice in the world. She'd merely reminded him of what he knew so well.

But, her reminder triggered an anger inside him, an anger that was so old and so firmly entrenched in his soul, that if Camilla had realized the strength of it, and the fury she was about to unleash, she'd have fled out the door.

Instead, she unwittingly persisted in probing the reaches of his bitterness. "You've already offended the sheriff by suggesting Barnabas is trafficking in illegal relics. If he thinks you have offended my virtue, he will not hesitate to mete out the proper punishment. Justice will prevail. That's what Godric always says."

"Ah, the proper punishment. I wonder, what do you really know about justice, dear girl."

"More than you can imagine, sir."

He laughed outright this time. She was nothing more than a silly girl. He'd been as wrong to trust Lady Camilla as he'd been to trust Sir Alfred those many years ago. Alfred, the man whose life he'd spared on the field of honor. Stevyn shuddered at the thought of the old man, left for dead in his bed, his life's force draining out of him. It was Stevyn's fault the old man had died in such a heinous fashion. Just as it was Stevyn's fault another woman had been raped and killed by Alfred's client.

But, Alfred had left a clue to the identity of his murderer, a tiny locket that opened to reveal a lock of Christ's hair. If Stevyn found another such forgery at Wickingham Castle, then he would find Alfred's murderer. And when he did, he would act as judge, jury and executioner in exacting justice.

"Justice?" he whispered. "Before I was appointed to the king's bench, gel, I was a paid champion, a fighter hired by litigants to win their causes, to battle for their freedom from punishment. Do you know what that means?"

She hugged herself tightly. "Trial by combat. I have heard tell of it, though Godric does not favor that sort of thing."

" 'Tis a bloody path to justice, true enough. But, for those who believe the mighty are righteous and that truth will always win out, 'tis a sporting way to decide a man's innocence or guilt."

"You were paid to fight?" A slight shudder wracked her shoulders. Paid champions were known for their ferocity, their blood thirst and their cunning.

"Aye." He swallowed hard, but the knot in his throat merely lodged itself in his chest. The image of Alfred on the battlefield was as painful to him as the one of Alfred dying in his bed. Badly wounded, Alfred had begged for mercy, and Stevyn had foolishly given it. Given mercy to a combatant who fought on behalf of a murdering rapist. Given mercy, ultimately, to the murderer himself.

So that the fiend could murder and rape again.

"You should go now," Stevyn said, his voice as rough as gravel. But, she remained at the foot of the bed, staring at him with her righteous little expression of moral superiority. Well, perhaps she was morally superior, he thought. She would have to be. He'd been bereft of morals for years, ever since his misjudgment had precipitated a horrendous miscarriage of justice. Even a harlot was morally superior to him.

But, be that as it may, he would not allow another travesty of justice to occur on his watch. Not if he could help it. He would not let his emotions or his pity interfere with his intellect ever again. If there was a job to be done, he would do it. Never mind who got trampled in the process. Never mind who was offended. Never mind what pretty little woman got her feelings hurt because he dallied with her body, but refused to give away his heart.

Camilla's voice drew him back to the present. "Do you have nothing else to say to me?"

"What would you have me say, woman? I have done nothing to offend you. If you want to report this incident, with your own embellishment, to Godric, then go ahead. Perhaps he will throw me in the dungeon. Perhaps he will put an arrow through my heart. I care not."

She stared at him a moment longer, her lips slightly parted. "You're not afraid of Godric?" she said quietly, at length.

He threw his arms over his face, shutting out the dim light of the candlelit chamber, shutting out the sight of Camilla's lovely face. "No, I do not fear Godric." For God's sake, he had more to fear than a power-hungry sheriff. He had his own demons to worry about, and they were far more ferocious than Godric could ever hope to be. Stevyn's demons were like fire-breathing dragons that lived inside his head, invisible monsters he fought each time he closed his eyes.

"Well, then, may God be with you, sir. For you have tweaked the nose of a giant."

"Godric is a giant in these parts?" Stevyn peeked at her from beneath his arms. "I find that amusing, gel."

A worried frown, then a flash of anger, marred her pretty features. "Reckless man! You storm into Wickingham Castle like a cyclone, then dare to announce you are investigating Barnabas, one of the most respected men in this shire. And to make matters worse, you have the audacity to trifle with Godric's future daughter-in-law!"

"If it is so important to you that I be blamed as the aggressor in our encounter, then I will confess my crime in the morn." Stevyn grinned, but his mockery was pure theater. He wouldn't allow Camilla to think their lovemaking meant anything to him. In London, he made it a practice to impress upon his lovers that he was not interested in marriage. Sir Stevyn Strongbow might be a legendary lover, but he did not want to be depended upon, leaned upon or loved too dearly. That sort of intimacy was far more threatening to him than Godric's animosity.

She stared at him through narrowed eyes. "If you tell a soul what happened in here this night, I shall . . . I shall . . ."

"You shall what, sweetling? Kill me?" Stevyn sneered. "So I now have your wrath to fear as well as Godric's?"

"I pray that you are prepared for the consequences of your reckless actions," she bit out, turning on her heel.

Stevyn's smile vanished, and an overwhelming coldness gripped his bones as Camilla crossed the threshold.

But, before she pulled the heavy wooden door shut behind her, she paused and looked back at him. "And I hope you don't regard my indiscretion as a measure of my esteem for you, sir. Because what happened here tonight will never happen again."

"You may change your mind. And if you do,

my door is always open to you, my lady."

For a moment, she stared coldly at him. Then, she slammed the door shut with such force that Daisy whimpered, scrambled to her feet and shuffled to the side of Stevyn's bed.

"Crawl in, old girl, and sleep beside me. You are the only woman I'll ever trust in my bed. And if I were wise, the only one I would allow in it."

Daisy got into bed, trampling the counterpane and making several circles on the mattress before she finally settled down. As she slept, she snuggled closer to Stevyn, until she nearly pushed him off the bed. He gave the dog a shove and turned on his side, staring at the wall with a blankness born of hurt and anger.

Camilla would do well to hate him, he thought. At the very least, she should realize what the limitations of caring about him were. He had no intentions of loving her, and never would. If she expected anything more from him than physical pleasure, she would be mightily disappointed. If she expected him to love her, she was a naive little mooncalf.

He wouldn't mind enjoying more bed play with her, though. Lady Camilla was sweet and innocent, if not virginal. Pleasuring such a repressed little minx was a reward in itself. Camilla clearly needed the physical release brought by lovemaking as much as he did. God, but he was irritable when deprived of it!

Moreover, if Camilla was engaged to Risby, she couldn't expect Stevyn to make any sort of emotional investment in her. Their relationship, *if* she returned to his bedchamber, would be based on a mutual need for physical pleasure. There was nothing wrong with a purely physical relationship. It was healthy. And it was necessary if he meant to keep his mind focused on his work.

After several sleepless hours, Stevyn got out of bed. Daisy lifted her head and sighed as he returned to his desk. The paper and ink that awaited him, the sheaf of parchment letters stowed in his leather valise and the thick journals he so painstakingly kept, soothed him. Stevyn could always lose himself in work. If he had a mission, a job, a task to accomplish, then he had something to focus on rather than his guilt and his loneliness.

Taking up his quill, Stevyn dipped the tip in a small jar of ink and scratched out the day's events. Chronicling the happenings of his stay at Wickingham Castle would assist him in organizing his thoughts. Noting every observation, marking every detail brought to his attention, would ultimately aid him in his investigation of Barnabas.

Hunched over his desk, he wrote until his shoulders ached and his vision blurred. As dawn broke, he stumbled back to his bed. Drained, he fell asleep the moment his head hit the bolster. He slept fitfully though. While he'd consciously banished Camilla from his thoughts, she slipped inside his imaginings on a dream.

A scant hour later, he awoke, more restless than he'd been the night before. Rubbing sleep from his eyes, it occurred to him that tweaking Godric's nose might be tantamount to committing suicide by sheriff. But, staying away from Camilla was going to be slow torture, more savage a punishment than anything an executioner could inflict upon him.

Tossing off the counterpane, Stevyn's senses

came alert. Something was wrong. Sitting on the edge of the bed, he looked around.

"Daisy?"

There was no answering whuffle or growl, no responding thump of her huge tail. Lunging to his feet, Stevyn scanned the guest bedchamber. Daisy was nowhere to be seen. But, the door to the corridor was open and the shriek that sounded from above stairs gave him a right good clue as to where she had gone.

Chapter Four

Having been awake most of the night, fretting about Sir Stevyn and the impossible mission Godric had assigned her, Camilla slept straight through morning devotions and well past the first meal of the day. Her mind ached from the threat posed by Sir Stevyn's presence in the castle, and her body ached from . . . well, her body ached in places she had forgotten existed.

As sunlight filtered in through her window, Camilla rolled to her back and flung one arm over her eyes. Remembering the events of the night before brought an unbidden heat to her cheeks. Stevyn's skill at pleasuring a woman left her amazed and bewildered. Not only had he touched the most intimate parts of her body, he also seemed capable of reading her thoughts. It was as if he had seen right through her, recognized her inhibitions and fears, then stripped her naked of them.

"But, that is ludicrous, Bramble." Camilla's foot nudged the hound's head. With a heavy sigh, the dog rearranged himself amid the covers at the foot of the bed. "Men do not care what women feel. Men care only about their own pleasure. Barnabas has said as much in his sermons."

Bramble answered with a yawn and a stretch, followed shortly by the soothing sounds of his snores.

Camilla lay awake trying to make sense of the night before. The sensitivity Sir Stevyn had shown confused her. Men were not expected to care whether their bed partners were satisfied; women were not supposed to like lovemaking. Yet, Stevyn seemed to know more about what Camilla liked than she did. He anticipated what excited her, and pleasured her without demanding anything from her. He took pleasure in *her* pleasure.

Perhaps that was what Camilla found so confusing. She wasn't accustomed to such dealings with men. Her experiences with men had always involved some bartering. Wasn't that how she ended up in Wickingham Castle? No man had ever done anything for her, or shown her an ounce of affection, without expecting a little piece of her soul in return.

She hadn't any reference point from which to judge her own reaction to Stevyn's lovemaking abilities. Her short marriage to Gavin McGavin evoked memories of quick, sweaty rutting carried on in the dark beneath the coverlets. Camilla had been a dutiful wife, but far from enthusiastic in her physical responses. As a widow, she disregarded, even *denied* her needs. But, Sir Stevyn, with his brooding intensity and deep, velvety voice, had awakened a bud of desire in her. And Camilla wasn't at all certain she liked that.

The mere thought of him warmed her flesh. A shiver rippled up her spine as she recalled their lovemaking the night before. Shaking her head, she attempted to banish him from her thoughts, so she could pull herself from bed and face the day.

At her vanity, she sat before a polished glass and ran a comb through her hair. Behind her, Bramble padded about the rushes, sniffing and whuffling, eager to get outside. Dropping her tunic over her head and belting her girdle, Camilla watched him paw at the door. His unusual agitation wasn't entirely surprising. After all, the dog was amazingly attuned to Camilla's moods, and she, too, felt a sudden compelling urge to escape the castle confines. She opened the door and he ran ahead, bounding down the stairs. By the time she made it to the Great Hall, he was yelping for his release.

Their routine was set. While Bramble enjoyed his morning constitution in the inner bailey, Camilla visited the kitchens. There, she found Hilda and Bertha awaiting her descent and the morning's orders. The servant women filled a tub with hot water, and Camilla enjoyed a quick half-bath behind the screen in the corner. Then, she returned to the hall, opened the door and called for Bramble. When the hound heard his name, he turned and made for the castle keep, flew through the door, up the steps and into Camilla's bedchamber.

She followed slowly, ascending the steps with a slice of hard bread in one hand, her skirts clutched in the other. Entering her bedchamber, she shrieked.

In the middle of the room, locked together in what appeared an impossibly awkward mating position, Bramble and Daisy gave vent to their animal impulses.

"Merde!" Camilla dropped her bread and lunged toward the dogs.

But, strong hands grasped her upper arms, holding her back. "Try to separate them now, and you are likely to lose a finger. Or worse."

Looking over her shoulder at Sir Stevyn, Camilla felt her stomach knot. She wasn't ready for this, for *him*. She'd spent the night, and most of the morning, attempting to make sense of what had happened between her and Stevyn. Despite Godric's fiat that she befriend Stevyn, she had hoped to avoid him during his first full day at Wickingham.

"Let me go!" She jerked her arms against his restraint, but her struggles were useless.

"I do not want to see you hurt, my lady."

"Bramble would never bite me."

Stevyn chuckled. "Well, then, Daisy might. She appears to be enjoying herself."

"Bramble, stop!"

But, the yellow hound only quickened his movements. Daisy, meanwhile, was hunkered down in a most unladylike position, ears flat, the hair on her back bristling. Her throaty growls disturbed and embarrassed Camilla even though this was far from the first time she'd seen dogs mating.

Stevyn held her snugly against his hard chest. "I strongly advise against interfering. They are locked together now. Bramble might be injured if you force an end to his lovemaking."

Camilla snorted her disdain. "That is hardly what I would term lovemaking, sir."

"Some women like that position. I have heard that it produces quite a different sensation from the traditional male-on-top position."

Camilla drew in a sharp breath. "How dare you speak of such things to me? 'Tis unseemly!"

"You are not shocked. You said yourself that you have devoted yourself to working with unwed mothers. Surely, you must have heard the other women discuss such matters. They didn't get pregnant doing needlework, Camilla."

"Nice women do not discuss the details of their physical intimacies with men."

"That is not altogether true," Stevyn replied.

"And nice women do not attempt to enhance their pleasure in bed by . . . by . . ."

"Trying new positions?" His voice dropped a sultry octave. "Dear girl, you *are* repressed, aren't you?"

The trace of amusement in his voice irritated Camilla. Rankled, she shrugged out of his embrace and folded her arms across her chest. But, she did not step away from him and she made no effort to escape his nearness. "In the short time I have known you, sir, I have noticed that you have the insufferable habit of believing you know more about a woman's physical needs in bed than most women."

He stood directly behind her, his breath warm against her neck. "In the short time I have known you, my lady, I have noticed that you suffer from the unfortunate belief that women are not supposed to enjoy lovemaking."

"It is for making babies."

"Do you believe that Daisy is thinking of puppies just now?"

"Daisy is a bitch, sir. She is acting on an animal impulse, that is all. But, God gave every woman a brain and a conscience and the ability to resist temptation."

"You didn't resist it yesterday when I met you in the royal hunting fields. And you didn't resist it last night when you shared my bath with me."

"So, I sinned. I will ask God's forgiveness, and he will give it. And I will never sin again."

"Do you believe that finding pleasure with a man is always sinful? Do you truly think that God is that humorless?" Stevyn's arms encircled Camilla's waist, and he drew her closer to him.

Unable to look at Daisy and Bramble, Camilla averted her gaze. But, when she turned her head, she found that her cheek was pressed to Stevyn's shoulder, and the scent of his body, uncommonly clean and leathery, filled her senses.

"I believe that you would be wise, sir, to release me," she managed to get out, despite the fluttering of her heart. "I told you last night, and I will tell you again, I want no part of your seductive games. I am engaged to Risby, Godric's son, and I intend to remain true to him."

Stevyn nuzzled her neck. "Good. You keep your heart true to Risby. I am more interested in other parts of your body."

"What are you doing?"

"What am I doing?" Stevyn's hands roved from the flat of her belly over her rib cage to cup her tingling breasts. "I am making love to you. God, but you are beautiful!"

He stroked her nipples, softly at first, then harder.

A hot blast of pleasure shot through her. Stevyn's teasing aroused an ache that made her weak. Leaning back, Camilla clutched Stevyn's muscular biceps for support.

She was aware only of Stevyn's hands on her body and his lips against her neck. Every nerve she possessed sang beneath his touch, and Camilla experienced an insatiable hunger for the pleasure he offered. Before yesterday she had not even imagined her body could have such longings. She simply hadn't known that men existed who were able or even willing to make a woman feel so good. She had never heard tell of a man so knowledgeable in the art of lovemaking.

His breathing grew ragged and his manhood hardened against the small of her back. Turning in his arms, Camilla faced him, lifted her face to his and wound her arms around his neck.

Suddenly, his gaze went black as midnight. Camilla shivered beneath the intensity of Stevyn's expression; his features took on a sort of drunken ferocity. He kissed her savagely, then gently, then savagely again, his hands cradling her head, his palms framing her face. Then, he pressed his forehead against hers, squeezed his eyes shut and swallowed hard.

She thought he was trying to compose himself or to rein in his aggressive impulses. But, then he pressed his lips against her ear and whispered something so shockingly intimate she nearly collapsed in his arms.

"No!" She drew back, tossing her head. " 'Tis wrong to say such things! Your mouth is filthy, Stevyn! I am a lady. . . . You cannot speak to me in such a manner!"

He held her face in his hands, staring at her. "Why? It is true, everything I have said. I want you that way. . . ."

"It isn't right," Camilla practically hissed.

"You want it too—"

"No!" But she did, and there was no sense denying it. "I may want it, too. But, I am not going to betray my promise to Godric and Risby. I must be pure when Risby returns from France."

"You are not pure *now*," Stevyn drawled. "Your thoughts are not pure. I know you, Camilla. Twice now, I have touched you intimately. You *liked* it."

He had a point. "Well, then, I must be . . . careful. I must be careful to avoid temptation. I must be careful to maintain the dignity of my position in this castle. I must be careful not to bring embarrassment to Godric's household."

"You must be careful not to get pregnant," Stevyn said. "I have told you before, I will be careful in that regard, too. A baby would truly complicate my life."

"A babe is more than a *complication*, Stevyn."

"I might as well tell you, Camilla, that my work is my life. I am not looking for a woman to spend the rest of my days with. I do not need, nor do I desire, to be married. I haven't the time."

"Most men *make* time for a family when they fall in love."

"I am not *most* men. I do not plan to fall in love. I am completely devoted to doing the king's work and seeing that justice is done whenever I can. The responsibility of a family would only dull my sharp edge. Stay loyal to Risby, if you must. I will not interfere with your engagement to the lucky young lordling."

She sighed, incredibly frustrated and confused. Glancing at the door, she realized she should bolt and escape this man. Not only was he devilishly tempting, with his erotic talk and sweet kisses, he was enormously selfish. His career and self-advancement came before all else. Or was he fooling himself, she wondered. After all, even the king of England found time to fall in love.

But, her body thrummed beneath his gaze, and she was unable to wrench herself free from his embrace.

He tipped her chin, and made to kiss her.

She turned her head. "No, Stevyn. You must never touch me again. It is dangerous. Godric would kill you."

"I am willing to take that risk." He kissed her neck, drawing goose bumps to her flesh. "When Risby returns, I will leave you be. Until then, we can be lovers, Camilla. No one will be the wiser if we are discreet. It will be our secret. What we do together is no one's business, including Godric's."

A tiny fist of pain hammered at Camilla's ribs. Stevyn suggested that they sleep together purely for the physical pleasure of it. Did he think that when Risby returned from France, she could pretend nothing had ever happened? Was such a thing conceivable?

A sickening disappointment washed over her. Stevyn's offer was unequivocal; he would pleasure her, but he would not love her.

Given the reality of the situation, how could she expect anything else? She was, after all, engaged to be married. She had made it clear that she intended to marry Risby. Even if Stevyn were available *emotionally*, her status at Wickingham made it impossible for her to fall in love with him. Perhaps she should just take pleasure where she found it.

Surely, God wouldn't begrudge her a little happiness.

But, recalling Barnabas's frequent sermons, Camilla amended her thoughts. The wages of sin was death, or worse . . . pregnancy. And what Stevyn offered was stolen pleasure, guilty bed sport and nothing more. She was foolish even to consider such an offer. It was insulting, demeaning and dirty.

The notion of lovemaking without love, much less marriage, instantly sobered Camilla. Though her body still throbbed, her willpower returned. Her fear of offending God gave her renewed strength. She managed to press her hands flat against Stevyn's chest and push him gently to arm's length.

"I am sorry, Sir Stevyn. But, I have made a vow to marry Risby when he returns from France. And I would be committing an egregious sin were I to indulge in physical relations with any other man. In point of fact, I should not have allowed last night—"

He held up his hand to silence her. "I will not listen to any more apologies or excuses concerning last night, or about yesterday in the fields. We cannot undo what has been done. I feel no shame or remorse for what has passed between us, and I am sorry if you do."

Camilla hung her head. "I am sorry that I threatened to tell Godric that you raped me. I didn't really mean that."

"I know."

"But, I cannot encourage you further, sir. You must not expect to share any intimacies with me. From now on, we must pretend we have never even . . . kissed each other."

As Stevyn rubbed his chin, that infuriating

look of amusement returned to his expression. "Do you believe that you can do that?"

Camilla shrugged, unable to utter a truthful answer. At length, the sounds of Bramble's pathetic whining intruded. Glancing over her shoulder, she was grateful to see that the dogs had concluded their mating ritual. Daisy, tail tucked between her legs, fled the room. Bramble, looking sheepish and tired, threw himself onto Camilla's bed and promptly went to sleep.

"Now, that is the way *most* men behave, sir," Camilla said, attempting to lighten the moment and change the subject entirely.

Quick to take the hint, Stevyn put a respectful distance between them. Sweeping his hand through his hair, he released a pent-up breath. "If that has been your experience, my lady, I feel sorry for you."

Camilla stepped back even further, suddenly eager to widen the gap between her body and Stevyn's. What had she been thinking to allow this man to handle her body, manipulate her emotions and whisper *shockingly* graphic and lascivious things into her ear?

The weakness of her own flesh embarrassed her. She *must* pray for strength to resist this new temptation that had suddenly, in the last twenty-four hours, consumed her. She *would* pray about it. Later.

But, for now, she had work to do. *God's work.* And she'd already wasted half the morning, worrying about the pleasure this man afforded her, and then permitting herself to *be* pleasured by this wicked man. Barnabas would wonder where she was. In his kind, gentle way, not knowing where she'd been or what she'd been doing, he would chastise her for putting her own needs ahead of those of the unwed mothers to whom they ministered.

"I must go now, sir. The abbot is waiting for me."

Stevyn's brows arched. "Oh? You are heading toward the sanctuary?"

"Yes." She grabbed a light cloak, threw it over her shoulders and patted her hair. Sweeping from the room, she was careful to give Stevyn's disturbing male presence a wide berth.

"Good, then. I shall go with you."

Halting, Camilla turned on the threshold. "What did you say?"

"I said, I shall go with you." A slow grin spread across his handsome face. "Did you forget why I came to Wickinghamshire in the first place, Camilla? I am here to investigate your abbot's relic-selling enterprise. Certainly, there is no use in delaying my meeting with Barnabas. Indeed, it is only fitting that you introduce me to him."

A finger of ice stroked Camilla's spine. In her moment of passion, she had forgotten why Stevyn was at Wickingham Castle. How stupid of her!

But, now she remembered.

He was there to undermine Godric's authority. He was there to poke about in business that was none of his concern. He was there to jeopardize the future operation of Barnabas's Sanctuary for Unwed Mothers.

"Come then," she said tersely. "The day is already half gone."

And, she thought, as Sir Stevyn Strongbow followed her down the steps, he was there to wreak havoc on her heart.

* * *

Stevyn emerged in the courtyard surrounding the keep, his sense of pride slightly wounded. He couldn't recall when a woman had last spurned an offer such as the one he'd made to Camilla. The ladies in London, particularly the highborn ones, clamored to get in his bed. At times, their entreaties had even been a nuisance.

But, none of that seemed to matter to Camilla this morning. She'd made a bargain with Godric and despite yesterday's transgressions apparently she meant to remain celibate until Risby returned.

For a small woman, Camilla had an amazingly brisk stride. As he scanned the inner bailey, searching for Daisy, Stevyn hastened to remain abreast of the blond-haired little minx who had piqued his ire. His breathing was harsh and shallow by the time they reached the town gate. Passing over the drawbridge and beneath the raised portcullis, he gave her a sharp look.

Her bottom lip formed a sultry pout. Her shoulders were squared, and as she walked, her hips swished provocatively. Perversely, Stevyn was both amused and slightly aroused by her show of arrogant defiance.

"I wonder if we could pause a moment to look for Daisy."

"I have no time, sir. If you wish to remain behind, feel free."

Stevyn threw one last glance over his shoulder. There was no visible sign of Daisy in the courtyard. Sighing, he crossed the bridge with Camilla, and followed her down a dirt track that bordered a low Roman wall, nearly reduced to rubble. He didn't like leaving his faithful dog behind, especially in her condition.

But, as he rounded an outcropping of leafy

trees, Steven forgot about Daisy. The sight of Barnabas's monastery, its rose-colored sandstone walls rising atop a grassy hillock, drew him up short.

It was *not* a modest operation. Falling a pace behind Camilla, Steven gaped at the fortified compound. Passing through the gates, he met the cold stares of two guards clad in blue and crimson, the same colors painted on the pennants that flapped above Godric's castle ramparts.

"I hope they are not the monks," Stevyn muttered under his breath.

Camilla nodded at the thugs and smiled. Stevyn had the distinct impression that if he hadn't been accompanied by her, the guards would have detained him, interrogated him and quite probably tortured him to within an inch of his life just for the sport of it.

Inside the walls of the monastery, he was arrested by the grandeur of the stone chapel, its rare glass windows sparkling in the sunlight, its ancient Celtic cross reaching for the heavens. A multitude of people—mostly women—moved busily about the monastery's inner courtyard. As Camilla threaded her way through the crowd, she exchanged friendly greetings with many of them.

"Well, what do you think?" she asked, pausing before the door of the largest building in the compound.

"I feel like I am in Florence," he replied. "Where are the moneylenders' stalls?"

Frowning, she pushed the door open and gestured for him to precede her.

Steven stood inside the doorway, gazing at his

surroundings. The building was one large hall, filled with cots—all occupied—that lined the walls. Scanning the chamber, Stevyn counted at least two dozen pregnant women, some resting, some moaning in the throes of their labor.

Thick tapestries on the walls blocked the noise of the outside world, and, on many occasions, Stevyn thought, muffled the screams of women in childbirth. In one corner stood a refectory table laden with frightening-looking forceps, scissors, leather straps and other accoutrements of childbirth. Sweet-smelling candles scented the air, while servant women scuttled about, cleaning chamber pots and changing sheets.

Surely, there was not another monastery, teaching hospital or university in all of England that boasted a birthing center as sophisticated as this one.

The cleanliness of the place, the fragrant freshness of the rushes on the floor and the white crispness of the counterpanes that draped the bulging bellies of the pregnant ladies were stunning. But before Stevyn was able to assimilate the meaning of his observations, a small, stoop-shouldered man with a monk's tonsure and an ingratiating smile stepped forward.

"Good day, Sir Stevyn."

"Barnabas, I presume." Stevyn bowed in deference, surprised by the man's unassuming appearance. In brown woolen tunic and blood-stained smock, the abbot was anything but ostentatious in his own person. The prosperity of his sanctuary was a curious contrast.

With her head ducked, Camilla edged around the men, and headed toward one of the beds.

"Wait, child," Barnabas said. "What has kept

you so long from the sanctuary? Was something wrong in the castle keep?"

"No, Father." Camilla froze in her tracks. Studiously avoiding Stevyn's gaze, she looked unduly discomfitted by the abbot's question. "I was not feeling well this morning. I stayed in bed longer than usual as a result of my, er . . ."

"Ah." Barnabas smiled benevolently. "You are having your menses. But, there are many women here who would gladly trade their misery for yours, Camilla. Next time you are tempted to stay in bed, you should think of that."

Her cheeks turned scarlet. "Yes, Father."

"Go quickly, now. Wynifred has been having contractions at five-minute intervals for some time now. I believe her time is soon at hand."

"Yes, Father." Camilla turned and scurried away.

"Was that necessary?" Stevyn asked when Camilla was out of earshot. "You humiliated her!"

Barnabas smiled indulgently, as if at a dimwitted child. "I have known Lady Camilla for five years, sir. I believe I know what is best for her far better than you do."

"And what sort of talk is that, asking a woman if she is having her monthlies?"

"It is the sort of talk one hears all day in this place, sir." Barnabas steepled his fingers together, like a supplicant. "Forgive us if we do not adhere to the niceties of courtly conversation, but we are running a sanctuary for unwed mothers here. We have grown accustomed to speaking openly about such things as menstruation, ovulation, conception and pregnancy."

Stevyn's skin crawled as he listened to this litany of female concerns. Feeling like a rooster who had wandered into the henhouse at egg-laying time, he shook his head in disgust. "Well, I don't want to hear about such things."

"I am surprised. I was of the distinct impression that you *liked* women," Barnabas said.

"What makes you say that?"

"Courtly manners may be beyond our grasp, but courtly gossip is quite readily within our reach. Sir Alfred was a great friend and supporter of our sanctuary, you know."

"Alfred appears to have made many friends in Wickinghamshire," Steven said thoughtfully. "But I am puzzled. Why would Sir Alfred ever have mentioned my name to you?"

"You are a justice on the king's bench, sir. You are widely respected for your opinions. And, from what Alfred said, you are widely envied for your prowess with women."

"I didn't know Alfred was such an admirer."

"He was well loved and much admired in Wickinghamshire, sir. As you will be, I hope."

"I am afraid your hopes may not be realized. I do not expect you to welcome me with open arms, Barnabas." Stevyn thought he might as well be honest with this odd little man. It had long been his belief that a man under criminal investigation was entitled to know the nature of the charges made against him. It was only fair. "The king has authorized me to look into your relic-selling practices. That is why I am here, to see whether you or any of your agents have broken the law. And, if so, to conduct a trial."

Barnabas's expression tightened almost imperceptibly. "I am a man of God, sir. I have nothing to hide."

"Does that mean I can expect your full cooperation?"

"Of course."

Stevyn didn't believe it. "Good, then. I should like to begin by asking you some questions."

"We will talk while I make my rounds, sir. There is much to do here, and I cannot afford to spend the day wagging my tongue, even with you. I am certain you understand."

"Of course." Steven followed the little man as he went from bed to bed, holding hands, patting brows and tummies, murmuring words of consolation and dispensing prayer.

A young woman whose belly was grossly distended and whose face was deathly pale grasped the abbot's hand. "Please, Father," she cried. "The monks say I will die if the babes don't come soon! You must help me!"

Barnabas bent low over her face, whispering softly. Embarrassed by the woman's pitiful cries for help, Stevyn backed away. He heard her beg for forgiveness and, assuming she wanted to make a deathbed confession, he tried not to listen. The words *intercession* and *virgin* wafted to his ears, but he attached no particular significance to them. The entire scene left him sad and depressed.

"Poor thing," Barnabas muttered as they left the woman's bedside. "I hadn't the heart to tell her, but one of her babes is already dead. Even if the other one makes it out alive, she will never survive the ordeal of childbirth."

Stevyn shuddered, unnerved by the sight of so many women in agony. He'd been on many battlefields, and in many fighting arenas, but he'd never seen as much pain and suffering as there was in Barnabas's Sanctuary.

But, not once, as they made their way around the room, did Stevyn see Barnabas offer to sell an illegal relic to any of the women lying there.

When the abbot had finished his rounds, he and Stevyn were standing in the same spot in which they had begun. "Well, sir, did you see anything today that would support a finding that I am engaged in any criminal activity?"

"I saw nothing but good works," Stevyn said. "I must admit, I am impressed by your facility. It appears that you are doing much to improve the quality of life for these wretched women."

Barnabas smiled. "Thank you. I trust that you will soon be completing your investigation. And, please, send my warmest wishes to the queen when you return to London."

It was Stevyn's turn to smile, albeit rather grimly. "Oh, I do not think I will be leaving for London any time soon, Father. You see, I have only begun my investigation. I did not expect you to hawk illegal relics to your patients while I was overseeing you. Indeed, you would have been a fool to do so."

The abbot's expression went cold. "So, you seriously intend to pursue this investigation?"

"You are a man of God. I am a servant of the king."

"You are making a mistake by delving into matters that do not concern you, sir."

"Are you threatening me?" Stevyn asked quietly.

"Of course not." The smile returned. The abbot started to say something else, but before he did, a bloodcurdling scream pierced the air.

On the other side of the room, Camilla stood beside a low cot, her tunic splattered with blood, her expression a rictus of horror. For a moment, she seemed paralyzed with fear. Then, all at once, she came to life and the sanctuary burst into activity. Monks, their arms laden with clean towels and ewers of hot water, streamed through the room like ants.

And at the top of the din was Camilla's voice, clear and strong, shouting orders, telling everyone what to do, saving another woman's life.

Chapter Five

Camilla had just leaned down to press a cool cloth on Wynifred's forehead when the pregnant woman shrieked in pain. Staring wildly at Camilla, she whispered, "Do not let me die without the abbot's intervention! My family will pay dearly!" Then, her eyes rolled back in her head and she lapsed into a deep sleep.

At first, Camilla thought the woman was having a normal contraction. But, a peek beneath the coverlet set Camilla's heart to racing.

Blood was everywhere, soaked into the thin moss-stuffed cot, streaming down Wynifred's legs and pooled beneath her buttocks. Something was dreadfully wrong. If Camilla couldn't staunch the woman's hemorrhage, Wynifred would quickly bleed to death.

Only dimly aware of Stevyn's presence in the room, Camilla began barking out instructions. There didn't seem to be enough hot water in all of Wickinghamshire to rinse the blood from Wynifred's body, but what disturbed Camilla more was that the blood kept flowing. And a close inspection of Wynifred's body revealed that the baby was nowhere close to being born.

"We'll have to take it," she said to Barnabas, grateful that Wynifred was too senseless to understand what was going on.

"We can try," the abbot replied. "But, it is risky. She might die." To one of the monks, Barnabas said, "Bring an *escrevien,* quickly!"

"A scribe?" Sir Stevyn echoed, clearly confused. "What for?"

His question emphasized his status as interloper. Camilla would have told him to get out, but Barnabas did it for her.

"This is no place for you," the abbot said mildly. "Go now, if you please."

"I will stay," Stevyn said stubbornly.

The monks surrounding the bedside tensed, and for an instant, Camilla thought they might carry out the abbot's wishes by physically removing Stevyn from the sanctuary. But, after an apparent reconsideration, Barnabas said, "All right, you can stay, sir. We cannot waste time arguing. A woman's life is at stake."

At that moment, Wynifred's eyes flickered and she fixed her gaze on Barnabas. "Please, Father, I must go to God as a virgin."

"You will." The abbot patted her hands. "Do not worry, my child, you will." Then, as Wynifred slipped into a coma, he said softly, "Someone hand me the knife."

The next half hour seemed an eternity. Barnabas made a noble effort to save Wynifred and her child, but in the end, he could save neither. As the scribe sat uselessly at the foot of the cot,

Wynifred died without regaining consciousness.

Exhausted, her clothes caked in blood, Camilla kissed the nobleman's daughter on her cold cheek. Drawing the sheet over Wynifred's head, she told the monk named Phillip to remove the corpses to the morgue in the rear of the sanctuary. There was no point in returning the two lifeless bodies to Wynifred's family. They had already explained their daughter's absence from London by telling friends and neighbors she was visiting relatives in Scotland. Now, they would complete their deception with a tale of brigands on the highway. Lady Wynifred's humiliating pregnancy and tragic death would never be made public. And in exchange, her family would make a very large donation to Barnabas's Sanctuary.

A sudden wave of revulsion washed over Camilla. That Wynifred died so young was tragic. That she was estranged from her family at the time of her death—simply because she had the misfortune to get pregnant out of wedlock—was pathetic.

"Come, child, there is much work yet to be done." Barnabas's voice, normally so soothing and calm, unnerved Camilla.

"I need to get out of here," she replied, for once unable to obey the abbot's orders.

Suddenly, her knees felt weak beneath her skirts. Looking across the cot, she met Stevyn's penetrating gaze, and shuddered at the deception she was perpetrating on him. He probably thought all the women in the sanctuary were poor peasant women with nowhere to go.

Well, some of them were. But, some were from wealthy families whose lucre paid for God's forgiveness . . . and for clean linens, food and clothing, medicines and supplies. It was Barnabas's relic-selling and dispensation franchise that kept the doors of his Sanctuary for Unwed Mothers open.

But, that was something Sir Stevyn Strongbow need never know.

Nausea gripped Camilla's stomach and fluttered in her throat. She needed fresh air. She needed to get away from the smell of pregnancy, blood and, at that moment, death. Brushing past Barnabas, she skirted the end of the cot and stumbled across the room. But she never made it to the door.

As blackness closed in on her, one strong arm closed around her waist while another hooked beneath her knees. Strangely, and despite the fact that they were on opposite sides of the law, Camilla felt absolutely safe falling senseless into Stevyn's warm embrace.

Ignoring Barnabas's instructions to place her on a cot, Stevyn carried Camilla outside and gently laid her on a soft patch of grass, shaded by an apple tree.

His bones creaked as he sat beside her, his spine pressed against the gnarled trunk. He wasn't as young as he used to be; his body was beginning to protest these grueling days without sufficient sleep. But, duty demanded that he devote every minute of his day to doing the king's work and searching for an ever elusive justice.

Studying Camilla's parted lips, he was surprised that Barnabas didn't object to his sweeping her out of the sanctuary the way he did. The little abbot had merely stared in disapproval as Stevyn scooped Camilla into his arms and stalked out. One of the monks made to follow, but Barnabas held him back.

"Let them go," the abbot said, as Stevyn crossed the threshold into fresh air.

If he could erase the previous half hour from his mind, the setting he now found himself in would be bucolic. A cool autumn breeze cooled his skin and lifted the strands of blond hair falling loose from Camilla's bun. The horizon was green hillside flush against a clear blue sky. In the distance, cattle lowed, and, overhead, birds chirped.

And, if he could pretend that the beautiful woman stretched on the ground beside him was not Barnabas's protege, Risby's fiancée and Godric's future daughter-in-law, he could fall in love with her.

If he could fall in love with *anyone,* that is.

But he couldn't. Duty demanded his complete attention and all his efforts. The law was a jealous mistress. And falling in love, if Stevyn recalled correctly, was a time-consuming endeavor. He didn't have time for home, hearth and babies at this point in his life. He had to stay focused. His duties as a justice of the king's bench prohibited him from going all soft and mushy over a woman.

But, he couldn't deny that Lady Camilla was beautiful.

She shifted restlessly, and her lashes fluttered. A tiny moan escaped her lips, but she did not rouse. Impulsively, Stevyn drew her next to him and laid her head in his lap. His coarse leggings and woolen tunic were hardly a soft cushion, and even as he tenderly stroked the side of her face, he realized he was acting more in his self-interest than hers, but he couldn't help himself. Just because he wasn't going to fall in love didn't mean he had to live his life like a monk.

Mesmerized, he traced the curve of her lips. With a sharp inhale, she closed her lips around the tip of his middle finger. A streak of fire ran up Stevyn's spine. Now was hardly the time to get aroused, but his physical response was unbidden and uncontrollable. When Camilla gently sucked his finger into the warm softness of her mouth, he leaned his head back against the tree, closed his eyes and swore softly.

Her sudden movement startled him. With a jerk, he looked down into her wide blue eyes.

She'd awakened to find herself outside the sanctuary, with her head in Stevyn's lap and his finger in her mouth. A moment of silence yawed, while Camilla, her eyes glazed and confused, stared up at him, and Stevyn's body grew harder beneath her head.

Then, her gaze still locked with his, she sank her teeth into his finger.

"Merde!" he yelped, yanking his hand back.

"Don't touch me!" She tried to sit up, but her face instantly paled, and she fell back into his lap. "Oh, God! I do not feel very well."

"You didn't have to bite me!"

Squeezing her eyes closed, she swallowed hard. Then, after a long hesitation, she looked at him. "You took advantage of me when I fainted. If Godric found out, he would do far worse to you than I did. Are you *trying* to get yourself killed, sir?"

"I did not take advantage of you. I would *never!*" Stevyn examined the row of tiny teeth marks imprinted on his flesh, then shook his throbbing finger in the air, and cursed again. "I cannot believe you bit me!"

She struggled to her elbows again, but the defiant expression on her face quickly vanished, and in its place, a queasy sickness smeared her features. Lying back on his lap, she said weakly, "Let me go, Stevyn. I do not want to be here."

"I am not stopping you from going anywhere, my lady."

"You know that I am sick. I cannot move."

"'Tis my point." He shrugged. "I thought I was doing you a favor by taking you out of that place. Barnabas would have had you go back to work immediately. I perceive that the good abbot believes resting is a sin."

Camilla pressed the back of her hand to her forehead. "Among other things."

"I do not like it that he works you so hard."

A small smile tugged at her lips. "Are you not the man who told me he was too busy to fall in love, and too focused on his career to assume the responsibility of having a wife or family?"

Hearing his words repeated back to him made Stevyn's manhood soften. He *was* too busy to fall in love, but it sounded so silly when Camilla said it. Defensively, he said, "Our situations are entirely different, my lady. I am doing the king's work."

"And I am doing God's work." She winced through her chuckle. "Which do you think is more important, sir?"

"Let us talk about something else, shall we?" Resisting the urge to gather the ashen-faced Camilla in his arms and kiss the color back into her cheeks, Stevyn said, "Where precisely does Barnabas store these relics that he sells?"

A tiny groan escaped her lips. "Oh, I don't know!"

"But, I think you do," he said. "In fact, after

witnessing the degree of familiarity between you and Barnabas, I believe you know as much about his operation as anyone."

"I know that Barnabas is a good man. He has saved many lives, sir."

"I thought only God could save lives."

His jibe evidently piqued some of the spunk back into her. Through narrowed eyes, she glared at him. "Why did you come here, Sir Stevyn? I mean, why . . . *really?* There is more to your motivation than the simple desire to do the king's work. No man is so devoted to his sovereign that he shuns marriage and happiness in favor of obeying orders. What do you want from the people of Wickinghamshire? Why don't you just leave us alone and return to London? Tell King Edward that Barnabas is a good man! He is not a criminal!"

"I came here to investigate an alleged illegal relic-selling operation. If my sources tell the truth, then your friend Barnabas is making a very handsome profit selling fraudulent relics to unwitting penitents. And Godric is protecting him, probably in exchange for a share of the ill-gotten gains."

He was angry now, too. It was none of Camilla's business why he was *really* in Wickinghamshire. She didn't know that he worked himself to the point of exhaustion because his guilt would incapacitate him if he didn't. She didn't need to know that he felt responsible for Sir Alfred's death. And she *certainly* didn't need to know that he was looking for a killer, as well as a mountebank.

"You are wasting your time," she said. "Go home."

"I always finish what I start, Camilla. I am

sorry if my investigation inconveniences you, or interferes with your tidy little life."

"Tidy little life?" She sat bolt upright, grimacing against an apparent streak of pain. But, this time she did not succumb to her discomfort by falling back into Stevyn's lap. This time, with her blue eyes snapping, Camilla unleashed a volley of barbs. "How dare you belittle me! You do not know me, nor do you understand the importance of the work I do. Do you believe that you are the only person on earth who has answered a higher calling? Do you believe your work is more important than mine?"

Though he would later regret it, Stevyn shot back with all the firepower he had. "I ask *you*, gel, is *your* work so important that the king should ignore allegations of criminal activity, which if they are true, are taking place right beneath your nose?"

"I'll say it again, Stevyn. Barnabas is helping women! If it were not for this refuge, these women would have no place to go. Their babes would be born in shame and squalor. Many of them would die at birth."

" 'Tis a noble cause, this sanctuary. I allow you that. But, that does not deter me from investigating Barnabas. If the man is innocent, he has nothing to fear. And neither do you."

"And if you find that he is involved in the commerce of illegal relic selling? What will you do then, sir?"

"If the evidence supports an indictment, I will arrest him—and all of those who have conspired with him, or helped to cover up his criminal activity. Including you, Camilla, if you are guilty of such."

She drew back, stung. "Are you threatening me, sir?"

The sudden urge to tower over her compelled Stevyn to his feet. "I am promising you that I will avenge justice, Camilla. No matter who gets hurt in the process."

She scrambled to her feet, then, brushing leaves from her hair and smoothing her blood-stained tunic. With her fists planted on her hips, she pinned a furious stare on Stevyn. "You will rue the day that you accepted this mission from King Edward! I do not understand your motives, sir, but I know one thing. Barnabas is saving lives and, if you shut down his sanctuary, you will be destroying them. If you can sleep at night with that much on your conscience, then so be it!"

With that parting shot, she wheeled around and stalked back to the sanctuary.

In the sanctuary morgue, Camilla went about the task of preparing for the dual burials of Lady Wynifred and the infant taken from her belly. As she cleansed and wrapped the bodies, a somber mood settled over her. Two deaths at once were not as uncommon as Camilla would have liked. Childbirth remained a risky endeavor, and even under the most sanitary and sophisticated conditions, it often resulted in tragedy.

Moving about the small windowless chamber, she tried to make sense of all that had happened that morning. Strangely, Lady Wynifred's serenity in death was a calming influence. Away from the bustle of the castle keep and the stressful demands of the sanctuary, Camilla could collect her thoughts. And she was relieved to have something to do with her hands. As long as she kept herself busy, she could at least pretend she wasn't consumed with thoughts of Sir Stevyn Strongbow.

A silver locket strung around Wynifred's neck caught her eyes. She had not noticed the simple piece of jewelry before. She didn't recall Wynifred having worn it during the birth. Had one of the monks slipped it around the dead woman's neck?

Camilla's fingers closed around the tiny oval of dented silver.

Barnabas's sudden appearance at her side startled her.

"I didn't hear you enter!" Gasping, she released the locket.

The abbot's mouth curved in a small smile, and the liquid in his gaze rippled. "Your thoughts are elsewhere, child." He glanced at Wynifred's partially covered body.

"I will miss her." Gently, Camilla laid the tiny baby on Wynifred's bosom. It was only fitting that mother and child be wrapped in their winding sheets together. "She was a kind woman, and she would have been an excellent mother."

"She was a very generous woman, too." Barnabas lifted Wynifred's lifeless arm, and smoothly slid a bejeweled ring from her finger. "Her family's contribution will keep our sanctuary running for another six months, Camilla."

"And after that?" Averting her gaze, Camilla removed a jar of dried rosemary from the shelf above her and began making sachets to tuck in Wynifred's shroud. She knew money was necessary to keep Barnabas's Sanctuary operational, but it made her uncomfortable to see the abbot remove jewelry from dead bodies, confiscate valuables from patients or ask them to sign over their inheritances.

It made her even more uneasy to see him sell virgin cloths to debauched women, or heavenly dispensations to unwed mothers who hovered on death's doorstep and feared crossing the threshold without a guarantee of divine forgiveness.

The abbot shrugged. "We are dependent on the kindness of our patrons, child. That is why we must rid ourselves of this pox that has visited Wickinghamshire."

Camilla's body tensed. "What pox? I have heard of no recent outbreak—"

Chuckling, he patted her arm. "No, I am referring to this justice of the king's bench who is our midst. His investigation serves no useful purpose, Camilla. He will destroy us if he can. He has made it his life's work."

"Godric won't allow that, Father."

"Not if he can help it." Barnabas turned Wynifred's ring over in his hands, frowning. "But, this Sir Stevyn is not like Sir Alfred."

The memory of Alfred brought a wistful smile to Camilla's lips. She missed the kindly old man, and was saddened to learn of his murder. Moreover, his passing had brought Sir Stevyn into her life, and at the moment, Camilla couldn't imagine feeling anything but trepidation as long as he remained in Wickinghamshire.

"You do not trust this Sir Stevyn?" she asked at length.

The abbot hesitated, as if carefully choosing his words. "He holds himself out as a good man, intent on following the letter of the king's law. It would seem that his self-proclaimed integrity is his shield against all criticism."

"Are you saying he is self-righteous?"

"Child, it is not my place to judge Sir Stevyn." Barnabas preached against being judgmental. But, the censure in his voice was unmistakable.

"What if he believes that he is doing the right thing by investigating your ministry?" Camilla asked. "What if he believes in his heart that his calling is to seek out and eradicate corruption wherever he finds it? Would he then be an evil man even if his good intentions resulted in the closing down of the sanctuary?"

"Fanatics always believe that they are right, my child."

Camilla met the abbot's gaze. "Perhaps we are the fanatics. I would do almost anything to keep this sanctuary open."

"You are anything but a fanatic, Camilla." Barnabas gave her an avuncular smile. "On the contrary, you are a very wise and perceptive woman. I see that Sir Stevyn has impressed you by his good intentions. We must, therefore, give him the benefit of the doubt. Perhaps he believes that what he does is correct in the eyes of God. But, you know *we* are right, Camilla. Look at the many lives we are saving. More importantly, look at the souls we are saving."

Harkening back to her own ill-fated pregnancy, Camilla shivered. Though she hadn't a penny to her name when Godric's men arrested her in the hunting fields five years ago, Barnabas gave her refuge. Widowed, she expelled her still-born child in the sanctuary right above her head.

It was Barnabas's intervention, in fact, that resulted in Camilla's being given amnesty from prosecution for poaching. And it was Barnabas's negotiations that culminated in her being promised in marriage to Risby, Godric's absentee son.

Barnabas was right. The work they did at the sanctuary was more important than Stevyn's investigation.

But, it was all so confusing. And the man she'd spent the last five years working with, the man she'd regarded as a paragon of virtue, suddenly was bathed in shades of gray.

"You have a great responsibility," he said quietly. "Godric has asked you to watch this man Sir Stevyn and report all that he does. You are to be Godric's eyes and ears."

"Sir Stevyn has already begun to ask me questions."

Nodding, Barnabas said, "I am not surprised. He thinks you are weak because you are a woman. But, it is *he* who is weakened by his physical urges. It is said that at Edward's court he is like a bantam cock in the henhouse. Turn that to your advantage, gel. Perhaps you can even persuade Sir Stevyn that he is wrong about me, and that his actions will only bring devastation to the sanctuary and to this county."

Heat pinched at Camilla's cheeks. Did the abbot and Godric already know that she had permitted Sir Stevyn to touch her? Feeling transparent, she turned her back and busied herself with ripping a length of cheesecloth into tiny squares. "I will do what Godric has asked me to do, Father. And I will keep myself virtuous, have no fear."

"It never occurred to me that you wouldn't. You know too well the consequences of giving in to the temptations of the flesh." Barnabas fell silent a moment, then said quietly, "You don't want to wind up like poor Lady Wynifred here."

That thought was as comforting as an arctic blast. As she jerked a twine knot around the top of a lavender sachet, Camilla's resolve hardened. Barnabas spoke the truth. Sins of the flesh resulted in tragedy. Sir Stevyn was wrong in his stubborn refusal to drop his investigation. And she owed it to herself—and to Lady Wynifred—to combat the forces of evil that threatened to shut down Barnabas's Sanctuary.

Stifling the sob in her throat, she vigorously nodded her agreement. "Sir Stevyn will not destroy us," she finally managed to whisper.

She could feel the abbot's relief and picture his satisfied smile, but Camilla could not bring herself to turn around and look at Barnabas.

"God bless you," he said as he slipped quietly out of the morgue.

As the tears slid down her cheeks, Camilla tucked a packet of herbs inside Wynifred's winding sheet. "Help me, sweet Jesus," she prayed out loud. For, she had no illusions about the strength of Sir Stevyn's masculine appeal. If her moral duty required her to stay close to him, she might as well pray for forgiveness in advance.

Alone beneath the apple tree, Stevyn watched Camilla march toward the sanctuary. Camilla's uncanny perception of his inadequacies made his gut twist. He probably *would* regret the day he accepted this assignment in Wickinghamshire. And as for being able to sleep at night, Stevyn's rest came as a result of physical and mental exhaustion, certainly not as a balm to his conscience, which could only be described as troubled, at best. Camilla had no idea how right she was about that.

Grimacing, he hoped she would never have the satisfaction of knowing. The air of moral superiority that she exuded grated on his nerves.

Unfortunately, even as he resolved to emotionally distance himself from her, he realized he wanted her. His loins throbbed for Lady Camilla, and that, coupled with his need to knock her off her high horse, was a dangerous combination.

After a while, Stevyn slowly turned and made his way back to the road. Though he had many more questions to pose to Barnabas, he hadn't the fortitude to reenter the sanctuary and face Camilla . . . or see the rows of pregnant woman, all struggling bravely through their pain.

Slowly, he followed the old Roman wall, his mind distracted by thoughts of Camilla. Though he was loath to admit it, he wished she didn't have such a low opinion of him. And that, alone, was shocking in its novelty. Outside of wanting to please a woman in bed, Sir Stevyn Strongbow hadn't cared about a female's perception of him in years.

But, something about Lady Camilla was different. She wasn't like the other women he'd bedded. Her mind worked differently.

Which meant he would have to use a different tactic to get her into his bed. Camilla would have to feel as if it were she who was in control of their relationship. She would have to want Stevyn worse than he wanted her. And she would have to be the one to take the initiative and play the seducer.

The thought of turning the tables on Camilla greatly excited Stevyn. The prospect of playing with her mind was more titillating than that if playing with her body.

He faltered only for an instant. Mental gamesmanship with a woman, by definition, required an intellectual familiarity that went far beyond carnal knowledge. Everyone's emotions were at risk, Stevyn's included. He knew he was entering dangerous and uncharted territories; he was liable to get his own heart broken. But, suddenly Stevyn was determined to shape Camilla's opinion of him. He was determined to make her want him. He was determined to maintain total control of his increasing lust for Camilla.

Truth be known, Stevyn was somewhat in awe of Camilla's abilities. Her courage was daunting. He didn't think he would ever forget the sight of her calmly and efficiently marshaling her army of monks to try to save Wynifred's life. Nor would he forget the serene grace she'd shown in the face of Godric's rudeness the night before. Or the brave recklessness with which she threw herself between Bramble and Daisy. . . .

Daisy! Loose within the castle walls, there was no telling what kind of trouble that dog was in. The thought gave Stevyn a burst of energy, doubling his pace. Instantaneously, a gust of wind ruffled his nape, and a shiver danced along his skin. At first, Stevyn thought the sensation was a physical reaction to his concern for Daisy, or, more likely, his fear that Lady Camilla was getting beneath his skin. It wasn't until he reached up to smooth his hair that he discovered a nick on his neck and blood on his fingertips.

Someone had fired a longbow, and barely missed planting an arrow in Stevyn's head.

Chapter Six

He found Godric dismounting his destrier on the jousting green. Striding past the clusters of men and horses who awaited their turn at the quintain, Stevyn shouted, "Godric! I must have a word with you!" Then, he shouldered aside the small coterie of armor-clad warriors perennially surrounding the sheriff.

One of the sheriff's knights, a ruddy-faced man in mail shirt and scarlet gambeson, withdrew a small dagger and thrust his own body in front of Godric's. "Stand back, sir! Or I will cut your entrails out!"

"Back down," grumbled Godric, giving his protector a shove. Shedding his gauntlets, the sheriff met Stevyn in the center of the tournament field.

As Stevyn and the sheriff confronted each other, a stillness fell over the curious onlookers.

"Someone tried to kill me!" Stevyn touched

the back of his neck, then displayed his blood-soaked fingertips.

"Let me see!" Grasping Stevyn's shoulder, Godric turned him half around and peered at the wound. "Where? I see nothing more life threatening than a fleabite!"

The male laughter that erupted infuriated Stevyn. But a show of anger would give the sheriff more pleasure than a lusty wench. Staring into Godric's deep-sea blue eyes, Stevyn tamed his temper and said smoothly, "My would-be assassin was a poor archer, and thus did little damage. For that, I am grateful."

The tension thickened. "What reason have you to believe an assassin aimed an arrow at you? There are many men who hunt these woods for food."

"I was under the impression that the fields surrounding Wickingham Castle were royal hunting grounds. Anyone hunting on them would require a special license issued by you. To be sure, the arrow that nicked me appears to be from your arsenal." From his belt, Steven produced the broken shaft he had found on the side of the road. A bit of crimson paint beneath the nock identified the arrow as belonging to Godric. Or to one of his men.

"Haven't you heard of poachers, sir?" Godric said. "Perhaps a starving beggar stole a quiver from my storeroom, then went in search of food, and fired an arrow at a rabbit."

"Rabbits do not stand six feet tall," Stevyn said.

Assuming a sporting air, Godric chuckled. "No, I suppose they do not. But, I do not believe anyone tried to kill you, sir. And you are not injured. So, what would you have me do about it?"

"You are the chief law enforcement official in this county," Stevyn replied. "At the very least, I would expect you to launch an investigation into the crime I have just reported to you."

Godric's eyes twinkled. "I *was* the chief law enforcement official in Wickinghamshire. That was before you arrived, though, Sir Stevyn. I believe you outrank me now. Isn't that what King Edward said? So, if you want to investigate this crime, go ahead. I do not know how you will have time, however, given your determination to brand the abbot as a villainous criminal."

Derisive chuckles rumbled through the ranks. Resistance to Stevyn's investigation was deeply embedded in the creed of Godric's liege men. "I did not come to Wickinghamshire to ruin one man," Stevyn replied. "I came here to investigate an allegation of illegal relic selling, a corrupt practice with the potential to injure and swindle countless innocent people."

"You have accused Barnabas," Godric countered. "Let us not mince words. It is the abbot whom you are investigating."

As Stevyn clamped his jaw shut, a muscle in his cheek flexed. His fists clenched at his sides, and his blood ran hot. But, now was not the time to fight. "There is a saying, Godric. *'When you are the anvil, you bear. And, when you are the hammer, you strike.'* I will not always be the anvil. One day, I will be the hammer. And you had better hope you are not within my striking distance when I am."

"Are you threatening me?" Godric asked quietly.

Stevyn held the man's gaze. "If I find evidence that anyone in this county is subverting my investigation, then I will pursue charges of obstructing the king's justice."

"You would bring charges against me?"

"If the evidence warranted it."

Godric's straight white teeth flashed. "You would bring charges against *anyone* who refused to cooperate in your investigation?"

"I would show no mercy." A split second later, Stevyn turned on his heels and strode toward the keep. The day was growing late, and Daisy remained at large somewhere within the castle walls.

"Bramble?" Camilla sensed his absence the moment she stepped inside her bedchamber. Scanning the rumpled bed covers, her pulse skittered. She should have locked the randy hound in her room, or at the very least, tethered him to a piece of furniture. The poor dog was as weak as she when it came to resisting temptation.

On the other hand, they had both been confronted with seemingly irresistible temptations. At least Bramble had his animal instincts and canine impulses to excuse his behavior. Camilla could only claim momentary insanity as an excuse for her outrageous flirtation with Sir Stevyn.

An angry shout from below stairs exploded the silence. Pivoting, Camilla flew down the steps, through the corridor and across the threshold of the guest chamber.

The scene she encountered drew her up short. Frozen, she gaped at the sight of Sir Stevyn standing in the middle of the floor, Daisy clutched in his arms. He held the big wolfhound as high off the floor as he could, turning and dodging while Bramble leaped in the air like a bouncing ball, nipping at Daisy's toes and the tip of her feathered tail. When the absurdity of the situation sank in, Camilla burst out laughing.

"You think this is funny?" Stevyn's expression was pure frustration. "Can't you do something about that rapacious hellhound of yours?"

Stifling her laughter, Camilla grabbed Bramble's collar and gave him a stout tug. With a whine and a growl, the dog relented and heeled, sitting nervously at her side.

"I don't appreciate your calling my dog names," she said staunchly. "It takes two, you know."

"Oh, does it? Are you suggesting that Daisy's physical urges are as lusty as Bramble's?"

"Of course. Bramble can't be held solely responsible for his actions. He's just doing what comes natural to him. He's a dog, after all, and Daisy is clearly in heat. Bramble can't help himself."

With a sigh, Stevyn placed Daisy on the floor, looped a length of hemp around her collar and secured her to the leg of his work desk. Turning to Camilla, he gave her a quick head-to-toe appraisal, which did nothing to calm her nerves.

She supposed, judging from his frown, that her blood-spattered tunic did nothing to pique his ardor, either. After a morning in the sanctuary, she always looked a fright. She was hardly the sort of elegant London woman Sir Stevyn was accustomed to meeting at court.

In fact, Camilla wondered why he wanted her so badly when, according to the abbot, Stevyn had beautiful ladies waiting for him in London. And in the meantime, he could have any wench in the castle to satisfy his needs. A man as handsome and virile as Stevyn would have no difficulty finding willing bedmates. So, why would he place his life in harm's way just for the pleasure of *her* company? Why would he risk angering Godric for a bit of bed sport?

The heat in his gaze scorched Camilla's nerves. She lifted her chin in a show of bravado, but her insides were mush. Sensing her nervousness, Bramble growled empathetically.

"So, Bramble can't help himself, is that it?" Stevyn drawled. "Does that logic extend to our situation? Do you think that I cannot control my impulses?"

"Stop!" Camilla knew which road this conversation was going down. "I told you that I am engaged to marry Risby and I do not intend to cheat on him before I have ever laid eyes on him!"

"If you have never laid eyes on him, I do not think it would be regarded as cheating. But, I suppose that is beside the point." Stevyn chuckled. "Upon reflection, I believe you are correct in spurning my affections, Camilla. I respect your decision. Now, if you don't mind, Daisy and I would like to be alone."

"You are dismissing me?" Taken aback, Camilla retreated a step.

He gestured toward his desk, strewn with papers and journals. "I have much work to do. And I am certain you are eager to rid yourself of those soiled clothes. You probably want to go and soak in a hot bath."

She held her breath, waiting for his invitation. His gaze was wolfish, his lips curving slyly. He wanted to invite himself into her bath. He was imagining her submerged in an oaken mazer of hot herb-scented water, her naked flesh glistening and wet, her body arching into his touch; she knew how his mind worked now.

But, he didn't utter one untoward word. Instead, he shrugged, and said, "Thank you for taking me to the sanctuary. I was most impressed. Perhaps we can meet later this evening. Despite Barnabas's admonition, my investigation is not complete, and I have some more questions for you. But, for now, I must write in my journal."

"Your journal?" she stammered, stalling for time, wondering what happened to dull Stevyn's desire for her. She pointed to his desk. "Is that your journal?"

He glanced at the leather-bound volume lying open on the worktable. "Yes. Now, if you don't mind—"

She loosened her hold on Bramble's collar. "Stay!" To her relief, the dog obeyed her command. Crossing the room, she brushed past Stevyn, absorbing the warmth of his nearness, inhaling his masculine smell. She expected him to reach for her, encircle her waist with his arm and draw her tightly to his hard chest. Instead, he clasped his hands behind his back, and watched her.

Standing beside his desk, Camilla absently ran her finger along the page of his journal. There were too many words on the page to make sense of what he'd written, at least in the quick perusal Camilla allowed herself. But she was struck by the elegance of his handwriting, the small neatly inked words that tilted to the right as if they were striving forward and the flourishing, almost feminine strokes that flowed from the crosses on his *t*'s like a crusader's standard rippling in the wind.

Her fingertips stilled on the page. There was

something amazingly erotic about touching the words Stevyn had written.

"I am afraid that journal is for my eyes only," he said, his voice as thick as honey. Moving around her, he closed the book just as she removed her fingers from the pages. "I am meticulous about recording the progress of my investigation."

Camilla's ears pricked. "You keep a diary of your activities?"

"I try to write down everything . . . conversations that I have had with witnesses, my imprcssions of their credibility, bits of evidence that I accumulate. Oftentimes a seemingly insignificant detail turns out to be an important part of the puzzle." His fingertips rested on the leather-bound journal. "I like puzzles."

An unexpected smile came to Camilla's lips. Staring at Stevyn, she saw him as a boy, full of curiosity and eagerness. "You are an unusual man, Stevyn," she said softly. "Most men regard their work as a series of battles. You think of yours as a puzzle."

"I would rather solve puzzles than kill men."

"Most men use swords or arrows to combat their enemies. You use words as your weapons."

His features softened as he looked at her, but his gaze remained intensely hot. "When I was a paid champion, I fought for justice with swords. I find that words have more meaning for me."

An unearthly quiet settled in the room. Camilla stared into Stevyn's eyes, searching for a sign of the man who'd once been a paid champion. It was hard to imagine this intelligent, gentle man wielding a bloody sword. . . .

But, perhaps it wasn't such a stretch of the imagination. Camilla watched in fascination as

Stevyn's pupils enlarged, flooding his gaze with blackness. She'd seen that transformation before. She recognized the alteration of Stevyn's mood, his departure from civility, his simmering emotion, his barely restrained violence. An erotic thrill rushed through her veins. Longing blossomed in her loins. She wanted him. She feared him. She needed him.

And he needed her, too.

Stepping forward, she lifted her face. Her gaze fastened on his lips, and her bosom strained for his touch. But, he didn't touch her.

Stepping back, he said, "You told me you were engaged to Risby, and that you intended to honor your promise to him and to Godric."

His words felt like fists pummeling her belly. "I-I thought you wanted—"

"I have had some time to think things over. I agree with you. We should not yield to the temptation of an illicit love affair. 'Tis far too risky a proposition. If Godric were to discover us, he would kill me. God only knows what he would do to you."

"That did not concern you last night."

"That was last night. Today someone tried to kill me on the road outside the castle walls. Luckily, my assassin's arrow missed its mark, but only by a hair. Next time, the shooter will aim more carefully. Godric claims he had nothing to do with the attempt on my life, but I do not believe him."

"Godric is not a killer," Camilla breathed, reeling from the double blow she'd just been dealt. Not only had Sir Stevyn rejected her, he had also accused her future father-in-law of conspiring to murder him.

Stevyn shrugged. "For your sake, I hope you

are right about Godric. But, for now, I believe you should go, Camilla. As I said, I have work to do."

Camilla didn't know what to say, and when she finally did speak, her words sounded incredibly foolish. "So . . . you no longer wish to make love with me?"

"I respect you, Camilla. You are a good Christian woman and Risby is lucky to have you as his intended bride. Upon reflection, I feel that it would be wrong of me to cuckold my host's son. 'Twould be selfish and reckless. Neither of us has anything to gain by embarking on such a dangerous course."

Swallowing hard, Camilla backed away. Her pointed slippers moved quietly through the rushes until she stood beside Bramble, her fingers digging into the scruff of his neck for support. If she didn't have him to lean on, she feared her knees would collapse.

For a moment, she stood, staring at Stevyn, half expecting him to retract his shocking words. When, after an awkward silence, it was clear his mind was made up, she squared her shoulders and met Stevyn's gaze. Humiliated, she blinked back the tears in her eyes. "I suppose you think me a silly girl, throwing myself on you one moment, declaring my virtue the next."

"I admit, you seem a bit indecisive."

"So do you, Sir Stevyn."

"I have made my decision now. And I intend to adhere to my principles," he said.

Wounded, Camilla felt the urge to strike back. Aiming for the chink in his armor, she said, "Principles? Do not make me laugh, sir! You are no more principled than a horny billy goat! You pride yourself on your ability to live without love, yet you take your pleasure where you find it. What sort of man does that? A coward, that's what!"

"I am not a coward," Stevyn said through clenched jaws.

His agitation fueled her emotions. "You may be fooling yourself, Stevyn, but you are not fooling me. You are afraid to fall in love, and so you push away any woman who might fall in love with you."

"You do not know me," he said menacingly.

"No, but I have heard tell of men like you. I would wager that in London, you prefer the married women over the unmarried ones."

"Enough!"

"I'll bet you tell them when you first meet them that you have no intention of falling in love with them. Do you drop hints about some mysterious tragedy in your past, some horrible love affair gone awry that has scarred you for life?"

"I won't listen to this!"

She let out a haughty chuckle. "That's it, isn't it, Stevyn? My, you've carved quite a niche for yourself. *The brooding knight who can never fall in love!*"

Without warning, Stevyn closed the distance between them, grasping Camilla's upper arms and staring down at her with black passion blazing in his eyes. The little shake he gave her was frightening not for the tiny pain it caused, but for the underlying threat of what Stevyn could do if his anger got the better of him.

Still, Camilla could not bridle her tongue. "You extol your own honesty because you do not lie *to* the women you lie *with*. You pat yourself on the back for all the integrity you possess. But a truly honorable man wouldn't trifle with a woman's emotions, no matter how vigorously she proclaimed her independence. Because a woman cannot lie with a man and feel nothing for him, Stevyn. And if you say that she can, then you are surely the worst liar I've ever encountered."

The veins at Stevyn's temples pulsed. "Stop. I am warning you."

"Love is not a game any more than justice is a puzzle, Stevyn. Until you learn that, you know nothing."

His fingers dug into her flesh, and he held her so tightly that her toes nearly left the ground. Peering into her eyes, he whispered harshly, "You do not realize what you have done, Camilla."

Suddenly, she was frightened. Beside her, Bramble shuffled in the rushes and growled. Pressing her palms against Stevyn's chest, Camilla pushed away. What had she done? The recklessness of her arrogant little speech appalled her. She hadn't meant to alienate Sir Stevyn completely. She wasn't supposed to make an enemy of the man.

What would Godric say now? How would Camilla monitor the movements of a man who couldn't stand the sight of her?

And why had it been so important to wound Stevyn's pride, and bring him down a notch or two? Why did she have to insult his integrity? Why did she attempt to disabuse him of the notion he was an honest man, when clearly his honesty was the one characteristic on which he prided himself?

She knew the answer. It was because she wanted to hurt Sir Stevyn as badly as he hurt her. Camilla had enough insight into her own personality to recognize that she lashed out at Stevyn because he questioned her loyalty to Barnabas, threatened her life's calling and rejected her romantic advances. He'd insulted her more gravely and on more levels than any man ever had, and she was determined to get even.

But, after all her angry venting, her clever barbs and vitriolic indictment, all she'd really accomplished was the estrangement of a man she'd been instructed to befriend.

His rasping breath was hot on her neck. The violence simmering beneath the surface of his anger could boil over any second. What had Camilla been thinking, to have infuriated Sir Stevyn so? With a shudder, she wrenched herself from his embrace. The quicker she got out of his sight, the better. She'd be lucky if she escaped before he exploded.

Tugging Bramble by the collar, she beat a hasty retreat.

"That's right! Run away!" The menace in his voice was breathtaking. "Who is the coward now?"

She was, and she wasn't afraid to admit it. Sir Stevyn's fury filled the room like a storm cloud, repelling her even as it raised the hairs on the back of her neck. As she stumbled over the threshold, he came after her.

His movements were lightning quick. Camilla tripped over her gown and fell out the door, pulling Bramble with her. The hound's hair bristled and his lips pulled back in an ugly snarl. Straining to lunge at Stevyn, Bramble nearly pulled Camilla back into the room.

She scrambled to her knees, stood and struggled against the forward drag of her dog. Digging in her heels, she leaned back, pulling against Bramble's weight until she tilted precariously. Then, Stevyn slammed shut the door, Bramble went still and she toppled over, landing hard on her derriere.

When Bramble realized he'd been shut out, he trampled Camilla's skirts, licking her cheek and whining.

Stroking his ears, Camilla pressed her cheek against his soft yellow fur and sighed her relief. After a moment, a bitter sob racked her body and she pressed her face against Bramble's neck to muffle the sound of her crying. The last thing she wanted was for Stevyn to hear her cry. He had called her a coward and he was right. But, she didn't want him to know that what she truly feared was running him off.

She didn't want him to know how upset she was at the thought that he might hate her.

And she certainly didn't want him to know how wounded she was by his rejection.

Work would take his mind off Camilla. At his desk, head aching, Stevyn focused on his investigation. In his journal, he noted his impressions of the sanctuary. Superbly outfitted and sparkling clean, it was a maternity hospital unmatched in its modernity. If his own wife were pregnant, he would, without hesitation, commit her to the care of Barnabas and his highly trained staff of monks for her lying-in period.

Not that he ever intended to have a wife, much less a pregnant one.

Stevyn recorded the details of his conversation with Barnabas, then sat for a moment, idly chewing the end of his quill pen. The abbot's request for an *escrevien* during Wynifred's ordeal was strange. He found a loose sheet of parchment among his papers, and quickly scribbled a note. He asked the scribe to come to him for an interview. He wanted to know what role the *escrevien* fulfilled in Barnabas's operation.

As he sprinkled sand over his letter, he stood. His back and shoulders ached; every muscle in his body felt tense and knotted. Reaching above his head, Stevyn yawned and stretched. Then, he folded the letter, sealed it and tucked it in his belt.

At his feet, Daisy scrambled to a standing position and shook herself.

"Poor old girl," Stevyn said, bending down to unleash her from the desk leg. "You're going to be needing a home for unwed mothers yourself in a few months."

The dog trotted at his side as he descended the stairwell and skirted the Great Hall, already filling with weary knights and harried serving girls. Stevyn and Daisy passed behind the screens and through the corridor that led to the kitchen. There, Stevyn found an older woman willing to give Daisy a trencher of meaty bones and offal.

"Thank you, ma'am." Stevyn reached to take the platter from her hands.

But, she jerked the food away. "I think the beast had better eat outside," she said, heading toward the door that led to the rear courtyard and the herb gardens.

Intrigued, Stevyn had no choice but to follow the woman. Outside, the early evening contained a chill wind. But, the cozy sound of cowbells in the meadow warmed his heart while the piquant odor of the chicken coop, just meters away, tickled his nose. The woman barely lowered the food to the ground before Daisy attacked it.

"She seems to like me cookin'." In the dim glow of twilight, the woman's smile revealed a lifetime of poor dental hygiene. "I threw in a quarter of a mutton shoulder when the cook wasn't lookin'."

"That was very kind of you. Is that why you didn't want Daisy to eat in the kitchen? Were you afraid Cook might see what you had done?"

The woman's gray and frizzled nimbus bobbed nervously. "No, sir, not exactly. Might I ask ye a question, sir?" She wrung the end of her apron as if it were a wet washcloth.

"Of course. What troubles you, woman?"

"I hear the king sent you to Wickinghamshire to investigate Barnabas's Sanctuary."

"Yes. Specifically, the abbot's relic-selling business. Do you know anything about it?"

She looked ashamed, as if she had disappointed him. "Wouldn't matter if I did. Them sorts of things are dear and cost more money than I could ever hope to have."

"You did not answer my question."

Hilda's shoulders sagged. "I'm a poor woman, sir. If it weren't for the abbot, me dear daughter wouldn't have had a place to go when that rascal got her with child."

"You daughter was in the sanctuary?"

" 'Twas nearly seven years ago, now, before Lady Camilla came. When Sir Alfred was the circuit judge of Wickinghamshire. Her name is Teresa-Marie. My daughter, that is. You might have seen her, she's working the rotisserie this night."

The blast of a hunting horn startled them both. Overhead, in the turreted watchtower that rose above the castle ramparts, a lookout sounded his alarm.

"Someone is approaching the castle gates," Stevyn remarked.

The woman made the sign of the cross and muttered something Stevyn couldn't hear. She pivoted, and would have run back to the kitchen had he not grasped her bony arm and held her still.

"Have you something to tell me, ma'am? Something that has to do with my investigation?"

"Nothing, I suppose." She gave him a watery, apologetic smile. "I shouldna troubled ye, sir. I'm awfully sorry. Please don't tell anyone I spoke to ye."

"No, of course not." Stevyn released her, and she scurried back to the kitchens. For an instant, he considered pursuing her; his instincts told him he should. But, another horn blast from the watchtower startled him from his musings. The creak of the portcullis and the thunder of horses' hooves in the inner bailey announced the arrival of an important party. "Come, Daisy." Tapping his dog on the head, he made his way down the corridor and to the front steps of the castle keep.

There, a half dozen men dressed in Godric's colors, and looking as if they'd been riding for days, slid from their mounts and stamped their dusty boots. Men swarmed from the hall and surrounded them, clapping their backs and thrusting mugs of ale into their hands. Clearly, this party was welcome at Wickingham Castle, though Stevyn had no idea who they were.

Turning, he gazed back toward the kitchen. Hilda's furtive effort to confide in him still niggled at his suspicions. Perhaps, the old woman knew something material to his investigation. He would have to visit her some place where they could speak privately and candidly. Tomorrow morning, he would make arrangements to interview her again. Then, he would find out what poor Hilda and her daughter knew about Barnabas's Sanctuary for Unwed Mothers.

"Looking for someone?"

Stevyn was surprised to find Frederick the bailiff at his elbow. The man's smile revealed a lack of grooming, his solicitousness belied explanation.

"No, thank you," Stevyn replied. "I am learning my way around quite well."

With a shrug, the bailiff fell into step with a group of men entering the hall. Stevyn looked after him, a dart of wariness pricking at his neck.

He left the castle grounds through the northern gate, and spent the next half hour in the sanctuary, searching for the scribe who'd been summoned to Lady Wynifred's bedside by Barnabas.

"Do you mean Hotard? Look in the chapel, sir," advised one monk.

Another said, "I believe I last saw Hotard in the manuscript room, sharpening his quills."

But, Hotard was nowhere to be found. Frustrated, Stevyn strode through the sanctuary, ill at ease among a roomful of women all suffering to bring life into the world. In the tiny vestibule was an elderly stoop-shouldered monk staring at him through narrowed eyes. Stevyn had the distinct impression the man wanted him to leave.

"Do you know where Hotard can be found?" he asked.

The monk spoke with a pronounced lisp. "His duties are finished for the day. He has most likely gone home."

"Do you know where he lives?"

"In the village. You follow the south road from the castle, as if you were going to London."

"When will he return?" persisted Stevyn.

"He will return on the morrow. Is there something you wish to discuss with Hotard? Perhaps I can be of some assistance."

Mentally, Stevyn ticked off his options. At last, he withdrew his letter and handed it to the monk. "Will you see that he receives this? 'Tis a very important summons regarding the investigation I am conducting on behalf of the king's bench."

Nodding, the monk said solemnly, "Then I shall personally see that your letter reaches the proper person."

"Thank you." With a shudder, Stevyn stepped into the brisk night air. Leaving the monastery grounds, he had the feeling that a bug had crawled up the leg of his breeches and into his small clothes. He could not say why, but something about that elderly monk disturbed him.

Chapter Seven

In her bedchamber, Camilla peeled off her nasty, blood-encrusted clothes and threw herself on the bed. Bramble, exhausted from the day's excitement, stretched out on the floor and fell asleep in a trice. His snoring calmed her nerves, but nothing alleviated the sharp pain in her breast. Camilla had committed an egregious mistake.

She'd spoken in anger and made an enemy of a man she genuinely admired. That Stevyn's mission was to destroy her way of life did not detract from his personal integrity; she meant to debate that theological conundrum more thoroughly with Barnabas. That Stevyn didn't want to share his bed with her didn't make him loathsome or hypocritical. And, the fact that he was hell-bent on ruining the good names and reputations of the two most important men in her life, Barnabas and Godric, didn't make him a bad person.

Or did it?

Who was good, and who was bad?

"Merde!" Camilla pounded her fists into her mattress. Perhaps she was wrong to blur the distinctions between good and evil, right and wrong. But, Camilla simply couldn't make herself believe that Barnabas was a criminal because he financed the women's sanctuary with donations made by wealthy families in exchange for virgin clothes or dispensations. Barnabas saved more lives than anyone she knew, with the exception of Jesus Christ.

And she couldn't make herself believe that Stevyn was wrong for wanting to do the king's work and carry out the letter of the law.

Miserable and confused, Camilla fell into a deep sleep. While she napped, maids tiptoed in with buckets of steaming water. When the sun finally dipped beneath the hills and the castle was drenched in silky blackness, Bertha shook her awake.

"The evening meal will be served within an hour, child. And forgive me fer sayin' so, but you smell like you've spent the day in a charnel house. Get in the bath, now, and then I'll come and help you dress and comb yer hair."

Struggling to her elbows, Camilla inhaled the soothing scent of verbena steaming up from the surface of her bath. Groggily, she stumbled to the tub as Bertha gathered up her soiled clothes and left the room. Lowering her body into the fragrant water, Camilla moaned with pleasure. An unexpected sense of serenity washed over her.

It was a calm that didn't last for long. The

sound of heavy boots stomping up the steps lit a fire in Camilla's belly. Stevyn's booming voice hammered at her ribs. Camilla looked around the room, and a cry of panic squeezed her chest.

Bramble was gone again.

Stevyn had only let her out of his sight for a split second. But, when he turned around, Daisy was gone.

His frustration and anger was such that his entire body pulsed. Black spots danced before his eyes, and he hammered his palm with his fist. *Damn that bitch!* He was beginning to think the shaggy wolfhound taunted and defied him on purpose.

There was only one place she could be, of course. And that was wherever Bramble was . . . which was wherever Lady Camilla was. And, considering the lateness of the hour, that meant Stevyn had no alternative but to pay a visit to Camilla's bedchamber.

He turned and charged through the front doors of the keep. The party that had just arrived paid no notice as he stormed past them and pounded up the stairwell. Their celebration had apparently begun the moment they leapt from their saddles. Already, as Stevyn reached the first landing, he could hear them yelling for more beer and food. By the time he reached the second landing, the bawdy cries of wenches and the clangs of tankards on trestle tabletops had commenced.

Well, they could just enjoy their night of debauchery, whoever they were. Stevyn paused at the end of the corridor that led to Camilla's room. The scent of lemon and mint, punctuated by gentle splashes, drew him like a siren. The mental image of Camilla in her big oaken tub, naked, struck him like a bolt of thunder.

He hesitated, uncertain whether to approach or flee. The temptation that would present itself were he to intrude during Camilla's toilette might well prove irresistible. To succumb to his passions would be the ultimate humiliation. No matter his other failings, Sir Stevyn Strongbow prided himself on his willpower.

He had told Camilla just hours before that he had no intention of ever touching her again. He'd feigned a lack of interest in seducing her. He had applauded her virtue and self-righteously rebuffed her advance. Of course, his indifference had been a falsehood, designed to fuel the fires of her wanton lust. But, if he entered Camilla's room now, while she was bathing, he knew he would be unable to resist her, and she would know he had been lying earlier. She would know him for what he was, a fraud.

Releasing a heavy sigh, Stevyn stood against the rough stone wall, his anger at Daisy's disappearance swiftly being swallowed by his self-disgust. *What sort of man was he,* Camilla had asked. Inhaling the aroma of her bath, imagining the taste of her skin and aching for the comfort of her warm embrace, he asked himself the same question.

The answer his conscience provided tipped his soul empty. He was a man who craved to be loved, yet ran away from anyone who showed signs of loving him. He was a starving man, refusing to eat. He was a fraud.

Stevyn's head lolled back and the impact of the stones against his skull hurt. A flood of memories burst free from his brain, drowning him with phantom aches and pains. His throbbing jaw reminded him of a fall from a horse. The blazing pain behind his eyes recalled an opponent who had landed an almost fatal blow to the bridge of his nose. The constant hurt in his shoulders and neck brought back memories of the near fatal encounter he'd had with Sir Alfred, many years ago.

His body was a map of past battles and trials. Yet, it suddenly occurred to Stevyn that despite his cocky speeches about *justice,* and his pat little homilies about what was wrong with the world, Camilla was right about him. He didn't know anything.

He was a failure, and, as Camilla had so aptly described him, a liar. The worst part of it was, he had lied to himself for the better part of his adulthood. And he was miserable. Absolutely miserable.

In the end, it was the stillness emanating from her room that lured him away from the wall. He gently eased the door partway open and stood on the threshold, watching her, holding his breath, wondering if he dared utter her name. Camilla's eyes were closed, her neck resting on a towel draped over the edge of the tub.

Fragrant steam curled off the surface of the water; the gentle swell of her breasts was visible, and the skin of her slender neck, exposed and vulnerable, was slick, as if it had been oiled. Stevyn's mouth went dry. This woman affected him like no other. If he had a single brain in his head, he would turn around and escape. Otherwise, he might never get free from the powerful attraction he had for her.

It took every ounce of willpower he had to quietly retreat. She hadn't heard him. She would never know that he'd stood at her bedchamber door and gazed at her like a mooncalf. She would never know that, while in combat he had been the most fearless fighter in all of England, in love he had the soul of a deserter.

Stealthily, Stevyn crept down the corridor. He descended the steps and emerged in the Great Hall, only to be knocked aside by a drunken soldier chasing a half-naked woman. He jabbed another man's arm, and said, "Pray tell me, what is the cause for this celebration?"

Grinning beneath a beer-foam mustache, Frederick the bailiff replied, " 'Tis a welcoming festivity for Risby's advance party."

"Advance party? You mean the band of men who just rode in?"

"Aye, Risby always sends a reconnaissance party before him, to rid the road of brigands and highwaymen. If the weather holds, they expect their lord to be in Wickinghamshire within a fortnight. To be sure, Godric is monstrous happy, and there'll be a wedding to celebrate, too, once Risby is arrived."

A wedding. A bitter taste filled Stevyn's mouth. Yes, there would be a wedding. Camilla's prodigal husband was on English soil and would soon be in Wickinghamshire. She'd marry the man, live happily ever after and forget she'd ever once considered enjoying a dalliance with Sir Stevyn Strongbow.

As well she should.

For, Stevyn was *not* in the market for a bride. Nor was he in the least bit concerned about whether he ever got married, or had children and a family. The last few minutes he'd spent feeling sorry for himself had passed without event. His self-pity vanished. He tamped down his need. He hadn't humiliated himself, thank

God. Camilla would never know how close he'd come to retracting everything he'd said to her that afternoon and begging her to make love to him.

He was glad now that he'd controlled his impulses and reined in his emotions. The news that Risby would return within a fortnight affirmed Stevyn's decision to remain aloof from Camilla emotionally. She was nothing more to him than a witness in a criminal investigation. He'd learn what he could from her, and when he left Wickingham Castle, he would never speak to her or think about her again.

That's what he thought.

This news of Risby's return insured Camilla's unavailability; the added distance it put between them meant that Stevyn didn't have to worry about Camilla falling in love with him. She was a grown woman, and she could take care of herself. If she wanted to share his bed with him, so be it. If she didn't want to, that was fine, also.

That's what he told himself.

All the way back up the steps and down the corridor that led to Camilla's bedchamber.

Her eyes flung open at the sound of angry boot steps pounding up the stairwell. She realized Bramble was gone at the same time the door to her bedchamber crashed open. Sir Stevyn stood in the doorway, his handsome face dark with fury.

"What in bloody hell do you want?" Even she was surprised by the husky hostility in her voice.

His brows jerked up, but there remained in his gaze that slightly arrogant gleam, that trace of amusement that Camilla found infuriatingly arousing and insulting at the same time. "I'm looking for Daisy. What else?"

"Well, as you can see, sir, Daisy is not here."

His black eyes scanned the room. "Where is Bramble?"

"Wherever Daisy is, most likely." Camilla's tone was decidedly arch, drawing a hard look from Stevyn. Aware of her nakedness, she sank a little lower in the tub, until her chin touched the surface of the water and just the tops of her shoulders and knees were exposed.

"You have no idea where our wayward hounds have gone?" His voice fell lower in his throat as his gaze roamed over the surface of the water, taking in the visible parts of her body.

Camilla shook her head, unable to speak above the constriction in her throat. It didn't matter, anyway. The dogs could be anywhere within the castle walls. A mad search might unearth them, but they would eventually wander back on their own. Stevyn knew that.

"They've swyved so many times now," he drawled, "I suppose it is useless to try to keep them apart."

"I would thank you to watch your language, sir," she managed.

He closed the door behind him and dropped the latch, locking out intruders. Then, he stood, appraising her from across the room.

Her voice was strangled and girlish, her protest infantile in its weakness. "No, Stevyn, we must not. . . . You said so yourself. . . ."

A sly smile curled at Stevyn's lips as he slowly crossed the floor. Damn him! Damn the way his slender hips moved beneath his leather belt, the way his muscular thighs moved beneath his snug hosen. Camilla closed her eyes against his advance and tried to ignore the pounding of her heart. She felt him standing beside the oaken tub. She felt the power of his hunger roiling through the room.

"Look at me, Camilla."

"I cannot."

"You must." It was a fiat, issued sympathetically, as if he knew how badly she wanted him and how deeply she feared him.

But, it was still a command. Camilla opened her eyes and met his gaze, searching desperately for reassurance.

"I am here, sweetling, and I will never hurt you," he said, answering her unspoken fears. "I only want to make you happy. If you want me. . . ."

"I did not mean what I said this afternoon—"

"I know. I did not mean what I said."

"I'm sorry," she started.

He bent over and pressed his fingers to her lips. She saw the stubbled growth along his jawline, the worry lines that bracketed his eyes. A gentleness flowed from his presence, wrapping her protectively in the embrace of his nearness. The first dull throb of need awakened in her loins. A sense of urgency stole her breath. Wanton yearning robbed her of her inhibitions.

She kissed his fingertips before he drew his thumb along her cheek and traced the outline of her mouth. The sounds of a raucous celebration in the Great Hall trickled up the stairs, but dissipated in the air like the steam rising from Camilla's bath. The world seemed suddenly very far removed. Nothing existed outside of the secret intimacy Camilla shared with *him*. Nothing existed beyond Camilla's need.

He stood up very straight, then, and without

taking his gaze off her, unhooked his belt and tossed off his tunic. She'd never watched a man disrobe so deliberately before. He watched her, too, gauging her reaction as he revealed his well-formed body. When he'd stripped off the last of his clothing he stood at the side of the tub, unashamed.

There was no hurry. Leisurely, Camilla studied the cords of muscle in his neck, the sinews in his arms, the hardness of his chest and belly. Her gaze traced the pattern of dark hair that tufted his pectorals and pelted his lower body. There was not an ounce of fat on Sir Stevyn Strongbow. Even his hipbones, jutting provocatively, fueled Camilla's imagination.

She never knew anyone could be as comfortable in his own skin as Stevyn was. She never knew any man could excite her the way he did.

Boldly, she met his gaze. His slightly amused look now held an element of curiosity and wonder. This time, she smiled in return, vaguely wondering if other people smiled during lovemaking. She was amazed at her lack of self consciousness around Stevyn. It was as though his confidence transferred itself to her.

Rising, she stood before him, naked and dripping. He grabbed a towel, wrapped it around her and lifted her over the edge of the tub. Wordlessly, he carried her across the room and laid her on her bed. Then, he lay beside her and pressed a kiss against her neck.

Camilla's breathing altered and, as he tasted her mouth, she gasped against his lips. She touched his chest and clung to his arms and caressed his back. She inhaled his scent and smiled against his kisses. When his hand moved between her legs, she pressed her body into his palm and moaned.

He slipped his finger inside her, stroking her toward release. They found a rhythm and moved together. Camilla's legs were spread wide apart, one thrown over Stevyn's hips as he explored her. Her hips bucked against him, and he deepened his touch, quickened his movements to keep pace with her.

And all the while, he whispered in her ear, telling her what he wanted, describing how he felt, promising to kiss her in places she'd never imagined being kissed, threatening to drink her up and never let her go.

He told her shocking, graphic things, putting words to feelings Camilla was embarrassed to admit she had. But, his whispers excited her, and created an intimacy between them that in itself was shocking and that Camilla knew she would never share with another man.

She pressed her lips against his neck and told him she was near her release.

And, he told her he wanted her to let go, to give in to the sensations she felt, to revel in her loss of control.

Stevyn's words propelled her past the point of no return, and her inhibitions melted. . . .

So that her release, when it came, was so intense it wracked her body and shook the breath out of her.

Rolling on her side, Camilla snuggled into his embrace and kissed the throbbing pulse in his throat. His arms enveloped her and he drew her snug against his body. Their breathing slowly synchronized while their legs entwined and the perfumes of their flesh mingled. The room fell silent except for the distant clatter of beer mugs and the occasional swell of laughter.

Camilla sighed, content. "It sounds as if Godric is throwing a party tonight. He must have done well on the jousting field today."

Stevyn's body tensed, and his arms around her tightened. His Adam's apple bobbed against her lips. "No, 'tis a welcome party for the band of men who just rode in."

"Oh, and who would that be?"

"Risby's advance men. They say he is less than a fortnight behind them."

Coldness swept through her. "Risby," she whispered woodenly, stunned.

"Yes, they say there'll be a wedding soon."

She hid her despair in the crook of his neck. "Stevyn . . ."

"What, love?"

She didn't have the words to express her feelings. She wasn't nearly as facile with words as Sir Stevyn Strongbow. He couldn't expect her to be.

But, he expected more from her than tears and silence. "What, Camilla? Tell me, what are you thinking? How do you feel knowing that Risby is approaching and Godric expects you to marry him, a man you've never seen before—a man you don't even know?"

"I don't know," she whispered. "I don't know how I feel."

"Are you going to marry Risby?" Stevyn asked, his voice taught, his embrace already loosening around her body.

A length of indecision and confusion passed in hurtful silence. Finally, Camilla rolled away from Stevyn and hid her face. "I have to," she murmured.

She felt him go still; she heard him swallow.

She didn't dare to look, but she felt him get out of bed and heard him putting on his clothes, hooking his belt and pulling on his boots. Her bedchamber door opened and closed very quietly, and he was gone.

Grief and pain clawed at Camilla's heart. She didn't want to marry a man she'd never laid eyes on, no woman would. But, five years earlier, she made a devil's bargain in order to save her life and that of her unborn child's. It wasn't Godric's fault that the child had been born dead. He arranged for Barnabas to care for her, and in doing so, saved her from prosecution for poaching on royal lands.

Everything she'd done since then had been in repayment of her debt to Godric. Everything Godric had done for her had been in consideration of their agreement.

She couldn't live with herself if she reneged on her agreement.

If she reneged on an agreement with Godric, she might not live at all.

He was a fool! Stevyn slipped out of Camilla's bedchamber and padded down the steps toward the hall. Bertha shot him a shrewd glance as he met her on the steps, but he had already passed the landing on the floor where his guest chamber was located, so she had no reason to suspect he had been in Camilla's room. Had he dallied there five minutes longer, however, he might have put his life and Camilla's at terrible risk.

The thought of what he had done sobered him. Bertha might easily have discovered him leaving Camilla's room and alerted the entire castle. Godric might have paid a surprise visit on his future daughter-in-law in order to inform her of Risby's imminent arrival. Anyone could have knocked on Camilla's door and, finding it locked, deduced that she had a visitor whose identity she wished to keep secret.

Had their tryst been revealed, Camilla would have forfeited her status as chatelaine of Wickingham Castle. Stevyn would have returned to London in disgrace. Or worse, he would have been roasted alive by Godric, whose word was clearly law among his devoted retainers. To take such a monumental risk for a few moments of pleasure was absurd. He must have been momentarily insane. The pressure of this relic-selling investigation apparently was affecting his ability to reason.

In the Great Hall, the festivities had begun. Strolling about the room was a small band of musicians, a harpist, lutist and trumpeter, whose noise competed poorly with the laughter of Godric's liege men and Risby's newly arrived retainers. Scullions, wenches and kitchen boys scurried about, refilling empty tankards, fetching bread and food. And at the far end of the hall was Godric, seated at the center of the most honored banquette, flanked by Barnabas the abbot on his right, and Frederick the bailiff on his left.

Resentment boiled up in Stevyn's blood. Godric's easy smiles, the abbot's congenial laughter, even the bailiff's conspiratorial snickering, seemed an effrontery to his manhood. They mocked him with their carefree attitudes. They dared him to challenge their authority in Wickinghamshire.

Godric offended Stevyn's sense of fairness, because he thought he *owned* Camilla. Barnabas repulsed Stevyn, because he profited from the fears of others. Everything about the goings-on at Wickingham Castle made his stomach roil. Yet, there was nothing he could do about it because Camilla was determined to marry Risby, and he had no intention of trying to stop her.

His interlude with her was nothing more than a few moments of pleasure. He didn't love her and he never would. He repeated that to himself because he had to believe it. He couldn't afford to fall in love. A wife would only complicate his life and interfere with his work and his ambitions. Camilla didn't care for him, and he didn't care for her. He felt nothing more for her than all the other women in London whom he'd swyved. He just needed some fresh air and a little time alone, and he'd be his old self again.

Deliberately, he headed for the door. But, Godric had spied him and, from across the hall, bellowed, "Sir Stevyn! Come join us for a toast!"

Heads turned, accompanied by a lull in the din. Every hair on his body rose in wariness, but Stevyn had no choice. Forcing a small smile to his lips, he casually approached the sheriff's table. Godric could not know how deeply Stevyn despised him; the time was not ripe for Stevyn to disclose his true feelings.

"Are you recovered from your misadventure of this afternoon, sir?" Godric, blue eyes twinkling, dipped his greasy fingers in the tiny water bowl beside his trencher.

Stevyn gave the sheriff a self-deprecating grin. "I apologize, Godric, for my hastiness in accusing one of your men. There was no basis for such a conclusion."

Taken off guard, Godric's eyes narrowed assessingly. "An apology? From the inestimable Sir Stevyn Strongbow? Do my ears deceive me?"

"I was angry," Stevyn said, swallowing the bile

that surged up in his throat. His distaste for Godric and his grinning minions grew. "I withdraw my accusation."

Absently, Godric dried his fingers on the overcloth laid beneath his trencher. One bushy black brow arched in frank appraisal of Stevyn's motive. "Your apology is accepted, sir. As I told you, the arrow that nicked your neck could have come from anywhere."

"Agreed. In fact, had the arrow been aimed by one of your archers, Godric, I am certain it would have found its mark." Stevyn's smile was charming and genuine, his demeanor as relaxed as Godric's. He'd been rash when he accused Godric of masterminding a plot to assassinate him that afternoon. His investigation was far from complete, and it did no good to make an intractable enemy out of the sheriff.

Barnabas spoke up. "I did not hear about this incident. Pray, someone tell me! What happened?"

"Sir Stevyn said someone tried to kill him. An arrow flew past his neck as he was walking the road that leads to the castle."

Barnabas frowned. "Did you see the archer?"

"No," Stevyn replied. "It could have been a poacher hunting in the woods."

"A poacher in these parts would be arrested and hung," Frederick said. "That is the punishment for such a crime in the royal fields surrounding Wickinghamshire. There are no exceptions."

Noting the glance exchanged between Godric and Barnabas, Stevyn thought they *knew* it wasn't a poacher who'd fired an arrow at him. "At any rate, I am not seriously injured," he said.

Godric waved over a serving girl. "Give this

gentleman a mazer and fill it to the brim!" As she poured, Godric beckoned for Stevyn to lean closer. In a whisper, he said, " 'Tis good Gascony wine, sir. You will be pleased by my drink, as well as by my generosity. I am not unwilling to reward you should you perform your job to my satisfaction. The king himself would not be as fair, I assure you."

Stunned, Stevyn straightened.

Godric lifted his own jeweled mazer. "Here's to you, Sir Stevyn. I trust that we have put our disagreements behind us."

Barnabas drank, too, then added, "You see, then, that the people of Wickinghamshire are peaceful and pious."

"This is a lawful county," Frederick said. "Sir Alfred rarely tried a case here. Indeed, he likened sitting on the bench during assize term in Wickinghamshire to taking holiday."

Stevyn took a sip of the offered libation. "The wine is excellent," he commented. Godric's sly expression only added to Stevyn's wariness. He set down his cup, and gave the sheriff a curt bow. "But, it is late, and my hound Daisy has gone missing. I must find her before bedtime. If you will excuse me . . ."

Godric smiled broadly. "Good night, Sir Stevyn. I trust that you will remain in Wickinghamshire until my son Risby arrives. If you think this is an opulent celebration, just wait until you see the feast I have planned for my son's return. It's been five years, you know. I am sorely eager to see his handsome face!"

"Congratulations are in order, Godric. I will pray for your son's safe return and celebrate with you when he arrives."

"Perhaps you will also stay for the wedding?" Godric said, chuckling.

"I hope my investigation is concluded long before that."

"I am certain it will be, sir. Especially if you accept my offer. As I said, you will be well compensated if you do not cause me any further trouble."

Stevyn's face hurt from smiling and the nausea that burned in his belly threatened to erupt. But, his speech remained smooth and his gaze direct. It wouldn't do to show this man how shocked he was by the offer of a bribe. And it wouldn't do to rebuff the offer in public, in the presence of Frederick and Barnabas. No, he would handle the situation more discreetly and in private. But, he needed time to clear his head and think. He needed to escape this crowded, smoke-filled hall.

He nodded, backed a few steps away from Godric's table, then turned. The chill air in the inner bailey hit him like a wave of icy water, rattling his teeth and sinuses. It felt good. His muscles ached from the effort required to suppress his anger. His encounter with Godric had been as frustrating as his foolish dalliance with Camilla. Edginess prickled at his skin.

Plunging into darkness, he set off in search of Daisy. Damn her mangy hide! But, at least his hunt for her occupied his time and busied his troubled mind. Idleness was his enemy. Work and activity would keep him from dwelling on thoughts of Camilla. Work was what kept him from going insane. Falling in love would weaken him and hinder his ambition.

He could not allow himself to love Camilla. He hadn't paid his penance. He didn't deserve her.

But, the thought of her lying in the arms of another man was unbearable. He could not fathom why she would marry a man she had never seen. Camilla Rosedown perplexed him.

Pounding one fist into his open palm, Stevyn vented his frustration. A puzzle was like an aphrodisiac to him. Once his curiosity was piqued, he would not be satisfied until he had pieced together the entire picture. What troubled Stevyn most was that the more he saw of Camilla, the more intriguing the puzzle became. If he wasn't careful, he would lose sight of why he had come to Wickingham Castle in the first place.

If he wasn't careful, he would lose his heart.

Chapter Eight

Bertha stood behind Camilla, combing her golden hair, then twisting it into tight, gleaming braids. "Did ye enjoy yer bath, m'lady?"

In the looking glass, Camilla met her maid's gaze. Bertha was no simpleton, and the tone of her voice asked more than her question. "It was very relaxing, Bertha. I thank you."

"And was yer sleep relaxing, too?"

"Yes. It was a difficult day at the sanctuary. Lady Wynifred died."

"Aye, I heard." The older woman nodded. "Childbirth is risky. I lost three babes meself before my little boy was born. Then, he died, too, before he even took a step. Me husband died shortly thereafter. The physic said he died of too much black bile in his blood. But, I always thought the grief had somethin' to do with it."

Camilla studied her maid's reflection. "You must have been grief-stricken, too, Bertha. I am sorry for your losses. I didn't know."

"That's why I came here five years ago." Bertha's expression, etched in hardship, set itself in a look of wistful resignation. "I couldna stand livin' there in that tiny village no more, seein' me sisters and friends with their babes and their husbands. So, I packed me bag and I headed south. Wound up in Wickinghamshire and got a job in the castle as yer maid. You remember, it was just a few weeks after you came here. I always wondered why the sheriff allowed a nobody like me to wait on ye. But, I was grateful, you know?"

"As I have been grateful to you, Bertha."

"Now, I don't have no place to say this, m'lady, but seein' as how I've grown to know and love ye, I feel it is me duty. . . ."

"Go ahead, Bertha. Speak freely."

Bertha nimbly wound Camilla's flaxen braids into tiny buns. "Seems to me that you've got a decision to make."

A light-headed sensation stole Camilla's breath. Her first impulse was to scold her servant and forbid such familiarity. It wasn't Bertha's place to advise Camilla. It wasn't Bertha's place to comment on Camilla's personal decisions. It was Bertha's place to comb her hair and draw her bath and dress her. Yet, Camilla needed female counsel, and she was desperate to bare her soul. Brushing away a tear, she said, "Oh, Bertha, I don't know what to do!"

"You made love to the man this afternoon, did you not?"

She couldn't bring herself to say yes, but her tiny, involuntary nod answered for her.

"And was it satisfyin', m'lady? Did ye enjoy his lovemakin'?"

Heat suffused Camilla's cheeks. At the sanctuary, she was comfortable with the constant clinical talk of women's bodies. She was well versed on subjects such as lovemaking, menstruation and childbirth. But, talking about her own activities was entirely different. Embarrassed, she closed her eyes.

Unfortunately, the pictures that danced behind her lids were even more evocative than Bertha's question. Burning liquid tingled in Camilla's feminine region as she recalled her afternoon with Stevyn. She imagined his fingers penetrating her golden thatch and recalled the shock she'd felt. She heard the words he whispered in her ear, and she shivered.

Good God, how could just the remembrance of their time together affect her so much? Her desire for Stevyn had reduced her to a wanton woman. She was pathetic! How in the world was she going to control her wicked longings now that she had sampled the exquisite pleasures Stevyn had to offer her?

"Are you all right, m'lady?" Bertha chuckled.

Sighing, Camilla opened her eyes. "Yes. No. Oh, I don't know!"

"He had somethin' that no other man has, doesn't he? At least, as far as you're concerned."

"I don't understand."

Bertha's sympathetic look was reflected in the polished glass. "Is he the most handsome man you've ever met?"

"His cheeks are a bit pocked, not badly. His nose is too big, and his hair is thinning. He might be bald when he is old."

"But, you find him attractive nonetheless."

"What woman wouldn't? He has a certain appeal. I cannot explain it." But, even his smell aroused her, and she knew that if she were ever in the same bedchamber with him again, she would not be able to constrain the heat that flowered between her legs.

"Is he the most intelligent man you've ever met?"

"He is clever, but Godric is equally intelligent." Camilla paused. "I think that Sir Stevyn is the most intense, hardworking man I've ever met. I do not comprehend what drives him so."

"Is he humorless?"

"No, he is distracted. But, when he turns his attentions on me . . ." Her voice faded. She couldn't describe the intimacy that she and Stevyn shared. The things he whispered to her were too secret, too private, to repeat.

"Does he excite you in bed?"

Tension knotted in Camilla's stomach at the thought of how much Stevyn excited her in bed. Her mouth went dry, and she pressed her lips together.

"Does he?" Bertha pressed.

"Lovemaking is not enough to ground a man-woman relationship on, Bertha."

"No, but a man-woman relationship without lovemaking is groundless. If you love him, and he excites you in bed, gel, you must follow your heart."

"What are you saying to me? That I should forget my vow to marry Risby, and run off with the one man who could destroy everything I've worked for these past five years?" Camilla's confusion took the form of irritation. She didn't mean to sound so testy.

But, Bertha, soundly reprimanded, saw that she had stepped out of her place. "Pardon me fer speakin' me mind, m'lady. I had no right."

Cheeks darkened, she anchored Camilla's buns above her ears with pins, then stood back to survey her work. "Ye look beautiful. Godric will be pleased."

Camilla stood, her back straight, her body aching from having to contain her desire and frustration. She squeezed Bertha's arm and murmured her apologies, then hurriedly left the room and made her way below stairs. There was no use avoiding the Great Hall or the festivities surrounding the announcement of Risby's imminent return. She might as well face her destiny. She might as well get used to the idea of being married to Risby, a man she'd never met, didn't know and couldn't possibly love.

She might as well forget about Sir Stevyn Strongbow and the way he made her feel.

"Good evening, daughter. Sit here, on my left, in Frederick's place. I fear he has gone to the latrine, and will most likely be there for quite some time." Godric stood and kissed Camilla on the cheek.

She sat beside the sheriff, her nerves jangling, her stomach rolling at the sight of a trencher piled high with roast peacock, squab and pheasant, all smothered in brown gravy and accented with precious spices like pepper, nutmeg, galingale and cloves.

"Barnabas tells me you had a difficult day, child. I am sorry for Lady Wynifred. She was from a good family. But, we have much to celebrate this evening. Risby's advance party has arrived and he will be in Wickinghamshire before a fortnight is up."

Forcing a smile to her lips, Camilla lifted her mazer and drank deeply of the good red wine she had learned to appreciate. "I am pleased, sir. I look forward to meeting my future husband."

As Godric leaned toward her, even the gray in his beard seemed to sparkle. "You do not look so pleased, my child."

Camilla's gaze flickered to his. She wondered if Risby were as handsome a man as Godric. "I am nervous, sir—"

"Call me Father. Soon, I will be as family to you."

"Fa–Father. I cannot help but be apprehensive. What if Risby finds me unappealing? What if he has fallen in love with another?"

Godric's voice gentled. "You are a beautiful woman, Camilla. Trust me, he will find you attractive. And I know that he is not in love with another. His retainers assure me that he is most eager to enter into matrimony with you. They say he has been as celibate as a monk these past few years. He's long since given up his rakish ways. He's been saving himself for you, dear."

Head dipped, she held back her tears. "When shall the wedding take place?"

"As soon as possible. I want an heir, Camilla."

An heir! The idea of marrying Risby, much less conceiving a child with him, seemed to Camilla a stroke of madness. She felt as if she were trapped in a never-ending nightmare. "I will try my best to give you a grandchild, Godric."

"A *grandson* would be nice," he drawled.

"Yes." A weak smile trembled at her lips. "A grandson."

After a length, Godric touched her cheek. "How are you getting along with Sir Stevyn Strongbow?"

She drank more deeply than she should have,

then set down her cup with a heavy clank. "He is a most unusual man. I would ask that you relieve me from the responsibility of monitoring his activities. I do not like him. He makes me . . . nervous."

"How so?"

With the tip of her finger, she wiped a drop of wine from her lips. "He says one thing, then does another. Ask Barnabas. He is pushy, overly inquisitive and not to be trusted."

Barnabas leaned past the sheriff. "No, he is not to be trusted. But, that is why you must continue to befriend him, Camilla."

"He must not be allowed to wander around the castle grounds unaccompanied," Godric said.

"Nor must he be permitted to invade the sanctity of the sanctuary, Camilla." Barnabas's entreaty tugged at her heart. "The women who are there have had enough tragedy and hardship in their lives. It does them no good to be ogled and scrutinized by a man such as Sir Stevyn. I don't care that he is on a mission from the king. My duties are to God and to the poor women He sends me. I will not brook any interference from Sir Stevyn."

"I cannot control Sir Stevyn's actions," Camilla said weakly.

"No, but you can watch him. Stay close to him. Tell us everything that he does." Godric patted her shoulder. "What did he think of the sanctuary, for example? Has he told you?"

Camilla searched her brain for details of her conversation with Stevyn. "He said he was impressed." He'd also said he did not intend to lie with her, but that had turned out to be a falsehood. She wondered whether she could believe anything Sir Stevyn said.

"Impressed?" Godric and Barnabas echoed in unison.

Chuckling, Godric murmured, "I should imagine that he is. There is not a hospital in all of England, or on the continent, for that matter, that can compare to Barnabas's Sanctuary."

"Has he said anything to you about Sir Alfred?" Barnabas asked.

"Sir Alfred?" Camilla was puzzled. "Why would he mention Sir Alfred to me?"

Barnabas shrugged. "I find it a strange coincidence that poor old Alfred, who would never have questioned Godric's integrity, or mine, was murdered in his bed one day, and the next day, we are being investigated by some overly ambitious, upstart from the king's bench."

Barnabas's insinuation was so gruesome, it defied a response. Reaching for her wine cup, Camilla fought against the urge to bolt from the table. She needed to be alone, to think through all the conflicting information being fed to her. She didn't know whom to believe anymore. If what Godric and Barnabas said was true, then Sir Stevyn Strongbow was, at best, a liar, and, at worst, a murderer. If Sir Stevyn told the truth, then Barnabas was a mountebank, and Godric a thief.

"You must ask him questions, gel." Godric's tone held a trace of admonishment. "You have not succeeded in gaining his confidence. You must be sweeter to him. Use your feminine charms, if you must—"

"But, what about Risby?" Camilla blurted. "With all due respect, sir, would not my future husband object to my becoming so familiar with another man?"

Barnabas steepled his fingertips, as if in prayer. "I believe that Risby would expect you to do your duty in this matter. You would dishonor him by refusing to obey Godric's instructions."

"No one is asking you to *lie* with Sir Stevyn," Godric said roguishly. "We are only asking you to find out what he knows, and to watch him, and tell us everything that he discovers. You don't want him to prosecute the abbot for illegal relic selling, do you?"

"You don't want him to close down the sanctuary, do you?" Barnabas added.

Camilla shivered. "No." The women's sanctuary was a holy place. Anyone who threatened to close it down had to be stopped.

"Then, go." Godric stood, drawing Camilla to her feet with a gentle grasp at her forearm. "Get some rest, child. There is much to do on the morrow. And we haven't much time. When Risby returns, there will be a great celebration . . . and a wedding. But not if Sir Stevyn brings an indictment against Barnabas or me. That man must not be allowed to ruin our way of life, *your* way of life, Camilla."

Barnabas smiled up at her. "God be with you, my lady."

Woodenly, Camilla crossed the floor of the Great Hall and tread the steps leading to her bedchamber. Her determination to save Barnabas's Sanctuary was rekindled. Despite her attraction to Sir Stevyn, he was not a man to be trusted. Barnabas, whom she had long regarded as a father figure, and Godric, who would soon be her father through marriage, regarded Stevyn as an enormous threat to Wickinghamshire. So, she would do her duty and obey Godric's orders.

As she made the first landing, her mind flashed on the journal Sir Stevyn kept in his bedchamber. Pausing, she silently debated. Should she obey Godric and betray Stevyn? Or should she respect Stevyn's right to privacy and defy Godric?

Slowly, she stole down the corridor. Standing outside Stevyn's bedchamber, Camilla listened for footsteps in his room, the sound of Daisy whining or shuffling in the rushes, the scratch of a quill on foolscap.

But, all she heard was silence. Perhaps he was asleep, though that seemed unlikely, considering the raucous dinner festivities going on below stairs.

"Stevyn?" she called out, pushing open the door.

The dim light from a wall sconce revealed an empty room. Quickly, Camilla tiptoed to Stevyn's worktable. Stevyn's journal lay closed on its surface. A written record of all Stevyn's thoughts and impressions, Godric would be ecstatic if she read it and reported her findings. Barnabas would be proud of her. Risby would be honored by his future wife's clever ingenuity.

She picked up the book and ran her fingers over the leather binding. Guilt gnawed at her stomach while the sensation of possessing Stevyn's private musings thrilled her. Flipping open the journal, she saw his distinctive handwriting, and her pulse quickened. How could a man's script, his written letters and words, excite her so?

His hands had touched these pages and his fingers had moved the pen across the paper. The smell of him drifted up to her, and she couldn't help herself. . . . She lifted the book to her nose and inhaled deeply. Memories of Stevyn's kisses, his erotic whispers and expert caresses flooded her imagination. For a long moment, she stood in his room, surrounded by his books, his smell, his belongings, and she *felt* him, felt his presence, felt his strength.

Then, his voice interrupted her fantasy, and she slapped the book shut only to see his silhouette looming on the threshold, fists clenched at his sides, shoulders filling the doorway. "What the bloody hell are you doing?" he growled.

Her heart dropped like a stone.

Stevyn kicked the door shut behind him and lit a taper. Then, he slowly walked toward her, his face a mask of censure and betrayal.

She opened her mouth to speak, but no words emerged. Terror exploded in her bones. Stevyn's fury seemed all the more dangerous for the tight control he held over it. She didn't want to see his anger released. She didn't want to confront him at all. At that moment, all Camilla wanted was to be anywhere else in the world except in Sir Stevyn Strongbow's presence.

Roughly, he took the journal from her hands and dropped it on the table. "I don't suppose you need answer me. 'Tis obvious what you were doing."

"I thought you were out," she stammered.

"I went out to look for Daisy. But, I could not find her. I thought she might have returned to my chamber."

She took a step, thinking to move around him and run for the door. But, his iron grip closed around her arm, halting her.

"Let me go," she whispered.

"Not until I am ready," he replied softly. "You have invaded my privacy. Now it is my turn to invade yours."

"Godric will kill you," she said, as he pulled her next to him.

He stared down into her blue eyes, his body reacting to her beauty even as his mind screamed that she was the enemy. Harshly, he released her, and she stumbled back against the table, cowering.

For once, he wanted her to fear him. "How dare you?" he whispered. "How dare you sneak into my room and read my journal!"

"I did not read anything." Her fear was obvious, but she met his gaze and lifted her chin.

"Am I supposed to believe you?" He let out a mean bark of laughter. "When you have made it clear to me that you consider me evil incarnate? When everyone in this entire damnable county considers me the Antichrist?"

"I never said you were evil, Stevyn."

"No, but I can see it in your eyes, and in everyone else's, too! That poor woman Hilda skittered away from me this afternoon as if I were demon possessed! You're just like Hilda! Whatever Barnabas and Godric say, you believe without question! Has it ever occurred to you, Camilla, that they might be telling you lies for their own evil purposes?"

"Barnabas is practically a saint, considering all the good works he does. And Godric rules this county fairly and with a firm hand. They have been good to me. They would not lie to me."

Stevyn propped his hands on his hips and stared at Camilla. Not for the first time, he wondered whether he was witnessing extreme naivete or skillful duplicity. At any rate, Camilla's allegiance to Godric and Barnabas was apparently unshakable.

On the other hand, he was an expert at cross-examination. Turning away from her, he allowed the silence to deepen, giving her time to think and worry, increasing her nervousness. When, at length, he faced her, his practiced expression was mild and inscrutable. "I would like to ask you a few questions, Camilla."

"I would like not to answer them."

"You have no choice."

"You cannot compel me."

"Oh, but I can. You see, as the king's justice, I have subpoena power over everyone in this country. You can answer my questions now, or I can take you into court and have you answer there, under oath, before an *escrevien*. If I discover that you have lied under oath, Camilla, I can indict you for perjury. Do you know the penalty for perjury?"

She swallowed hard. "No."

"Stoning. You would probably not survive."

"Godric would not allow you to do such a thing."

"No, but that is assuming Godric is still sheriff when my investigation is complete."

Her eyes widened slightly at that, and she gripped the edge of the desk behind her so hard that her entire body tensed. "I hate you," she whispered.

"I am certain of that. But, your feelings toward me are immaterial to this investigation."

"What do you want from me?"

"I want to know how much money Barnabas made last year selling relics."

"How would I know such a thing? I have no idea."

Appraising her, he thought she was telling the truth. It was highly unlikely, after all, that the abbot and the sheriff would share such information with anyone. "Do you know where Barnabas obtains the items he sells as relics?"

"Knights and monks returning from crusades, mostly."

"Have you seen these relics?"

Camilla shook her head.

He didn't believe her, so he waited.

At length, she offered, "I have seen the virgin cloths and some splinters from Christ's cross and a thorn removed from his crown."

Resisting the urge to chuckle, Stevyn said, "Pray, what precisely is a virgin cloth."

" 'Tis a snippet from Mary's winding shroud. If a woman has been debauched, she can pray to Mary to have her virginity restored. If she touches the virgin cloth, her prayers will be answered, and her maidenhead repaired."

"You don't believe that, do you, Camilla?"

Her blue eyes blazed. "Well, it doesn't really matter if I believe it, does it, Stevyn? If a scrap of dirty linen can restore a woman's self-esteem, then, in my eyes, a miracle has been performed!"

"Even if Barnabas is selling lies?" Stevyn thundered.

"I suppose that if a woman ends up pregnant, unmarried and giving birth alone in Barnabas's Sanctuary, she's already purchased a few lies from some other man. At least Barnabas is saving lives, not destroying them!"

"My God, are you that stupid?" Stevyn's anger boiled over. Pounding one fist into his palm, he took a step toward Camilla. He wanted to shake some sense into her. But, when she bent backward, flinching away from him, the sight of her terror sobered him.

Drawing himself up, he took a deep breath and pinched the bridge of his nose. "You are the most confounding woman I have ever met," he muttered.

"You, sir, are the most hateful man I have ever met. You should be ashamed of yourself for interfering with God's work."

Perhaps he *should* be ashamed, but not for investigating Barnabas and Godric. "Do you know how much the abbot charges for a virgin cloth?"

"No." Her bottom lip looked as though a bee had stung it.

"You wouldn't tell me if you knew, would you?"

"I am cooperating with your investigation, sir, by agreeing to answer these questions without a subpoena. If you doubt my veracity, you have the burden of proving me a liar. Otherwise, do not cast aspersions on my integrity. I do not appreciate it."

"Well done, my lady!" He laughed. "Keep it up, and perhaps you will be called to the bar yourself. Your tongue is sharp enough and your wit quick enough to recommend you as a lawyer."

"I would rather be a dung farmer than a lawyer."

"Many would say that shoveling manure is the same as practicing law. However, we are digressing, Camilla. I have but one more question of you. I want to know why Barnabas called for an *escrevien* when Lady Wynifred was attempting to give birth."

She looked away, giving the lie to her answer. "It is routine, sir, in the event Lady Wynifred desired to dictate a deathbed letter to her loved ones. On many occasions, a message such as that has meant a great deal to the bereaved families."

"I see." He stroked his chin. "*Lady* Wynifred, you say?"

Startled, her cheeks darkened. She looked at him as though she failed to comprehend his question.

"Did you say *Lady* Wynifred?" he repeated.

She nodded.

"I was under the impression that Barnabas provided shelter and medical attention to destitute women who have no other place to go."

"When a woman finds herself pregnant and unmarried, it doesn't matter whether she is rich or poor. More often than not, her family turns her out."

Stevyn smiled. He had found a piece of the puzzle, thanks to a slip of Camilla's tongue. "And do these wealthy women pay for the medical and spiritual attention they receive while in Barnabas's custody?"

Camilla's chin wobbled. "The sanctuary is funded by charitable donations. Many of the donations are made anonymously. I do not know where all the money comes from."

"Don't lie to me."

"I'm not lying! My duties at the sanctuary do not include meddling in Barnabas's financial affairs. If you want to know more, you'll have to talk to him."

"I will," Stevyn said. "Believe me, I will."

"I'm leaving now." Camilla pushed off the table, and edged her way around him, her eyes as round as trenchers, her lips slightly parted.

As she brushed past, Stevyn's passion flared.

He could not allow this little minx to sneak into his room, read his journal, then lie to him. He could not allow her to leave his room unchastised.

He cuffed Camilla's upper arm and drew her into his embrace. For an instant, they stared at each other, awareness charging the air. Then, Stevyn lowered his head and covered her mouth with his. She made a little moan of protest, but hungrily kissed him back.

"Do you still hate me?" he asked.

"I wish I could," she replied hoarsely.

"Should I stop? Do you *want* me to stop?" He needed the comfort of her body, but Risby's approach grew more vivid with each passing hour.

"Yes, you should leave me alone," she replied. "But, no, I don't want you to stop."

Pain ripped through his gut. Stevyn cradled Camilla's head in his hands, and gazed at her anguished expression. "You don't have to marry a man you don't love, sweetling."

"But, I do. I have to marry Risby. It is decided. I cannot refuse him now."

He rubbed his nose against hers. "Can you tell me why?"

A sob caught in her throat, but she quickly suppressed it. "No."

"Then, we are on opposite sides of the law, Camilla. I cannot help you if you refuse to reach out for me."

With her arms wrapped around his neck, she pressed her soft bosom against his chest and clung to him. "Yes, you can do something for me."

"Say it. Say anything. Name your deepest desire, tell me your most private secret. Perhaps I cannot satisfy your needs outside this room,

Camilla, but here, tonight . . . I will do anything that will bring a glimmer of a smile to your face."

"I fear that when I am married to Risby, my life will be over. All the excitement that I have shared with you will cease to exist. No man can ever make me feel the way you do, Stevyn."

"Then, let me make love to you."

"Please. I want it to be very . . . wicked."

He smiled against her lips. "You have a very wicked streak, Camilla. You are not meant to be married to a boring man. For Risby's sake, I hope he has a wicked streak, too."

"I hear he has been as virtuous as a monk these past few years."

"Poor Risby."

"Poor me."

"Tell me what you need, Camilla."

She sighed. "Redemption. Salvation. Punishment."

Desire weighted his loins. Nuzzling her ear, Stevyn whispered, "It was very wicked of you to betray me, Camilla. Yes, I believe you do deserve to be punished."

Her mouth was warm and wet against his neck, her voice small and girlish. "And how would you propose to punish me, sir?"

By the hand, he led her to the side of the bed, where he sat down, stretched out his legs and said very quietly, "Bend over."

Chapter Nine

Camilla gasped. She wanted something wicked; well, Sir Stevyn was going to give it to her.

"Do you trust me?" he asked.

"Beyond that door, sir, I do not trust you as far as I could throw you. But, in here . . . yes. I trust you completely."

He patted his thighs invitingly. After the briefest of hesitations, she bent over his lap, her derriere propped in the air, her head resting on the mattress. A feeling of empowerment shored up her boldness. She felt like an actress in a play, or an artist painting a picture. Whatever she wanted could become reality. Whatever she wanted Stevyn to do, he would.

He smoothed the hem of her kirtle up her legs. The chill air kissed her skin, and she shivered. For a long time, Stevyn patiently caressed the backs of her knees and thighs, calming her with loving words.

Then, without warning, he rucked her tunic and thin linen undergarment around her hips, exposing her bare backside. Naked and vulnerable, Camilla drew a sharp breath. Stevyn's fingertips traced delicate patterns on her flesh, drawing goose bumps and heat. The quick gush of liquid between her legs would have embarrassed Camilla in her marriage bed with Gavin McGavin, but now, here, she was pleased by the evidence of her own arousal because she knew it excited Stevyn, too.

He talked to her, his voice gentle, his words incredibly erotic. He told her she was naughty and she needed to be punished. He gave her a sound smack on her behind, then lightly rubbed her stinging skin with his open palm.

Robbed of her ability to speak, Camilla's fingers clutched at the bedclothes, and her breathing came in short little pants. The need to fill her body with his overwhelmed her. As if he could read her mind, Stevyn penetrated her with his finger, skillfully stroking the innermost reaches of her womanhood. A strangled cry of pleasure escaped her, and she reached her first release almost instantly.

Abruptly, he turned her over and tossed her on the bed. "I must have you now," he said hoarsely, standing beside the bed.

Eagerly, she watched him strip off his clothes. The sight of Stevyn's naked body renewed her desire. As he hovered over her, Camilla spread her legs and drew her knees to his underarms.

"God, you are beautiful," he whispered, covering her body with his, lowering his weight. Slowly, he entered her, moving inside her, watching her face, kissing her lips, gauging her reaction.

She smiled against his kisses, savoring her pleasure and his, too. A low moan escaped his lips, and his expression tightened. His excitement fueled Camilla's arousal, precipitating another round of contractions, drawing her toward another peak. She found release, not even trying to be quiet or ladylike, not even trying to stifle the keening that escaped her lips as she grasped Stevyn's shoulders, hugging him even closer to her, gripping him as tightly inside her body as she could.

He plunged even deeper inside her. Then, after a moment of thrusting, his muscles tensed, and his entire body went very still. Camilla's fingers caressed Stevyn's nape, and she lovingly whispered his name. He groaned and withdrew from her, spilling his seed on her belly in quick, shuddering bursts of passion.

At length, he lifted his head and smiled. His eyes were glazed with contentment, his brow unfurrowed. For once, Camilla thought Sir Stevyn Strongbow wasn't worried about his work.

"My God, woman," he growled. "You are incredible."

"No, Sir Stevyn. 'Tis you who are the expert."

She laughed with joy as his head nestled in the crook of her neck.

But, her laughter was snatched from her throat by the rude knock that suddenly sounded at Sir Stevyn's door.

"Sir Stevyn, come quick! You are needed below stairs!" The voice was that of a young boy, a porter or valet probably, but God only knew who stood behind the lad. If Godric had become suspicious and decided to investigate, he would find his future daughter-in-law in bed with the king's justice. In Wickinghamshire, such an indiscretion was sure to be a hanging offense, or worse.

"Quick, hide beneath the covers," Stevyn whispered, leaping from the bed. Ruffling through the pile of clothes he'd tossed to the floor, he found his belt and short dagger. Weapon drawn, he approached the door.

"Who are you?" he demanded through the thick slab of oak.

"I am Godric's page, sir. He said to come and find you. You must come quick, for there has been a murder inside the castle walls!"

"Tell Godric I was using the chamber pot. I will be there shortly."

"Yes, sir!"

Stephen released his pent-up breath as the boy's footsteps pattered down the hall and faded on the stairwell. Hastily, he stepped into his hosen and boots, then pulled his tunic over his head and cinched his belt. When he turned to Camilla, she was already dressed and waiting at the side of the bed. They stared at each other in awkward silence.

"Had that been Godric at the door, soldiers would be hauling us off to the donjon even as we speak." She twisted her fingers in nervous agitation.

"It was not Godric. We are to be thankful for that."

"This—" She gestured helplessly at the bed. "This does not change anything, Stevyn. I must marry Risby. I have no choice."

Stevyn's impulse was to disabuse Camilla of that ridiculous notion. She was not bound by law to marry any man. She was no one's slave or serf. She was a free woman, as far as he knew.

On the other hand, he had nothing to offer her even if he did succeed in disrupting her marriage plans. He'd spent the last five years believing that his work was his life, and that he did not deserve to be in love, much less married. He had done more than a fair job of convincing himself that he would never attach himself to a single woman. What right did he have to talk Camilla out of marrying Risby when he had no intention of marrying her himself?

"Yes." He held his hand out for her. "I understand that you intend to honor your agreement to marry Risby. If that is what you wish to do, I will not stand in your way."

She laid her smaller hand in his. "Thank you."

"Come. You must wait here until I am safely below stairs. After a sufficient length of time has passed, you may return to your bedchamber. Just be certain that there is no one in the corridor when you leave this room."

"You trust me?" Her voice quavered.

At first, he didn't know what she meant. Then, he realized he was leaving her alone—with his journal.

"You said that within this room, you trusted me completely, Camilla." He pulled her snug to his body, and kissed her lips. "Now, I must trust you."

A tear sparkled on her pale lashes. Stevyn pressed a fleeting kiss on Camilla's eyelids, then turned and slipped out the door.

The celebration in the Great Hall had not stopped, despite the news that a murder had occurred in Wickingham. If anything, Stevyn thought, the party had grown more rowdy. Risby's advance men were so deep in their cups several of them had fallen asleep at the trestle tables. The ones that remained upright were noisy and rude, grabbing at the skirts of serving women, singing at the top of their lungs and generally making fools of themselves.

Indeed, they behaved far more crudely than Godric's men. Vaguely, Stevyn wondered where Camilla got the idea that Risby had been living like a monk these past few years.

At present, however, Risby was not Stevyn's problem. Stalking the length of the cavernous room, he eyed the targets of his investigation with distrust. Together with Frederick, Godric and Barnabas sat huddled at the table of honor, laughing and slapping one another on the back. Nothing about their behavior suggested they were the least bit concerned that someone had been killed within their jurisdiction.

Stevyn stood before Godric while the sheriff ignored him, continuing instead to recite a bawdy story to Frederick and Barnabas.

After a moment, Stevyn interrupted. "You sent for me, Godric."

The sheriff looked up, feigning surprise. "Oh, there you are! Yes, Stevyn, there has been a murder."

"What has that to do with me?"

"Considering your investigation, sir, I thought you would like to know."

"I believe such crimes fall within your bailiwick," Stevyn replied.

"Just so." Godric's lips twisted, as if he were trying to suppress a smile. "Therefore, it is my unpleasant duty to inform you, Stevyn, that you are under investigation."

"What the devil are you talking about?"

Godric mugged a somber expression. "It

seems you were last seen talking with the murdered woman. Naturally, that draws you into the web of suspicion."

Stevyn felt his scalp tingle with rage. Yet, he met Godric's gaze with cold equanimity. "Who has been murdered, Godric?"

"The old woman, Hilda. 'Tis a shame, she was an able baker. Anyway, she was found by her daughter, poor wretched thing, in the alleyway that runs between the hall and the kitchens. Her throat was slit with a dagger. . . . But perhaps you already knew that."

"Christ on a raft! Surely, you cannot believe that I had anything to do with that old woman's murder."

Godric shrugged. "As I said, you were seen talking to her this evening, shortly before she was found dead."

"Just about the time Risby's men rode into Wickingham," Frederick the bailiff added, squinting at Stevyn.

"So what?" For the first time since he'd been in Wickinghamshire, fear tiptoed up Stevyn's spine. He *was* on Godric's turf. The fact that he was an emissary from the king meant nothing. If Godric and Frederick accused him of murdering Hilda, there wasn't a jury in Wickinghamshire that would acquit him.

Godric sighed. "As a show of good faith, Stevyn, I am not going to arrest you now—despite the evidence weighing against you. But, I suggest that you conclude your investigation quickly, sir, and get out of Wickinghamshire. Before I decide to initiate my own investigation into Hilda's death."

It was blackmail, pure and simple—intimidation at the highest level. Bribery hadn't achieved the result Godric had hoped for, now he was resorting to blackmail.

Stevyn returned Godric's stare and chuckled. "You are playing deep, sheriff."

"You are a worthy opponent," replied the older man.

Stevyn gave an abbreviated bow in mock obeisance. "May the best man win, Godric."

Frederick laughed nervously, but Godric and Barnabas remained tight-lipped as Stevyn exited the Great Hall.

For Camilla, the night passed in episodes of fitful sleep and fevered dreams. In the morning, she awoke with a sense that something was wrong. Realizing that Bramble was not in her room, she hurriedly threw on a pair of men's breeches and a short tunic. After a quick search of the kitchen, the bailey, and even the corridor outside Stevyn's room Camilla knew Bramble must be outside the castle walls.

Inside the castle's arsenal, located in a small squat building adjacent to the stables, she found a quiver, arrows and a birch-wood bow. With her weapon slung across her back, she quickly made her way to the aviary, where her prized falcon was perched on a pedestal inside a huge wicker cage.

"Good morning, Atalanta," Camilla cooed, pulling a thick leather gauntlet over her hand.

The bird willingly leapt to her wrist, and Camilla deftly slipped a leather hood over the bird's head. She tied Atalanta's jesses around her wrist and set off. While the bird's weight would have stiffened the arm of a court lady, Camilla gave her bird a sturdy limb on which to travel. Following their usual route, they departed the lower bailey through the southern gate, setting out on the old Roman road.

Less than a mile from the castle walls, Camilla left the road and plunged through the high weeds and gorse, arriving at Bramble's favorite hunting field with a beating heart.

"He must be here." She scanned the countryside. The sky was cloudless and as shiny gray as a new coat of arms. A gentle breeze fanned her face, ruffling the wisps of hair sticking from her woolen cap. Had Bramble been at her side, it would have been a perfect morning.

"Find him, girl." Expertly, she untied Atalanta's hood using her free hand and her teeth. Then she loosened the bird's jesses and, with a gentle shrug, launched her skyward. As always, the sight of Atalanta airborne thrilled Camilla. Head tilted, she watched her bird float and soar and circle overhead. A flash of rabbit fur would surely catch Atalanta's keen gaze. But, Camilla hoped that the bird's instincts would also home in on Bramble.

She felt the pounding of a horse's hooves just seconds before she heard the rumble. Whirling, Camilla watched the bend in the road, eagerly awaiting sight of an approaching rider. Panic raced in her heart. Her mind flashed on the first day she'd been caught hunting in these fields.

Irrational though her fears were, she half expected to see Godric and Frederick galloping toward her, their faces set in malicious grins. Though she'd been arrested five years earlier, the scars of that experience had never truly healed. Despite the fact that Camilla's rights to hunt in the royal fields were secure, she still grew frightened at the thought of being mistaken for a poacher.

When Sir Stevyn Strongbow rode into sight, she nearly gasped with relief. Without thinking, her arm flew up in greeting. A welcome heat suffused her face, and the prickly dread that had burned in her chest seconds earlier quickly vanished.

Horse and rider slowed to a trot, then left the road and waded slowly through the thick brush. Sir Stevyn slid from his horse and, without even bothering to hobble his destrier, tossed the reins aside. Then, hands on hips, he stood a few paces away wearing the familiar, faintly amused expression that Camilla found wildly attractive.

Confusion flooded Camilla's senses. She didn't want to find Stevyn wildly attractive; in fact, she resented the surge of excitement that flowed through her as he stared. Surely, her inability to control her emotions was a serious character flaw. Hadn't Barnabas once preached an entire sermon on the virtues of discipline and self-control?

"A good morning to you, my lady." His voice was as smooth and spicy as mulled wine.

"What brings you beyond the castle walls?" she asked.

He glanced at Atalanta. "The same thing that brings you and your falcon here. I am in search of Daisy."

She sighed her exasperation. "Pray, tell me, Sir Stevyn, what are we going to do about those animals?"

"They do not seem to have the willpower to stay away from each other." He took a step closer to Camilla.

She inched backward. "Barnabas says that freedom of choice is what differentiates us from stupid animals. Barnabas says that the strength with which one resists temptation is a measure of his or her character."

"Does Barnabas find no joy at all in life?"

"Are you mocking the abbot?"

He shrugged. "Has it never occurred to you that temptation is not always such an evil thing?"

She folded her arms across her chest. "Temptation is Satan's way of inviting you to sin."

"Sometimes, temptation is God's way of saying that you take life too seriously."

Despite her determination to appear unamused, Camilla could not resist grinning. "Weren't you the man who told me his work was the most important thing in his life?"

"I also told you that I do not take myself very seriously. You should not take me seriously, either."

"Oh?" Looking up, Camilla noted that Atalanta was gliding in circles above a spot in the middle of the field, some fifty yards away. Facing Stevyn, she said, "Does that mean that I should question your credibility? Have you been dishonest with me?"

Something in his black gaze flickered. A frown tugged at his lips, and his laughing eyes grew somber. He started to speak; then his stare shot to Atalanta, and he murmured, "She has spotted something. Something that is not moving, or else she would descend and attack."

"Falcons often circle above dead animals," Camilla said.

"God's teeth." Stevyn's features hardened. "If anything has happened to Daisy, I shall never forgive myself!"

He ran as if he'd been fired from a catapult, strong legs whipping through the tall grass, arms pumping furiously. After an instant, Camilla realized his fear. Cold terror seized her. If Atalanta had succeeded in locating Bramble and Daisy, the dogs were not moving.

And, if anything had happened to Bramble, Camilla would never forgive herself, either—or Sir Stevyn, for that matter.

She ran after him as fast as she could. When he skidded to a stop, she slammed into his back.

"Dear God," he whispered hoarsely.

Camilla stared in shock. Acid burned her throat, and her stomach clenched. Turning, she fell to her knees and wretched.

The corpse had already been picked over by vultures and scavenging rodents.

Chapter Ten

Thankfully, she had not yet broken her fast. Camilla's belly twisted and her ribs ached by the time she was able to catch her breath. When the retching abated, she covered her face with her hands and sobbed.

Stevyn stood over her, gripping her shoulders and patting her back. "Are you all right, now?"

Nodding, she scrambled to her knees, then allowed him to pull her to her feet. Her gaze skittered to the man lying dead in the field, and she drew a quick breath.

"Do not look, sweetling," Stevyn drew her into his arms, and pressed her cheek against his chest. Her woolen cap had fallen off and her braids fell loose down her back. Stroking her hair, Stevyn said, "There, there, Camilla. There is nothing to be afraid of."

"But, there is!" Her tears spilled against his tunic. "Someone has murdered Hotard!"

Stevyn's body stiffened. "Hotard? The scribe?"

"Yes." Sniffling, she met Stevyn's worried look. "Do you not remember him from yesterday? He was called to Lady Wynifred's bedside—"

"Yes, I remember." Stevyn glanced over his shoulder. "But, how can you be certain that is Hotard? The vultures have got to him. His face is indistinguishable."

"Look at his fingers. The tips of them are black. Trust me, that is Hotard. He always looks as if he has dipped his fingers in an inkwell."

He nodded. "Well, that is very interesting. A dead man cannot tell lies, can he?"

"What are you talking about?" Reluctantly, she stepped out of Stevyn's embrace. She didn't want to become dependent on his nearness for comfort. Risby would soon be home, and the relationship she'd enjoyed with Stevyn would come to an end. Best not to rely on him for anything.

"I'm talking about the recent epidemic in Wickinghamshire Castle."

"Epidemic?" The very word made Camilla's pulse race.

"Of murders," he amended. "Last night, Teresa-Marie's mother was killed."

"Who is Teresa-Marie?" Camilla asked.

"She is a young woman who gave birth in Barnabas's sanctuary. Her mother, Hilda, was a kitchen wench."

"Hilda? Murdered?"

"Her throat was slit. Just like poor Hotard's. Your future father-in-law has suggested that perhaps I was the murderer."

"When was she murdered, Stevyn?"

"Last night, while Godric was celebrating the arrival of Risby's advance party."

"Then you could not have murdered Hilda. You were with me!"

Stevyn's lips quirked. "Are you willing to be my alibi, Camilla? Are you willing to testify in a court of law that I was with you when the unfortunate hag was murdered, and therefore I cannot possibly be guilty of the crime?"

Camilla's throat constricted. "I—I will not let them hang you for a murder you did not commit!"

"Even if it means you must confess you were enjoying a little bed sport with me while Godric was below stairs celebrating the return of his prodigal son . . . your fiancé?"

Stevyn's question was like a devouring worm, and her heart an apple core. Flustered, she said, "Surely, Godric does not believe you killed Hilda! Why would you have? What reason would you have to harm that little old woman?"

"I did not like the bread she baked?"

"Oh! Stop!" Stevyn's flippancy torched Camilla's self-control. Balling her fist, she threw a punch at his shoulder. "There is nothing to laugh about in this situation, Stevyn. Godric will have you on a rack before sundown if you defy him, and you'll hear your bones crackling like dry faggots! You do not know him, sir. His word is the gospel in Wickinghamshire!"

Stevyn's smirk vanished. "I would ask that you not strike me again, my lady."

His equanimity unnerved her. Did he ever show his emotion? Could anything or anyone wound him? Blood boiling, she retreated a step, both fists held up like a tournament brawler. "Oooh! I hate you!"

His gaze twinkled. "Might I ask why, precisely?"

"Because you have used me for your physical gratification, and you have toyed with my emotions. You have questioned my reasons for marrying a man whose intentions toward me are honorable."

"And?"

"And—" His nonchalance in the face of almost certain tragedy infuriated her. "And you have declared war on Barnabas, who is like my father, and Godric, who soon *will* be."

Wind rustled the top of the grass, and the air suddenly chilled. Camilla smelled rain and, looking up, saw that Atalanta's aerial circles were growing tighter and lower. The bird sensed a change in the weather, too, and needed to find a perch.

Stevyn's expression darkened. "Camilla, do you really believe that Godric and Barnabas are without fault in connection with the financing of the refuge for homeless women?"

"Of course, I believe they are completely blameless!" She had to. Otherwise, her life was a sham.

His intense stare bore into her, as if he were considering whether to educate her to some simple fact that even the village idiot should be aware of. After a moment, he shook his head. Apparently, he'd decided she lacked even the most basic powers of comprehension.

She hugged herself against the cold that clawed at her bones. "You think my loyalty to Godric and Barnabas is misplaced."

"I do not understand it," he admitted. "But, you have not seen fit to explain why you must marry Risby and so I cannot judge your reasons for doing so."

" 'Tis none of your business." She lifted her chin a notch. She had no intention of telling Stevyn that she had once been homeless and pregnant, or that she'd met Godric after being caught poaching in royal hunting fields. He might think her unwise for marrying a man sight unseen, but if he knew she entered that agreement in exchange for amnesty, he would consider her an immoral mercenary. She hadn't known Stevyn for a long time, but she knew him well enough to know that his moral code was stricter than hers.

"You are correct. 'Tis none of my business why you have chosen to marry Risby. But, Barnabas's unusual method of raising funds to finance his sanctuary is my business. And so are the deaths of Hotard and Hilda."

"How is Hotard's death connected with Hilda's?"

Stevyn arched his brows. "Hilda tried to talk to me yesterday, but I believe that the arrival of Risby's men frightened her off. I intended to continue our conversation today, but it is too late. Someone slit her throat last night."

Camilla clapped her hand over her mouth to suppress her nausea.

"As for Hotard," Stevyn continued. "I attempted to deliver a summons to him last night at the sanctuary. I wanted to interrogate him concerning his duties as Barnabas's scribe. When I could not find him, I asked another monk to deliver my letter to him. Today, Hotard is dead. Do you think it is a coincidence?"

"I do not know what to think. I do not know what I *should* think!"

"You must decide for yourself what is right, and what is wrong, Camilla."

"You would have me reject everything Barnabas stands for, and accept your version of what is just!"

"Keep an open mind, that is all I am asking."

"You don't understand," Camilla whispered.

He reached out and took her hand. Pressing it to his cheek, he said, "No, I do not. Why don't you tell me? Why don't you share all your secrets with me?"

"Because I do not want to be judged by you, Stevyn."

Her answer appeared to wound him. His fingers tightened around hers and his eyes squeezed shut. When he looked at her, he said hoarsely, "It is not my place to judge you, sweetling. But, I think you are a kind, loving, passionate woman. 'Tis only your dogged allegiance to Godric and Barnabas that I question. And I fear for your future. What will you do if my investigation unearths evidence of criminality? Who will take care of you then?"

She would take care of herself. She had done so before, and she could do so again.

"Are you all right?" he asked her.

"No." Her head ached, and her knees were wobbly. The earth seemed to spin in one direction while the sky spun in another. "I want to go back," Camilla said weakly. The edges of her vision darkened, and her voice sounded small and disembodied.

"Come, I will return you to the castle. You are a trifle green around the gills."

Confusion, along with a strange sense of weightlessness, overtook Camilla. Why didn't she want to return to the sanctuary for refuge?

Why did Barnabas's hospital suddenly seem a dangerous place to be?

Above her, Atalanta swam in dizzying circles as the sky rumbled ominously.

"The rain will be here any moment," Stevyn said. "I can see it on the other side of that hilltop."

"I have to bring Atalanta down." But, Camilla couldn't lift her arm to signal the falcon, and she lacked the strength to blow her whistle.

"Let me." Stevyn slipped the gauntlet off her hand and onto his. "Ho!" Then, he gracefully drew in the exhausted bird. After he'd hooded and tethered Atalanta to his glove, he took Camilla's arm and guided her toward the road where his horse waited patiently.

He tossed her on his saddle as if she were a feather. Amazingly, he mounted his horse with Atalanta clutching his arm. In Camilla's half-dazed state, the landscape wrinkled and curled like a parchment snatched from the grate, but she was not immune to Stevyn's body pressed against her back. And she was not unsusceptible to the little thrill that shot up her spine when he nudged his horse to a trot, and his thighs moved against hers.

But, her mind could not grasp the enormity of what he had told her. Someone had killed Hotard and Hilda because Stevyn wanted to interrogate them. Someone wanted to prevent Hotard and Hilda from talking. Someone had killed them in order to thwart Stevyn's investigation.

She felt as if she'd been stampeded by a rabid destrier. Was it possible that Godric and Barnabas were so fearful of Stevyn's investigation that they ordered the deaths of Hotard and Hilda?

No! She shuddered in disgust, and silently berated herself for doubting the two men who had rescued her from poverty. She had much to be grateful for, and Stevyn was a newcomer in these parts. She hardly knew him. He had not yet proved to her that Barnabas and Godric were criminals, or that her view of the world was warped.

She had no reason to trust Sir Stevyn Strongbow.

Yet, she'd been intimate with the man in ways she'd never known possible. She had taken him inside her body. She had allowed herself to be completely vulnerable. She *had* shared all her secrets with him. She hadn't held back.

And, he had proved to her that he could take everything she had to offer. In the bedchamber, he was not judgmental or rigid; whatever delighted her pleased him, too.

If that was not trust, Camilla didn't know what was.

Why, then, was she trying so hard to convince herself that he was untrustworthy?

Her head rested on his shoulder, while her hips fit comfortably between his legs. In her boyish attire, Camilla's voluptuous body was hardly accentuated, but when she pushed her bottom snug against Stevyn's groin, her feminine curves aroused him.

He held the reins in his one hand while grappling with Atalanta's jesses in the other. A more leisurely pace was necessary in order to calm the bird, so Stevyn slowed his horse. With the rain pursuing him, he should have been vexed by the awkwardness of his seat. But, Camilla's warmth, the feel of her weight leaning into him and the sweet perfume of her body made the ride enjoyable.

Droplets of rain started to batter their heads and shoulders. Atalanta spread her wings in a ruffle of agitation, but remained upright, much to Stevyn's surprise. She was a well-trained bird, and a testament to Camilla's talent as a falconer.

Inside the castle walls, they clip-clopped through the bailey and halted outside the aviary. Stevyn left Camilla clinging to the saddle while he dismounted and transferred Atalanta to her cage. Without warning, a sheet of rain fell from the sky. Stevyn dashed back to his mount just as a tottering Camilla lost her hold on the saddle and slid to the ground.

"Take my horse!" Stevyn yelled to a stable boy as he scooped Camilla in his arms. Then, he raced across the muddy earth to the Great Hall, barging through the front door and up the stairwell as if an army of vandals were at his heels.

Gently, he laid her on her bed. Rain dripped from his hair and splattered her face as he hovered over her. But, she didn't move. A burst of panic ignited in his chest. Touching Camilla's face, he was appalled at the chill in her flesh. Her eyes were closed and her teeth chattered uncontrollably.

Stevyn desperately stoked the kindling in the grate. When a healthy fire was roaring, he searched the wedding chest at the foot of Camilla's bed, grabbed an armful of quilts and pelts, then fitted them around Camilla's body. With her hand in his, he sat on the edge of her bed. He rubbed her cold, clammy skin, praying that she would revive quickly. The thought of Camilla suffering, even for a moment, was simply intolerable to him.

The thought of her marrying Risby, a man Stevyn knew nothing of, but instinctively disliked, was equally intolerable. A part of him rebelled against the idea of Camilla agreeing to marry a man she didn't know, much less love. And that part of him urged Stevyn to find out why she'd entered such a heinous bargain. Another part of him retreated from such chivalry; who was he to meddle in Camilla's marriage plans when he couldn't offer her anything more suitable?

Vaguely, somewhere deep in his heart, the thought of marrying Camilla himself took hold.

But, he quickly shook himself free from the clinging roots of that preposterous fantasy, and reminded himself that he had too much work to do to fall in love. It would be unfair to subject a woman like Camilla to the kind of lifestyle he led, always working, never focusing on his home life. If they had a child, she would be left to raise it alone. If she were ill, he might be far away and unable to tend to her.

No, it was best he didn't entertain such silly dreams as marrying anyone, let alone Camilla Rosedown.

"Is there somethin' I can do, sir?" The voice startled him.

Fully expecting to see Godric looming in the doorway, Stevyn's head snapped around. In his imagination, the sheriff's blue eyes twinkled merrily and his smug smile glowed. Stevyn blinked. And, when he opened his eyes, he saw instead that Camilla's personal maid, her eyes round with questions, stood on the threshold.

"Is m'lady taken ill?" the woman asked.

"I—I don't know." Stevyn felt peculiarly helpless. "She had a bit of a shock, then she caught a chill."

The gray-haired woman looked skeptically at Stevyn as she entered the room. She stood at the bedside and laid her hand on Camilla's forehead. "She'll be all right, sir. She needs some rest, is all. She's had much on her mind, of late."

"Yes, I suppose she has." Stevyn rose slowly, reluctant to surrender his authority. But, the serving woman's compressed lips told him he should leave. "Do you really think she is all right?"

"Yes, sir. If you'll go now, I'll strip these wet clothes off her, and put her night rail on."

Stevyn backed away from the bed. "Perhaps she needs a hot bath—"

"I'll see to it, sir."

"Or a warm posset. I will go to the kitchens—"

"No need, sir. I'll do it myself. Just as soon as she's alert enough to get anythin' down her throat."

Sighing, Stevyn turned and left the room, drawing the door shut behind him. His chest spasmed with frustration as he entered his own room. At his desk, he opened his diary and recorded the events of the previous twenty-four hours. Two deaths and news of a wedding. He didn't know which upset him more.

Rubbing his eyes, he groaned. It was official—Camilla Rosedown was not a passing flirtation, a temporary bed partner who would fade from his memory as soon as another woman warmed his bed. She was under his skin, and it bothered him. He didn't know how or why he had allowed himself to become emotionally entangled with her. But, he knew it wasn't good.

The distraction Camilla created interfered with his ultimate goal, which was to bring down Godric and Barnabas. Worse, Camilla was now his alibi. He had put her life at risk by sharing his bed with her. Liquid fire spewed up the back of his throat at that thought. If anything happened to Camilla as a result of his recklessness, Stevyn would never forgive himself.

A murky sea of voices lapped at the edge of Camilla's consciousness. She heard her name, and she struggled to swim to the surface. Then, in a burst of awareness, she broke through the sleep that submerged her, and opened her eyes.

Godric sat on a low stool beside her bed, his long legs crossed, his big leonine head tilted. Seeing that she was awake, he smiled. "Good afternoon, daughter. Did you have a good rest?"

"It is afternoon, already?"

"You had quite a shock, from what I hear. Sir Stevyn reported Hotard's death to Frederick, presumably in an effort to divert suspicion from himself."

Camilla pushed up on her elbows. "Why should he wish to do that? Who suspects him?"

"Why, dear, the entire population of this castle, the neighboring village and surrounding countryside suspects him! Who else would have murdered a simple kitchen wench and a pious scribe?"

"Why would Stevyn have murdered them?"

Godric spoke as if he were explaining elementary mathematics to a dumb child. "Because they did not tell him what he wished to hear."

Falling back on her pillows, Camilla gasped. "Are you suggesting that Stevyn killed a man and woman because their testimony would have ruined his case?"

"It has been known to happen."

"I do not believe it."

Godric's stare hardened. "Are you questioning me?"

A long moment stumbled awkwardly between them. Camilla met the sheriff's cold blue gaze, but she was the first to look away. Folding her arms across her chest, she said quietly, "No, sir."

"Eh?"

"No, sir," she enunciated.

His three-legged stool scraped across the floor as he moved nearer the bed. Taking her hand, he leaned over her. "Now, listen, gel, you do not seem to realize the danger that we—*you, me and Barnabas*—are in. This Sir Stevyn Strongbow has got it in his head that we are criminals, all of us."

"Me included?"

"You, too. After all, you practically run the sanctuary. When Barnabas is not present, aren't you the one who directs the monks' activities? And, aren't you the one who monitors the progress of each childbirth that occurs in the hospital?"

"Yes, but—"

"It is presumed you know everything about the daily operations of the sanctuary, including the relic-selling operation and the sources of funding that keep the hospital running."

"But, I do not participate in the selling of relics. Indeed, I have never—"

He placed his fingertips on her lips. "Shush. That is immaterial to a man like Sir Stevyn. You have had ample opportunity to apprize yourself of Barnabas's activities, and you are not a stupid woman. Therefore, Stevyn believes that you know everything. And if you know everything, you are equally culpable should Sir Stevyn be successful in obtaining indictments and verdicts against us."

Godric's news pushed Camilla deeper into her goose-feather pillows. Her heart kicked like an angry mule, and her hands felt numb. The fuzziness of her fainting spell instantly evaporated, only to be replaced by a tingly apprehension. She had to think about what Godric said. She had to analyze the situation for herself.

"Sir Stevyn is a very ambitious man," she murmured.

"Yes, it is said of him that all he does is work." Godric paused, then added, "Work and swyve, that is. I hear that he is quite popular with the court ladies in London. They say he possesses great skills in bed, and that his mattress is never without another man's wife to warm it."

Humiliation burned on Camilla's cheeks. Had she been made a total fool? Was Stevyn using her for bed sport . . . and information?

"He particularly likes other men's wives," Godric said.

Her mind reeled back to the night when he'd ravished her in this very bed. She trusted him, then. She trusted him so completely that she'd behaved like a wanton, and loved every minute of it.

"And, it is also said that women are attracted to him like moths to a flame," Godric drawled.

Her mouth went dry. She was a fool! She shouldn't have trusted Sir Stevyn. She shouldn't have considered believing what he told her about Godric and Barnabas.

Thankfully, Godric hadn't noticed her unease.

He changed the subject fluidly. "Have you learned anything about his investigation?"

She shook her head. "Very little. He tried to question Hotard and Hilda, but they were murdered before he was able to."

"That's what he told you?"

"Yes."

"And I suppose he suggested that I had something to do with the deaths of his potential witnesses?"

Camilla merely stared at Godric, unable to speak above the clot of confusion in her throat.

He laughed. "Yes, that is what I thought he would do. Clever bastard."

"You mean, he wanted me to believe that you—" She swallowed hard. "And Barnabas—"

"I should have known." Godric nodded sagely. "I should have anticipated that he would attempt to pit you against me. 'Tis very, very clever of him! I have to admire him for that! Ah, he is a worthy adversary, as sly as a serpent, Camilla. You must watch yourself, gel, lest you get bit!"

"Will you not allow me to leave him alone? I told you I did not like him. He frightens me."

Godric's smile vanished. "As he should. He frightens us all. He is a murderer."

"Dear God! Is there any evidence that Stevyn committed those murders?"

"Evidence? Have you become a lawyer now, too, Camilla? What sort of evidence is necessary when you know that I speak the truth? Isn't it enough that I tell you what I know?"

"Yes, but—"

"But, if you require evidence, then consider this. Where was Sir Stevyn last night when the murders occurred?"

"I do not know," Camilla lied, her fear leaping. "When was Hilda killed?"

"Her body was found in the alley shortly after Risby's advance men arrived, and just minutes after Stevyn was spied talking to her at the edge of the courtyard."

"And what about Hotard?"

"There is a monk at the sanctuary who is willing to testify that Stevyn was looking for Hotard."

"That doesn't prove anything."

Godric stood abruptly. "It proves that Sir Stevyn is a murderer, Camilla. And if he cannot prove where he was at the time of Hilda's and Hotard's deaths, then he shall be hanged."

"You're going to arrest him?"

"He is already under arrest. He is forbidden to leave these castle grounds. Frederick will make it known to him anon. In the meantime, Camilla, your instructions remain the same. Find out as much about Sir Stevyn's investigation as you can. Stay as close to him as you can, short of sharing his bed, of course."

She drew a deep breath, and opened her mouth to protest.

But, Godric quickly cut her off. "And don't forget, daughter. I saved your life once. It is only right that you return the favor now."

He stalked from the room, pulling the door closed behind him. Minutes later, Bertha appeared, her face etched in worry.

"You look a fright, Bertha," Camilla said, sitting up. She lifted her arms, and Bertha dropped a freshly laundered tunic over her head.

Camilla stood, sliding into her surcoat, stepping into her pointy-toed shoes. "Come, now, speak freely. What is on your mind?"

"It's the rumors goin' round, m'lady. They say Sir Stevyn killed poor old Hilda. And Hotard, too."

"Do you believe it, Bertha?"

"No, ma'am." The older woman lowered her eyes, as if she were afraid to speak. "I knows he didna murder those folks, not if they was killed last night while the festivities was goin' on."

"How do you know that, Bertha?"

"Because I know who the gentleman was with, m'lady."

Chapter Eleven

Stevyn's eyes stung with bitterness as he gazed at the pathetic little gathering attending Hilda's funeral. They were a ragtag band of wenches, laborers, farmers and scullery maids. A sudden downpour drenched their spirits, filled the shallow grave with water and turned the cemetery into a mud puddle. Thunder and a streak of lightning broke in the sky. The parish priest hurriedly crossed himself, then ran for the shelter of the monastery walls.

Two monks rolled Hilda's burlap-enshrouded corpse into the watery hole in the ground, then filled it in with black peat and mud. The crowd dispersed, with the exception of one young woman standing at the edge of the burial ground, her hair covered by a woolen scarf, her head bowed.

Icy needles of rain pricked his skin, but Stevyn

approached the lone mourner. "Teresa-Marie?" he guessed.

She looked up, her eyes round and watery. He had guessed correctly. In another twenty years, Teresa-Marie would look just like Hilda.

"I am sorry for your loss," he started.

Her eyes were quick and intelligent, but there was something about the serenity of her expression that disturbed Stevyn.

He was put off by her silence, and stammered the remainder of his condolence speech. "I should like to ask you some questions regarding your experience at Barnabas's Sanctuary," he said, at length.

Her gaze widened, and she glanced at the rain-slicked walls of the monastery. Frantically, she shook her head.

"Please, Teresa-Marie. Your mother tried to tell me something in the last moments of her life. I believe she may have known something about the goings-on at the hospital."

She drew her coarsely woven cloak around her and hunched her shoulders. Then, she turned and practically ran back to the road that led to the castle.

Frozen in surprise, Stevyn let her get a few paces ahead. Then, his senses returned and he bolted after her, grasping her arm and halting her progress just as she reached the old Roman wall. He touched her chin, forcing her to look at him.

"You can hear me, can't you?"

She nodded.

"Can you speak?"

She shook her head, then struggled to escape his hold.

"Christ on a raft!" Stevyn caught up with her

again, and, taking her by the shoulders, turned her to face him. "You found your mother in the alleyway. . . . Did you see who murdered her?"

She shook her head furiously, her features scrunched in a mask of fear. Something between a mewl and a grunt sounded from her throat, and she pulled to get away.

"No! You must listen to me! Your life may be in danger."

But, his words were cut short by the rumble of horses' hooves rounding the bend. Stevyn released Teresa-Marie, and she scurried to the other side of the road, slipping into the forest just as a burly soldier mounted on horseback galloped into view.

Frederick and Godric soon appeared on their own richly caparisoned steeds. The three horsemen drew up, halting in the middle of the road. The huge destriers snorted and stamped and fidgeted as the bailiff and the sheriff stared down their noses at Stevyn.

"You are under arrest, sir." Godric's voice boomed like thunder, even above the din of the rainfall.

"What for?" Stevyn demanded.

Frederick's voice, while not as certain as the sheriff's, carried an unmistakable note of smug satisfaction. "For the murder of Hotard the *escrevien,* and Hilda the serving wench."

"Absurd!" Stevyn yelled back. "What mockery of justice is this?"

"As sheriff of Wickinghamshire, Sir Stevyn, it is my duty to arrest all those accused of crimes against my citizens. I have reviewed the evidence against you, and it is sufficient to justify an arrest and indictment."

"You know that I did not kill Hotard or Hilda."

Godric threw his head back and laughed. "Of course, Sir Stevyn. But, all is fair in love and war, and if you thought I intended to sit by idly while you destroyed me, you truly were insane!"

"You will not get away with this, Godric."

"Don't waste your breath. You are remanded to the custody of Frederick the bailiff, and until such time as you are tried by a jury of your peers on these charges, you may not leave the walls of Wickingham Castle."

"You are lucky," Frederick inserted. "Godric has chosen not to commit you to the donjon."

"You will remain in your guest chamber," Godric continued. "Eric here shall guard your door," he said, gesturing at the bulky man seated beside him. "You will not be allowed visitors, with the exception of Camilla, my future daughter-in-law, who is my most trusted vassal, and who will report to me everything that you say and do . . . as she has already done." He smiled. "You see, Stevyn, I am not an unjust man."

Stevyn returned the sarcasm. "Thank you for your leniency, Godric. And for the privilege of my continued society with your future daughter-in-law. You are well advised to trust her. She is most obedient to you."

"My son will be here soon, Stevyn."

"I know."

"I do not want the unpleasantness of your trial hanging over my son's wedding like a black cloud. Therefore, I will grant you speedy justice."

Though anger coursed through his veins like lava, Stevyn remained outwardly calm and collected. "Ironic, isn't it, Godric? I came here to conduct an investigation for the king, and soon I am to be on trial for my life."

"That's what happens when you poke about where you shouldn't, sir."

"On the contrary, it appears I have poked about in precisely the right place." Stevyn began walking back to the castle. Godric, Frederick and Eric the guard would follow on horseback. There would be no ostentatious show of arresting the king's justice or taking him prisoner. Godric would want his people to believe that even murderers received fair treatment in Wickinghamshire.

Moreover, it wasn't necessary to toss him in the donjon and throw away the key. Stevyn wouldn't try to escape even if he could. His business at Wickingham Castle was far from finished. Godric could try as he might, but Sir Stevyn Strongbow would not be intimidated into abandoning his original mission. Godric's malicious persecution of him only made Stevyn more determined to bring the corrupt sheriff down.

By late afternoon, the rain slowed to a drizzle, and the sounds of industry within the castle walls resumed. The upper and lower baileys filled with merchants hawking their wares, housewives seeking the freshest vegetables and herbs, and grimy children darting among the crowds and hopping in mud puddles.

Camilla searched the aviary, the arsenal, the fletcher's hut, even the blacksmith's shop for signs of Bramble. No one had seen him, or the big shaggy wolfhound named Daisy. Exasperated, she exited the northern gate and took the road that led to the monastery. Why the dogs would venture so far from home she couldn't fathom, but dusk would soon descend and she had no intention of allowing Bramble to roam freely another night.

She passed through the gates of Barnabas's compound, then strode the courtyard and the surrounding grounds. She poked a long stick at bushes, looked behind storage sheds and asked every monk she encountered whether he had seen two frisky dogs, specifically, one yellow hound and a gray beast twice his size.

In her thoughts, she characterized Daisy as a seductive she-devil, solely responsible for the corruption of her innocent Bramble. No doubt the wench had absorbed the characteristics of her master. And, if she ever got her hands on that hellhound, she'd see to it that a canine chastity belt was forged specially for Daisy.

Behind the hospital, she followed the flagstone path that led through Barnabas's rose garden. A patient gardener, the abbot had cultivated a species of yellow roses that thrived in the peculiar combination of black earth and peat of Northumbria. But, in their autumnal hibernation, the bushes were bare and thorny, as bleak and forbidding as the gorse and scree that blanketed the surrounding hillsides. In its present state, the rose garden would not conceal a pair of randy dogs.

As her gaze scanned the stone walls, she saw a monk emerge from the greenhouse at the rear of the garden. He took a key from the belt around his waist, and carefully locked the door. Then, he turned in Camilla's direction, starting down the flagstone path with his head lowered and his bony shoulders hunched.

He almost stepped on her toes before he saw

her. "Dear God!" he gasped, stumbling back.

"I am sorry, Brother—"

"Igor," the elderly man breathed.

"Brother Igor. I did not mean to startle you. I am looking for my dog, Bramble. He is most likely in the company of a big shaggy hound named Daisy. Have you seen either one of them?"

Igor's shock faded, and he offered Camilla an avuncular smile. "Dogs? No, child, there are no dogs in Barnabas's rose garden."

"Perhaps you didn't see them if you were in the greenhouse. I'll just look around."

"No use, child. The dogs are not back here." He gestured for her to walk ahead of him, down the path and back toward the hospital.

"Probably not. But, I would like to look." Camilla refused to budge.

"You are wasting your time." Igor's lisp had a slightly sinister sound, and, for no explicable reason, a chill rippled on Camilla's skin. When he touched her arm, she flinched. "Come now, there is work to do in the hospital. Barnabas is displeased when I dodder about the garden all day."

"Go ahead," said Camilla, standing aside. "I won't harm anything, I promise. And Barnabas is not expecting me today. I do not work on Wednesday."

A flash of cruelty lit Igor's eyes, and the long, skinny fingers of his extended hand made a sudden grab at Camilla. But, she jumped sideways and shuddered, pulling her cloak tightly around her body. The monk, apparently suppressing his anger, quickly clasped his hands together, as if in prayer. An unnatural smile played on his thin lips, and he nodded.

"As you wish, child. Just remember, obstinance is the stumbling block to enlightenment. If your dog were here, I would have seen him. Your time would be better spent searching elsewhere. And, in the end, he may suffer from your stubborn refusal to heed my words."

"I will take my chances," Camilla replied tartly.

Head bobbing, the old monk shuffled back toward the hospital. Camilla watched him go, perplexed. Clearly, the monk meant to run her out of Barnabas's rose garden. Why? Because she wanted to search the grounds for Bramble and Daisy? It made no sense. But, nothing did, anymore.

The slam of the door, and the sudden scrabbling of toenails on flagstone gave her heart a jolt. Whirling, Camilla faced the greenhouse. Barreling down the path were two of the dirtiest, scruffiest dogs she'd ever seen. She didn't know where they'd come from. She thought the greenhouse door was locked, and there was nowhere else to hide among the rose beds. Stone walls surrounded the little plot of earth, and the only egress from the garden was either through the hospital door or through the tiny gate that led to the outer courtyard.

Bramble and Daisy skidded to a halt at Camilla's feet, then leaped and yelped and whuffled, apparently thrilled to see her. Camilla, despite her displeasure with her dog's behavior, couldn't resist bending down and hugging Bramble's neck.

Daisy took the opportunity to lick her cheek.

"Oooh, you are a bad girl," Camilla said, vaguely mindful of her earlier vow to insist the dog be locked up. Now that she'd found her

Bramble, her uncharitable feelings toward Daisy diminished. "Sir Stevyn is worried sick about you, girl. Come, now, if we hurry, we can get home before dark."

She practically ran from the monastery compound with both dogs tagging at her heels. Oddly, they seemed as eager as she to return to Wickingham Castle. Relief bubbled up Camilla's throat as she entered the huge double doors of the keep and passed through the Great Hall. Preparations were being made for dinner; for Godric, life seemed to revolve around wine, women and food. But, the servants paid little mind to her, except to wrinkle their noses at the disreputable-looking curs that trailed her skirts.

Their opinions meant nothing to her. She wanted to see the smile on Stevyn's face when she returned Daisy to him. After all, he loved his dog as much as she loved Bramble. And, a man so fiercely loyal to his dog possessed at least one redeeming quality. Despite their being on opposite sides of the law, Camilla did respect Stevyn's sense of loyalty.

Moreover, he had been kind to her when she fainted in the hunting fields. Camilla hadn't forgot the safe protection of Stevyn's embrace, or the warmth of his body, as he rode her back to Wickingham Castle.

Bounding up the stairs, she felt herself smile. But, at the first landing, she drew up short, gaping. The burly soldier standing guard outside Stevyn's room stared back at her. The happy reunion Camilla had anticipated would not occur. Godric, she was certain, had seen to that.

Daisy flew across the room and lunged at him. Knocked off balance, Stevyn couldn't help but laugh. With her huge paws resting on his shoulders, the wolfhound greedily licked his face. He ruffled the plume of fur on her head and hugged her, then he slipped a leash around her neck and tethered her to the leg of his desk. "You stink, girl."

She laid down with a huff, and happily thumped her tail on the floor.

Straightening, Stevyn said, "Thank you for returning my dog. Would you please leave us alone for a moment, Eric?"

Camilla stood in the open doorway, waiting. Behind her, the hovering guard made no pretense of hiding his interest in what went on between Stevyn and the chatelaine of Wickingham Castle. But, when Camilla turned and skewered the hulking Eric with a look of loathing, he slowly stepped back into the corridor and closed the door.

"You are most welcome, sir," she finally replied primly.

After a pause, Stevyn asked, "Where is Bramble?"

"I took him above stairs and tied him to my bedpost. From now on, I will not let the little gargoyle out of my sight."

"I suppose Daisy will be locked in here with me until I am tried. Would you be so kind as to stop in several times a day and take her for a walk?"

"Of course." She twisted her fingers nervously. "So, Godric has formally charged you with the murders of Hilda and Hotard?"

"Surely, you are not surprised."

"No."

"Godric says I shall have a speedy trial."

She ducked her head, refusing to meet his gaze.

He stared at her, amazed as always by her beauty, and by the puzzling conflicts that seemed to rage within her. They stood at the edge of the bed, alone, but not alone. Stevyn's need to touch Camilla was fierce, but his urge to protect her was stronger. So, he stood apart from her, his chest aching.

A little sob shook her body, and she covered her face with her hands.

"Do not fret, Camilla. I have no intention of using you as an alibi." Stevyn's fists coiled at his sides. Keeping his cool in the face of Godric's accusations was a simple task compared to controlling his emotions while Camilla stood before him and cried.

She ran her sleeve across her eyes and sniffled. "I am so sorry, Stevyn."

"You are not to blame. You have no reason to be sorry."

"You would not be on trial for your life if it were not for me." She looked at him with watery, red-rimmed eyes.

"Poppycock! Godric has it in for me. You know that. This trumped-up charge of murder is nothing more than retaliation for my accusation that he has conspired with Barnabas to profit from the sale of illegal relics. This has nothing to do with you, Camilla."

"You were with me when the murders occurred. Had you not been, had you been in the hall with the others, where everyone would have seen you—"

He couldn't stand it any longer. Closing the distance between them, Stevyn squeezed her upper arms and peered intently at her. "Listen to me. You are not the cause of my present predicament. Godric is. He, or someone on his behalf, went to great pains to make it appear that I murdered Hotard and Hilda. It didn't signify where I really was. In a trial, truth is not as important as the illusion, sweetling. I could have been in my own room, for that matter. Which, by the way, is what I intend to say."

"You intend to lie?"

"Would you have me tell the truth, that I was lying in bed with you?"

She shook her head. "No. Yes! Oh, I do not know."

"Think it through, Camilla. If we tell the truth, it still will not save me. Indeed, it will only damn the two of us."

"I don't care what happens to me! I cannot let Godric believe that you murdered two innocent people. He will draw and quarter you, and disembowel—"

"Yes, thank you." The last thing Stevyn needed was a reminder of the punishment in store for him. His gut soured at the thought of it. "But, you miss the point, Camilla. Godric does not believe that I murdered Hilda and Hotard. He knows that I am innocent."

Her mouth formed an oval of despair. "How does he know? How can he know if you refuse to tell him where you were?"

"He knows because he is responsible for the deaths."

"You are accusing Godric of murder!"

A blast of impatience shot through Stevyn. "Either you believe in Godric, or you believe in me, Camilla."

"Why should I believe in you?" she managed through the tears streaming down her face.

"Because I am telling the truth. And because we have been honest with each other, Camilla. I have seen every inch of your body, and I believe I have even glimpsed your soul. You trust me, sweetling. I know you do." Embracing her, he nuzzled her damp nose, then kissed her hard on the lips.

Her body reacted instantly, and she sighed against his neck. Hugging her tightly, Stevyn felt the roundness of her breasts, and the flatness of her belly. The warmth of her body fitted in his arms emboldened him. Holding her at arm's length, he said, "Tell me you believe me, Camilla."

Another sob racked her body, and she squeezed her eyes shut. Gulping for air, she trembled in his grasp, her face the picture of misery. At last, she opened her eyes and wrenched herself free of his hold.

Retreating a step, she stammered, "If I am to believe you, I must give up everything that I have worked these past five years to accomplish. I must reject the people who have declared their love for me. And I must sacrifice my future, perhaps even my life, for the uncertainty of loving you, a man who has declared his intention never to marry."

A breath caught in Stevyn's throat. He hadn't asked Camilla to love him, but to believe in him. He hadn't asked her to lie for him, but to disbelieve Godric. And he hadn't asked her to sacrifice her future for him, but to share his bed.

The words flowed from his lips so easily that he scared himself. "I am not the marrying sort, 'tis true. You wouldn't want me to lie about that, would you?"

She looked as though he'd slapped her. "Rapscallion! Cad! You ask me to believe in you, yet you are no better than your dog when it comes to satisfying your physical urges. You'll leave Wickinghamshire, and you'll forget you ever knew me!"

"That is not true," he said softly.

"And I will be left here to deal with the after-effects of your conduct! How can you be so self-righteous about your principles? How can you sermonize about justice and honesty and fairness when you have no compunctions about using a woman, then tossing her aside? Rationalize your behavior however you will, but you are not to be trusted, Stevyn!"

Stevyn felt as though he'd been slapped himself. He opened his mouth to protest, but Camilla was right in everything she said, with one notable exception: He was not going to leave Wickinghamshire and never think of her again. That was going to be impossible.

"I want you to know that you are more to me than just someone to share my bed."

She scoffed. "Then, tell me, Stevyn, what am I to you? Then, I will tell you whether I believe you are a good and honest man."

Time ground to a halt. Flashing before Stevyn's eyes was the history of his life, the years he spent training to be a paid combatant, then the many duels, fights and tournaments he participated in. He saw Sir Alfred's bloodied face, and heard the man plead for mercy. Pain stabbed him as he recalled the night he'd learned Alfred's client raped and killed again.

Closing his eyes, Stevyn heard the law professors drone. He relived the pride he'd felt at being called to the bar and appointed to the king's bench. Cases and disputes ruffled in his memory like the pages of an open book.

But, where was he now? Where had all his hard work and industry gotten him? He was a prisoner of the corrupt sheriff he'd been sent to investigate. He was a failure yet again, an impotent, insignificant cog in the wheel of justice. He didn't deserve the title of justice on the king's bench. He sure as hell didn't deserve to love a woman like Camilla.

Her blue eyes looked right through him. She was waiting.

He needed her succor, and the comfort of her arms; he needed her honesty and her integrity. He needed her testimony that he was with her when Hilda and Hotard were killed.

He loved her. Yet, he couldn't bring himself to tell Camilla that. Because if he did, she'd be bound to defend him by telling Godric she had slept with him. She wasn't the sort of woman who loved halfway. If he allowed Camilla to commit herself to him, she would insist on being his alibi.

And, the truth would be her death sentence.

She waited. But, when it was apparent that Stevyn would not respond to her question, she backed slowly toward the door. Her tears dried, and her breathing calmed. She was embarrassed at her show of emotion. She had not intended to reveal her weakness. Squaring her shoulders, Camilla resolved to be as cold and hard as Sir Stevyn Strongbow. If he maintained that their relationship was based solely on a mutual need for physical release, then so be it.

She tried for a businesslike tone of voice. "The guard tells me I am to be your only visitor."

"A strange move on Godric's part, don't you think?"

She shrugged. "Not so strange. As chatelaine of the castle, I am responsible for the comfort of its guests."

Stevyn chuckled. "If this is way Godric treats his guests, I shudder to think how he treats his enemies."

"I promise to take Daisy out at least three times a day. And if there is anything else you need, please inform the guard."

"I am not entirely certain that Eric will be a willing messenger boy. Besides, I would be reluctant to tell him what I need from you, Camilla." Stevyn's black eyes raked over her.

"I will not attend to your physical needs, sir. You have declared your true feelings, and so you must respect my decision."

"You have chosen to believe Godric over me?"

"You have chosen the law over me. At least, I don't lie to myself."

A muscle in his jaw flinched. "You think that just because I refuse to announce my love for you, I am lying to myself? Do not flatter yourself, gel. I don't need you, or anyone else. There are many willing lemans in this castle who can satisfy my lust."

"You can't get to them, now," she replied lightly.

His features tightened, then slowly eased. Other than Godric, Camilla had never seen a man control his emotions so masterfully.

He nodded, as if to concede the point to her. Then, he glanced at Daisy. "Where did you find the dogs?"

"They found me actually." Relief poured through Camilla. The whereabouts of their dogs was one subject they could discuss without artifice or the tension of trying to interpret each other's motivations. "I was at the monastery."

"You worked in the sanctuary today?"

"No. Barnabas insists that I take one day off each week. He says it is not good for me to be in the hospital all the time."

"I would have thought he believed hard work was good for the soul." Camilla ignored Stevyn's sarcasm. "I searched the monastery grounds, high and low. 'Struth, I almost gave up. But, then, I remembered the rose garden behind the sanctuary. The bushes are nothing but prickly branches, but I thought the dogs might have found a place to dig in the dirt, or a toad to play with."

"And did they? Find a place to dig, that is?"

"I don't know what they were doing in the garden. I didn't see them until they bounded up to me."

Frowning, Stevyn asked, "Was anyone else in the garden?"

"Just that funny old monk, the one with the lisp. He told me his name was Igor."

"Ah, yes. Hardly a candidate for sainthood, if congeniality is a requirement."

"I think I startled him. He emerged from the greenhouse and started down the path toward the hospital. He nearly walked right over me before he saw me. Then, he acted as if he'd seen a ghost! He almost jumped out of his skin!"

"What was he doing in the greenhouse?"

"How should I know?"

"Well, you said the rosebushes are bare. This time of the year, I wouldn't think there was much gardening to be done."

"Perhaps Igor grows hothouse fruits or exotic flowers in there."

"You would know, wouldn't you?" Stevyn's brow furrowed. "You know everything that goes on in that sanctuary. Have you seen any evidence of fresh tomatoes or cucumbers? I certainly haven't. Not at the meals I have attended below stairs."

Camilla frowned, too. "Well, whatever Igor grows there, he made sure no one was going to get into the greenhouse without his permission. You should have seen the care with which he locked up when he left."

"Why would he lock the greenhouse?"

"Things disappear, Stevyn. Even in a monastery. One can never be too careful."

"Has there been a recent rash of thievery at the monastery?"

"Not that I know of."

"It's very curious, Camilla." Steven rubbed his lower lip. Then, he moved to his desk, sat down and scribbled some notes in his journal.

After a length, Camilla felt she was intruding on his privacy. He was deep in thought, staring first at the words he'd written, then at some invisible spot on the wall.

But, as she turned to leave, he stopped her with a question. "You didn't see where the dogs came from, Camilla?"

Her fingers froze on the latch. Stevyn's question had significance; she knew that from the tone of his voice. But, she didn't dare speculate as to his insinuation.

"You are an expert interrogator, Stevyn. I know you remember precisely what I told you. No, I did not see where the dogs came from. I was looking at the back door of the hospital when I heard Daisy and Bramble behind me. When I turned, they ran down the path to me, and starting jumping up and down."

"Did they come from the greenhouse?" he asked in his velvet voice.

"Igor locked the greenhouse door. I saw him."

"Sometimes our eyes deceive us, Camilla. If you remember anything else, would you kindly let me know?"

"Sometimes our hearts deceive us, too, Sir Stevyn. And, if I remember anything else, I will do whatever is right."

The guard nodded deferentially as she swept out of the prisoner's chambers. Camilla lifted her chin, ascending the stairs as if she were in total control of her emotions. But, when she threw herself on her own bed, the floodgates opened, and the tears she hadn't wanted to shed in Stevyn's presence escaped.

I will do whatever is right! Her own words mocked her. She despised her inability to judge the characters of the men attempting to rule her. She had no faith in her ability to act wisely and to make well-reasoned decisions. She needed someone to tell her what was right, and what was wrong.

But, that someone didn't exist. Camilla Rosedown would have to rely on her own ability to ferret out the truth.

Chapter Twelve

In Barnabas's Sanctuary for Unwed Mothers, the atmosphere was tense. Camilla bent over the bed of a scullery maid barely old enough to understand how she'd become pregnant, and held her hand while the child struggled to give birth.

Turning to the monk assisting her, Camilla practically hissed, "Where is Barnabas?"

The young, wide-eyed man with sweaty tonsure and bloodstained apron stammered, "You have asked me that ten times at least, my lady! I tell you, the abbot is not to be found!"

Camilla could not imagine where the abbot might be. She'd informed him earlier in the day that the girl might begin her labor at any moment. He promised he would be on hand. The child's body was not mature enough for the strain of childbirth, and her ordeal promised to be a dangerous one.

And it was growing more dangerous by the

moment. As the girl panicked and her breathing grew more erratic, the baby made its way down the birth canal. In Barnabas's absence, Camilla took charge of the delivery, checking the dilation of the girl's body, instructing her when to bear down and when not to.

"Just a little while longer," Camilla said soothingly. But, she knew she lied. The girl's test was far from over.

After an hour, Camilla, drenched in perspiration, stood at the foot of the bed. Her patient was more exhausted than she, and appeared on the verge of giving up. But, just as Camilla thought the infant would never be born, the young patient gave a shriek. The baby's head crowned, and Camilla caught her as she slipped from her mother's womb.

"A little girl," Camilla whispered, in awe. "And a messy little thing, at that." Deftly, she snipped the umbilical cord just as she'd seen Barnabas do a hundred times before. Then, she gave the baby a quick washing and laid her on her mother's breast.

"Hold out your hands," she told the young monk assisting her.

Unwittingly, the man did as he was told, and Camilla handed him the mother's placenta. "Now, plant that beneath the apple tree on the far side of the compound. No, on second thought, plant it beneath Barnabas's roses. I believe it is only fitting, and it will bring both the baby and roses good health and prosperity."

"Then, I shall name my baby Rose," the young mother said.

Looking as if he might faint at any moment, the monk darted out the back of the hospital. Chuckling, Camilla thought he would most likely be gone for some time, but that was fine with her. She was happy that her patient's misery was over, and the baby was healthy.

Humming contentedly, she set about replacing the bedclothes and cleaning her patient's body. Optimism brightened her spirits. Surely, some grand revelation would come to her concerning her dilemma. She had to believe that. Witnessing a birth, especially a difficult one, always gave her a new perspective on life.

Barnabas's appearance at the bedside startled her.

"I didn't mean to frighten you, my child." He looked at mother and child, sleeping peacefully, both of them exhausted.

"I'm afraid my mind was elsewhere, Father." Camilla smoothed a counterpane over the scullery maid's body, and gave the pink, wrinkled little baby a pat on the behind.

"They look healthy enough," Barnabas said. "You did a good job, Camilla. I'm proud of you."

"I've never delivered a baby all by myself, Father. I was very afraid. The girl is so young . . . and toward the end, she seemed to be losing strength."

"All's well that end's well."

"Is everything all right with you?" she asked, wiping her hands on her apron.

"Why wouldn't it be?"

"I looked for you. I sent word when the girl's contractions began. Only an emergency would have kept you away."

He smiled benignly. "I knew you could handle the situation."

"But, I am not trained to handle complications. What if she had not dilated sufficiently? What if the babe decided to come into the world feetfirst? What would I have done then, Father?"

"The Lord would have told you what to do, Camilla. You must always trust in the Lord."

The abbot's lack of concern rankled. Camilla *did* trust the Lord. But, the Lord knew she wasn't equipped to handle a breech birth. Why didn't Barnabas understand that? Why had Barnabas made himself so scarce when the young scullery maid was undergoing a traumatic childbirth?

"Yes, Father."

Barnabas nodded pensively. "I was wondering if you have had any success with our prisoner, Sir Stevyn."

"You have heard of his arrest?"

"News of that nature does not remain secret for long, child." The abbot's voice held a coy note, disturbingly incongruous with his ordinarily beatific demeanor.

In the past five years, Camilla and Barnabas had discussed many extraordinarily intimate topics, but she found it necessary to screw up her courage in order to broach the subject of Stevyn's imminent trail. "Do you believe that he is guilty of the crimes with which he has been charged?"

"Who am I to judge? That is for the jury to decide."

For once, Barnabas's saintlike smile seemed sinister. But Camilla beat back her apprehension. With Stevyn telling her one thing, and Barnabas telling her another, it was natural that she viewed everyone with suspicion.

Barnabas had been good to her these past five years, she reminded herself. She was wrong to doubt his motivation now.

"Still, Father, do you think Sir Stevyn can get a fair jury in Wickinghamshire? Godric is revered in this county. His word is law. Once his accusation becomes known, general opinion will quickly turn against Sir Stevyn."

"Daughter, you sound as if you are sympathetic toward the scoundrel. Have you forgotten your loyalties to Godric? And, to me?"

Astounded, Camilla stammered, "No, Father. But, the man is entitled to a fair trial, is he not?"

The abbot's smile vanished and his features tensed. He looked like a man struggling to keep the lid on a pot of boiling water. He could not contain the anger in his voice. "Camilla, the man is a murderer!"

"He has not been convicted yet," she replied, her voice small.

Barnabas's voice boomed through the sanctuary. "Sir Stevyn Strongbow will be convicted of the murder of Hotard the scribe and Hilda the scullery wench! The evidence will prove it."

"What evidence? I know of none!" She regretted her retort as quickly as it escaped her lips.

The abbot's brows shot up, and his face turned red. He raised his pointed finger and jabbed the air as if punctuating some particularly righteous point in an otherwise bland Sabbath sermon.

"Listen to me, Camilla, and listen well! The man is evil! And like all demons, he has a silver tongue, one that will seduce you with lies and confuse you with fancy words if you are not vigilant in your faith. Godric has said the man killed Hotard and Hilda. That should be enough for you. If it is not, then . . . then, you are a fool as well as an ingrate, woman!"

For a moment, she thought he was going to strike her. Camilla squeezed her eyes shut and cowered. But, the blow she anticipated never came. A blast of silence echoed through the sanctuary, followed by the wail of babes awakened by Barnabas's outburst.

Inhaling deeply, she dared to look around. Monks frozen at the bedsides of their patients stared back curiously. Frightened women gaped. Startled infants continued to shriek and squeal.

At length, she looked at Barnabas.

Flexing his fingers, he moved away from her, as if he, too, were fearful that he might strike her. Eyes burning, he stood at the foot of the bed, and said quietly, "Godric has told you to befriend the man, Camilla. Your purpose is to find out what sort of scurrilous tripe Sir Stevyn intends to tell the king regarding my relic-selling enterprise. Are you nurturing the seeds of sedition in your heart, gel? Shall I tell the sheriff that you have pledged your allegiance to the enemy?"

Had he pounded her heart with a battering ram, Barnabas could not have wounded her more profoundly. "No! No, please! I love Godric. He has been more than kind to me. And so have you, Father. Please, forgive me. I didn't mean to—"

"Dear God, Camilla! A soldier must be able to engage the enemy without being pressed into service by him. Are you so weak that you cannot befriend Sir Stevyn without betraying Godric?"

"I have not betrayed Godric! I would not! Ever!"

Barnabas closed his eyes and drew in a deep breath. Serenity flowed back into his features, so that when he fixed his gaze on Camilla again, he was his old self, smiling benevolently, if not a trifle tightly, and exuding righteousness. "Godric loves you, Camilla. You are to be his daughter. The honor he has bestowed on you is not to be regarded lightly. In order to live up to the status you have been accorded, you must perform your duties, and perform them well."

"You mean I must continue to spy on him," she said dully.

"Are you unwilling to do this thing for Godric? And for me?"

Camilla hesitated. Twisting her fingers, she glanced uncertainly at the young scullery maid. The squalling din that surrounded her fairly accurately reflected her own feelings. But, she had to conceal her confused emotions. "Of course, I will do what Godric has asked me to do. I wouldn't dream of doing otherwise."

"God bless you, Camilla. And God help you to do what is right." The abbot turned and strode through the sanctuary, nodding greetings at the flustered monks, and murmuring blessings to the nervous mothers he passed.

"Thank you, Barnabas," Camilla whispered. Tears streamed down her cheeks as she held a cup of water to the scullery maid's lips. When the young girl and her babe had settled back to sleep, Camilla left their beside and returned to the castle. Ascending the stairwell, she paused on the first landing and met the speculative gaze of Eric, the guard standing duty outside Stevyn's door.

"Come to see the prisoner, m'lady?" he asked gruffly.

She wanted to. God, how she wanted to curl up in Stevyn's protective embrace and hide. But, her conscience wouldn't allow it. There was far too much work to be done, far too many mysteries to solve. Camilla had to figure out for herself who was right, and who was wrong. She couldn't rely on Barnabas and Godric to tell her the truth, she understood that now. But, she couldn't depend on Stevyn, either.

Camilla Rosedown would learn the truth for herself, and for no one else.

"No, Eric, I shall return later to take Daisy outside for some exercise."

"As you wish," the guard replied.

In her room, she lay down on her bed and stared at the ceiling. The wooden rafters above her head faded to a mental picture of Barnabas and Godric in the Great Hall, celebrating the arrival of Risby's advance men. She had a clear picture of them toasting Risby's return. Something was amiss in the scene, but she couldn't grasp what it was. She tried to make sense of all that had happened these past few days, but her mind was muddled and her thinking impaired. As she drifted to sleep, Godric's laughter echoed in her dreams, beckoning her, mocking her, challenging her to choose between him and Stevyn.

When she awakened, her room was cast in twilight's shadows. Faint steps on the stairwell announced Bertha's evening visit and the beginning of dinner preparations. Camilla rubbed the sleep from her eyes and yawned. A smile twitched at her lips. Sitting up, she rubbed her sore neck and stretched her limbs. Sleep had refreshed her. Her dreams had enlightened her.

She still did not known whom to trust. But, at least, she now knew whom to question and what to ask.

The sudden bark of orders outside his door, and the scrabbling of a key in the lock, startled Stevyn from his thoughts. Hunched over his journal, he lifted the nub of his pen and turned as his door crashed open. The guard named Eric crossed the threshold, while, behind him, Frederick the bailiff stood in the doorway.

"The sheriff has summoned you to appear below stairs," Eric said gruffly. "Frederick will accompany you."

"What time is it?" Stevyn rolled his shoulders, flexing the stiff muscles in his back and neck.

"Dinner has been under way for well over an hour," the guard answered. "Yet, I see you have not touched the plate of mutton I brought in to you this evening."

The thought of food made Stevyn's stomach rumble. He was hungry, now that he thought of it. Occupied with his journal, he hadn't eaten or drunk anything since the morning. His mouth watered as he glanced at the cold lamb waiting for him, but he didn't have time to worry about his physical needs; Godric wouldn't wait.

In the Great Hall, Stevyn stood before the table of honor where Godric dined. Barnabas sat at the sheriff's right hand, and Camilla occupied the space beside Barnabas. Having delivered the prisoner, Frederick took his usual place on Godric's left side.

The three men glared at Stevyn with an alarming mixture of malice and amusement, as if they truly relished the thought of seeing him convicted and hung. Stevyn returned their stares with cool equanimity. These local titans might, indeed, kill him, but they would never see him lose control of his emotions.

"How fare you, Stevyn?" Godric asked, his voice as creamy as butter.

"My accommodations are adequate, sheriff. The food is good and I am protected from the elements. As prisons go, Wickingham Castle is quite luxurious."

The men chuckled as easily as if Stevyn had just recited a bawdy rhyme.

Barnabas said, "Are you ready to confess your sins, son?"

"My sins are a matter of confidence between me and my Creator," Stevyn replied, "but I shall confess nothing to you. I am, after all, a lawyer. I must follow my own advice."

This reply drew less of a chuckle.

"Confess and you will receive mercy," Barnabas urged.

Stevyn shot a look at Camilla before he answered. "If the abbot's concept of mercy bears any relation to the sheriff's concept of justice, I should do better to take my chances with a jury. Thank you, Barnabas, but I have nothing to confess."

Camilla's color heightened, and she pursed her lips. Her gaze flickered from Godric to Stevyn, as if she were uncertain where to look. But, each time she did dare a glance at him, Stevyn's blood warmed. Even with his life hanging in the balance, Stevyn could not ignore her.

"Then you will be tried in the assize court of Wickinghamshire," Frederick announced, licking his lips.

Flipping his wrist foppishly, Godric said, "Oh, for God's sake, Freddie! We do not have a judge to preside over the trial! What shall we do?"

Frederick replied, " 'Tis a most unusual set of circumstances to have the circuit judge on trial for murder. I suppose we must attempt to locate a learned man of the law who can act as judge."

"Who would that be?" Godric asked, smiling slyly.

Barnabas spoke up. "I suppose it should be you, Godric."

"Do you think I can be fair and just?" Godric asked.

The sheriff's sarcasm knifed through Stevyn's body like a newly forged pike. Godric had no intention of granting Stevyn a fair trial. The trial would be a mockery of justice, and Stevyn would be sentenced to death. A dispatch would be sent to London informing King Edward that his trusted justice had killed two people, and was convicted by an impartial jury. No one at court would ever be the wiser. No one in Wickinghamshire was going to breathe a word.

Looking at Camilla, Stevyn's bitter anger deepened. She was a victim of the sheriff's villainy, too. And, though Stevyn didn't understand the exact nature of her relationship with Godric, he knew she hadn't agreed to marry Risby because she wanted to. Camilla was as much a prisoner of Godric's as Stevyn was.

Her chin wobbled as her future father-in-law revealed his scheme. Her agony was painfully apparent, but she kept her mouth closed, not daring to voice a protest. Her silence spoke for her. She might not have been threatening to ruin Stevyn's career and end his life, but her loyalties were pinned to the sheriff's quilted tunic like a badge of honor.

Stevyn looked away from her, uncertain whether he pitied or resented Camilla. He knew only one certainty: If Godric had his way, Stevyn would be buried in a burlap bag beside Hilda before the next sundown.

"It is decided, then," Godric said. "I shall be your judge, Sir Stevyn."

"And I shall prosecute the case," Frederick said.

"And since you are entitled to a jury of your peers, you shall choose any twelve of my soldiers to render a verdict," drawled Godric, grinning mischievously.

"*Your* soldiers? Do you really think *your* soldiers can be impartial?" For the first time, Stevyn was unable to suppress his disgust. "Why not put an arrow through my heart right now? Why bother with a trial? You intend to kill me, and everyone knows it!"

The blue in Godric's gaze turned to icy hatred. "I shall give you a fair trial, and when you are convicted, I shall send news of your sentencing and death to the king. It will not be said that I murdered the king's emissary."

"He will only send another judge to investigate you and Barnabas," Stevyn answered. "King Edward is determined to weed out the corrupt clergy who are preying upon innocent people. He will not give up simply because you have killed me."

"Then, let him send another justice," Frederick said in oily manner.

"Like Alfred?" Camilla blurted.

Godric's head snapped around and he leveled a quelling gaze at her. Barnabas and Frederick stared in astonishment. Cheeks scarlet, Camilla dipped her head and clasped her hands on the tabletop. Stevyn felt a smile twist at his lips.

She wasn't as naive as she appeared.

The clumsy silence at the table of honor was accentuated by the noise surrounding it. At the long trestle tables behind Stevyn, soldiers banged their tankards and laughed. Saucy wenches sat on men's laps and giggled. Dogs roamed the hall, fighting over bones tossed to the rushes.

A pair of mangy hounds wandered within kicking distance of Godric's feet. "Damme, woman!" Godric gave a well-placed stab with his boot, and the dogs yelped, then fled with their tails tucked between their legs.

Camilla flinched, but said nothing.

"Have I not told you?" Godric said through clenched teeth, "to keep your foolish little mouth shut unless I direct a question to you?"

She nodded.

"Well, then, do as I say, Camilla Rosedown!" The sheriff brought his fist down on the table-top, rattling mazers and salt cellars and the knives not yet removed by the pantler.

This demonstration brought the raucous cacophony in the background to a sudden stillness. Every head in the hall turned; all eyes were pinned on Godric. Food spilled out of soldiers' slack-jawed mouths as they stared. Not even a mouse rustled in the straw covering the floor.

The veins at Godric's temples pulsed, his nostrils flared and fury radiated from his imposing figure. He looked around the room, his eyes brandishing tyranny. Then, slowly, a smile spread over his face, and his expression eased.

"Well, I believe we have an understanding now," the sheriff said quietly.

"Yes, Godric," Camilla whispered.

"Everyone, back to dinner, then!" Godric cried, lifting his oaken cup in the air. He drank thirstily, then wiped his sleeve across his mouth.

A collective sigh went up throughout the hall. The soldiers went back to their feasting and drinking and wenching. Barnabas made the sign of the cross and whispered, "Thank God." Camilla, having seemingly forgotten to breathe, gulped for air.

Stevyn lifted his chin, and held her gaze. She'd spoken rashly, but she'd spoken her mind. And, in doing so, she'd provided another piece of the puzzle Stevyn had been working. The mention of Sir Alfred's name provoked the sheriff to rage. That could only mean one thing.

Godric didn't fear the king's next justice, or the one after that, because he knew eventually the king would send another Alfred, a man who could be bought or bribed or coerced into silence. Godric might have to kill Stevyn before he got another Alfred, but eventually he would. And Barnabas's relic-selling operation would once again be protected.

Camilla's eyes were full of questions. Stevyn tried to read her thoughts, but the sheriff interrupted with a shocking pronouncement.

"One other matter, Sir Stevyn. You are entitled to a representative to argue your case at trial."

Stevyn's nerves jumped. "You are granting me the privilege of being represented by a lawyer?"

Godric shrugged. "There are no trained practitioners in Wickinghamshire, sir. We are not in London. In these remote parts, any man who professes to know the law may represent another in court. Perhaps Barnabas can recommend one of the monks to you; many of them are well versed in the law. Some can even read and write."

"Thank you, but I would fain represent myself."

"You know what they say about lawyers who represent themselves, don't you, Stevyn?" Godric nudged Frederick's elbow. "You have a fool for a client, sir."

Frederick and Barnabas laughed obediently. Stevyn cut his eyes at Camilla.

Her worried look mirrored his own suspicions. Godric's offer of a representative was a troublesome deceit. There was not the smallest possibility that he intended to give his prisoner an advantage. Everything Godric did or said had an ulterior motive designed to ruin Stevyn.

"Choose a representative, sir," Godric said. "Or, I shall designate one for you."

"Igor would be perfect," Barnabas said.

"I do not believe his lisp will favorably impress the jury," Stevyn remarked drily.

Godric laughed from his gut. "Choose, Sir Stevyn! Now!"

Stevyn hesitated. There was only person in Wickingham Castle whose integrity he was sure of. Oddly, that person was on the opposite side of the law, and not to be trusted. Fixing his gaze on her, Stevyn said loudly, "I choose Camilla Rosedown as my counsel and representative. She will represent me at my trial. And I am confident that she will win my acquittal."

Barnabas gasped, and Frederick said, "Preposterous!"

Camilla's heart thundered like a herd of cattle. Staring at Stevyn always brought a rush of heat to her face, but now she felt as if her face were roasting. What the devil was he thinking, choosing her to represent him? Godric would never allow it, and even if he did, Camilla knew less about lawyering than she did about birthing breech babies. She was sorely tempted to echo

Frederick's sentiment. The idea *was* preposterous. Stevyn *had* to be joking.

Godric's voice was calm and deliberate. "You cannot be serious."

Stevyn's eyes glittered. "My life is at stake, Godric. I am deadly serious."

"She is but a *girl*."

"She is quick-witted and intelligent. There is no one else I want to represent me."

Drumming his fingers on the table, Godric looked at both Frederick and Barnabas. Then he shrugged, and said, "So be it."

The knot in Camilla's stomach tightened. No one even asked her whether she was willing. If she'd felt pulled apart by Stevyn and Godric before, she felt cut in half now. How dare these men use her so? How dare they toy with her for their own amusement?

In a blink, she considered all that she had done in her life, and all that had brought her to this place. Born just outside the market town of Hexham, she was orphaned at an early age when the plague swept through her village. Relatives in Haltwhistle took her in, and, anxious to rid themselves of her, arranged for her marriage to Gavin McGavin when she was barely fifteen.

When he fell from a horse in a jousting tournament, broke his neck and died, Camilla was homeless and penniless . . . *and pregnant*. Frederick arrested her in the royal fields outside Wickinghamshire where she was found hawking for food. Barnabas held her hand during the terrible ordeal of her infant's stillbirth. And Godric offered her amnesty in exchange for her agreement to marry Risby.

Now she sat in the Great Hall of Wickinghamshire Castle, all eyes upon her. Her heart was divided; she wanted to believe that the men who had rescued her from poverty were good and wise. But, Stevyn, the man she'd fallen in love with, had tossed down his gauntlet and challenged them all. Camilla felt like the quintain, waiting to be attacked from either side.

A lump rose in her throat. She did love Sir Stevyn Strongbow. Try as she might, she could not separate her physical attraction to him from her emotions. Perhaps their first encounter had been precipitated by lust and impulsive desperation, but in a matter of days, she'd grown to love Stevyn. Yet, her promise to Godric was written in stone. No matter what Camilla did, she would betray someone.

Stevyn stared at her with that vaguely amused look in his eyes.

She almost forgot that Godric, Frederick and Barnabas were there. "Do you fear nothing, Sir Stevyn?" she asked.

Godric gave a derisive snort.

Stevyn approached the table, stood before Camilla, then bowed slowly. When he straightened, he said, "Any man who tells you he is not afraid in battle is a liar."

"I am afraid for you," Camilla replied. Then, remembering Godric's presence, she added, "With me as your lawyer, your life is in mortal jeopardy."

Stevyn shrugged. "I trust you."

Stunned, Camilla merely stared as Godric clapped his hands and dismissed Stevyn from his presence. Frederick escorted the prisoner out of the hall and up the steps. Dinner continued as if nothing unusual had happened, Godric gnawing on a grizzled bone, Barnabas sipping his wine.

At length, Camilla folded her serviette and laid it on the table beside the trencher she shared with the abbot. "If you will excuse me," she said, standing. "I am quite weary and wish to retire to my chambers."

"You might want to visit with your client before bedtime," Godric teased.

Camilla's blood froze. Stevyn's trial was a farce, a form of entertainment for Godric and his cohorts. Her courage fortified by wine, she paused beside her chair, and faced the sheriff. "Why are you doing this, Godric?"

"Call me Father," he cooed.

"Why did you allow him to choose me as his representative?"

"What harm can it do?" The sheriff laughed. "You know nothing of the law, and cannot possibly represent his interests adequately. However, it will never be said that I denied him a lawyer of his choice. He picked you over Igor? Well, that is his poor decision, not mine."

"You should have denied his request to name me as his lawyer! He is entitled to competent legal counsel. I cannot defend him."

Chuckling, Godric stood and placed his hands on Camilla's shoulders. He tenderly kissed her cheek, then drew back and peered at her. "Child, I am proud of you. You have gained the man's trust, just as I have asked. Now, use the power you have over him, and find out who sent him this evil mission to destroy me and Barnabas."

"You know who sent him . . . the king!"

Barnabas leaned closer, so that when he whispered, Camilla smelled the rancid animal fat on his beard. "There is a spy within these castle walls. There must be. Otherwise, King Edward would never have launched such an investigation."

"Perhaps Alfred told the king about the relic-selling operation."

"Alfred was our friend, Camilla. He would never have testified against us."

Because he was being paid not to. The unspoken words hung in the air like smoke. Camilla's pulse skittered. If Alfred had not put a bug in the king's ear, who did? Nervously, she looked around, wondering who in Wickingham Castle possessed the motivation to shut down Barnabas's Sanctuary for Unwed Mothers. The mystery seemed unsolvable.

As did her own dilemma. "Godric, I do not want to represent Sir Stevyn," she stammered.

Smiling paternally, he patted her arm. "Do not fret, child. You can do no harm. Sir Stevyn's fate is already sealed. Your duty is to learn the identity of the traitor who accused Barnabas and me of wrongdoing. Can you do that?"

"I will try," she whispered, looking him straight in the eye.

His features hardened. "Do not *try,* Camilla. Do it. Your future, as well as mine, depends upon it."

"Yes . . . Father." She gave a little curtsy to show her deference and respect, then turned and left the table. Gliding past the rows of trestle tables, Camilla clenched her jaw and steeled her nerves.

She picked up her skirts and ascended the stairs, heart pounding. Her future was uncertain and her course of action undecided, but her mind was made up. Camilla Rosedown was no man's puppet. She would do what she believed was right, and to hell with what Godric or Stevyn told her.

When she discovered the truth, she would know what to do. Until then, her duty as a lawyer was to zealously defend her client. But, as a woman, she had only to be true to herself. A great feeling of relief and enlightenment flooded Camilla's heart as she greeted Eric. She might be Risby's bride within a fortnight, or she might be penniless and homeless again. It didn't matter. Pulled in opposite directions by the men who controlled her future, Camilla had finally found her center.

Chapter Thirteen

At the sound of the key turning in the lock, Stevyn looked up from his journal. Daisy, tied to the leg of his desk, lifted her head and thumped her tail on the floor.

"Thank you, Eric," Camilla said calmly as the guard opened the door. She waited in the center of the room until Eric retreated. Then, she crossed the floor and stood, arms akimbo, before Stevyn.

"Have you lost your mind?" she demanded, blue eyes flashing.

Stevyn stood slowly, stretching his aching muscles. The anger roiling off Camilla's body was daunting. Yet, her presence, and the fact that she hadn't refused to act as his legal representative, gave him comfort. "Mayhaps I have lost my mind. Are you thinking of pleading my insanity as a defense?"

"Oooh!" She stomped her foot, and shook her

head, causing Daisy to whine. "You are an evil trickster, Stevyn, if you believe that you can sway the jury by choosing me as your lawyer."

"The jury will be chosen from among Godric's soldiers," Stevyn replied. "I believe they will warm to you far more easily than they would to Igor."

"Igor! Of all the ridiculous—"

He cut her off. "Of course, it was ridiculous. Igor is in Barnabas's pocket, to be sure. Anything I said in confidence to him would be repeated to the abbot and the sheriff before my tongue ceased wagging. Whatever I say to you is strictly between us. I can trust you, can I not, Camilla?"

She clasped her hands in front of her. "I will not lie for you, or for anyone else, Stevyn."

"That is all I ask for, that you argue the truth on my behalf."

A look of anguish struck her. "You want me to tell Godric where you were when the murders took place? Why didn't you tell him yourself?"

"For the same reason I did not want Igor appointed my legal representative. I have no intention of using you as an alibi, Camilla. And as long as you are my lawyer, you cannot be a witness as well. Therefore, we have effectively eliminated that option as a possible defense strategy for our case."

"*Our* case?

The near hysteria in her voice reminded him of the first time he'd tried a case before the king's bench. His stomach had soured from nervousness, and just minutes before his case was called, he threw up. It was not uncommon for young lawyers, particularly the good ones, to anticipate trial with a mixture of eagerness and sickening dread.

"There, there," he said, struggling against the urge to embrace her. "You will catch onto this legal jargon very quickly, I am certain. By tomorrow, you will be more learned than Charlemagne in the procedures of English common law."

"I do not want to be a lawyer!" she wailed.

"But, I need you!"

" 'Struth, I believe I would rather be your alibi!"

Stevyn gripped her upper arms. "That would be the death of both of us, Camilla. I will not allow it. If one of us must die, it will be me. I will not allow Godric to destroy you as well. Now, you must trust me. I have a plan."

She brushed away her tears as he began to explain his argument. Bathed in candlelight, they sat at his desk, Stevyn making notes and diagrams, Camilla asking questions. He told her everything he'd done in pursuing his investigation. He described his conversations with Hilda and Teresa-Marie, his attempt to draw out Hotard. He recounted his arrest on the road leading from the monastery, and Godric's bold admission that he'd orchestrated Stevyn's ruination.

They worked for hours, going over courtroom procedure, the mechanics of empaneling a jury, the proper objections that could be made and the technical maneuvers she might expect from Frederick.

Stevyn scratched out a series of questions Camilla would ask him under oath. His case rested largely on his own testimony that he was wrongfully accused by Godric in retaliation for the investigation he'd begun. Even if he was convicted, Stevyn explained, there would be an official court record detailing Godric's corrupt practices. He might never make it back to London alive, but at least his death would not be in vain.

" 'Tis risky, Stevyn." Rubbing her tired eyes, Camilla glanced with alarm at the first rays of morning sun streaming through the window.

"I trust you, sweetling." He laid down his pen, and picked up her hand. Brushing his lips across the back of her knuckles, he sighed. "Whatever you do, you must never say that I was with you when the murders occurred."

"I told you I will not lie."

"I am not asking you to lie. I am only asking you to argue the greater truth, that Godric accused me maliciously in order to put an end to King Edward's investigation."

"And what if, after all my fancy arguments, you are still convicted of murdering Hilda and Hotard?"

"Innocent men are sometimes wrongfully convicted. You cannot blame yourself if that occurs. If I am convicted and sentenced to death, you must not feel guilty. You did not commit this crime, nor did you charge me with it. You did everything you could to try to obtain an acquittal. Ultimately, the decision lies with the jury, over whom you have no control."

"If you are convicted . . ." Camilla's voice trembled softly. "Will I have the opportunity to talk with my client before the sentence is carried out?"

"I expect the bailiff will take me immediately to the scaffold, Camilla."

"Then, this may be the last time—"

He put his fingers on her lips. "Do not say it." Stevyn's bones creaked as he stood, drawing

Camilla to her full height and enclosing her in his arms. He laid his head atop hers and breathed in the clean fragrance of her hair and skin. Her soft breasts and flat belly pressed against him. The warmth of her flesh enveloped him.

Despite his state of exhaustion, a heaviness tingled in his groin. He'd taken so much from Camilla, he should have felt guilty. But, fear clawed at his heart and made him needy.

Tipping her chin with his thumb, Stevyn lowered his lips to hers. "Dear God, I know we shouldn't, but I cannot help myself," he whispered hoarsely.

Her fingers tangled in the hair at his nape. Her breath was hot and moist on his neck. "Oh, Stevyn, I am so scared."

"So am I, love. So am I."

Camilla's heart raced. With Eric standing watch outside the door, it was reckless beyond belief to give in to their passions. But, the thought that she might never see Stevyn again after tomorrow's trial filled her with terror.

As they lay on his bed, however, a sense of peacefulness descended on them. Propped on his elbow, Stephen stretched out alongside Camilla, staring down at her as if she were some amazing object of beauty he'd never seen before. Amused, she watched him as he removed the pins from her hair. Toying with the flaxen braids, he tested their texture, inhaled their perfume, even held them to his lips. A slow smile spread across his face, and a sparkling veil of tears filmed his eyes.

She stroked his head. "Remember the first time we made love?"

"It wasn't so long ago," he said.

"Odd. I made love to you then because I feared my life was ending."

"And now you make love to me because you fear *mine* is."

Her fingers stilled at the side of his face. Outside, a rooster crowed the dawn's approach. But, in Stevyn's bedchamber, the world had ceased spinning and nothing existed other than Camilla's need for him.

His hands roved the length of her body, caressing the curves of her hips and legs. Finding the hem of her kirtle, he drew it up to her belt. His fingers brushed the sensitive flesh of her thighs and grappled in her soft curls.

Unhooking her girdle, Camilla tossed it to the floor. Then, she lifted her hips and allowed Stevyn to pull her tunic over her head. The rest of her garments—and his, too—were quickly shed. Naked, they lay in each other's arms, their mouths connected in a long, passionate kiss.

"I need you," she whispered as he hovered over her.

"Then you shall have me." Moving between her legs, he gently opened her up to him.

Camilla accepted the hard length of him inside her with a gasp of pleasure. Her inner muscles contracted, squeezing him, drawing him even deeper inside. They moved rhythmically against each other, their bodies melting together, their skin releasing the scent of their exertions.

Watching his expression, Camilla's arousal peaked. She loved to see Stevyn's hunger for her reflected on his face. His eyes burned feverishly as he gazed down at her. His cheeks darkened and his jaw set as he struggled for control.

Wave after wave of pleasure shook her body, but Stevyn had yet to find his release. His jagged breathing filled the room, threatening to alert Eric to their lovemaking. Then, suddenly, Stevyn reached beneath Camilla's bottom, and slid her lower in the bed. He rose on his knees, and grasped her ankles. Resting them on his shoulders, he entered her from a deeper angle, plunging inside her, filling her, reaching as far inside her as he could.

She bit her lower lip to keep from crying out as she reached her fulfillment. Stevyn found his release, too, moaning as he withdrew his shaft. Hot seed spilled on her belly. His body tensed and shuddered. For a moment, he seemed paralyzed, frozen forever with his slender hips wedged between her spread thighs. Then, with a sigh, he slowly moved away. His body separated from hers, filling her with *emptiness*.

In the hall below, soldiers stamped their boots and roared for breakfast. The squawk of chickens rose from the courtyard, while, faintly, the rattle of pots and pans wafted through the alleyway and through Stevyn's open window. Then, a new sound pricked at Camilla's ears; it was the dull thud of nails being hammered into oaken beams. The groggy pleasure throbbing in her veins disappeared. Struggling to her elbows, she listened.

"What do you hear?" Stevyn asked, his voice soft, like a lover's.

"They're building a scaffold, Stevyn." She turned to look at him, and before he could conceal it, she saw the flash of fear in his eyes.

Rolling away from her, he grabbed for his clothes. "You must go, Camilla. I will see you next in court."

She lightly touched his naked back, but he stood, moving away from her. Hurriedly, Camilla dressed and tapped on the door. She smoothed her hair as Eric let her out.

"Good luck," the burly guard said. "I hope he is acquitted."

Surprised, Camilla hesitated. "I should have thought you were on Godric's side. Doesn't everyone believe that Sir Stevyn is guilty of killing Hilda and Hotard?"

The big man shrugged. "I don't know what everyone else thinks. I only know what I have heard with me own ears, and seen with me own eyes. Eric isn't as stupid as the bailiff thinks he is."

Puzzled, Camilla turned and headed up the steps. Her mind grasped at bits of evidence, turning them over, piecing them together. Snippets of her conversation with Stevyn, and glimpses of Godric's smug expression, niggled at her subconscious. But, it wasn't until she was in her own bedchamber, stripping off her wrinkled clothes, that the revelation hit her.

Bertha helped her dress and comb her hair. Then, Camilla stuffed the papers and notes she and Stevyn had made into a leather pouch. She kissed her worried-looking maid on the cheek, and raced from the room. In four scant hours, Stevyn's trial would begin. And teaching her surprise witness how to talk before nuncheon was not going to be easy.

The Great Hall was filled with spectators, old and young alike. Godric had supervised the rearrangement of the furnishings, and now he sat at the far end of the room, enthroned on a huge, ornately carved chair. On his left, at the trestle tables bordering the walls, camped a platoon of soldiers, some of them still clad in chain-mail vests, others wearing less cumbersome quilted gambesons. Lining the walls were village citizens, tradesmen, housewives and servants, all eager to see the drama of Stevyn's trial, and, if they were lucky, perhaps a good hanging.

And, in the center of the room, directly in front of Godric, were two long refectory tables borrowed from the monastery, one reserved for Frederick and his witnesses, the other meant for Camilla Rosedown and her client.

As the noon bells tolled in the monastery tower, Godric banged a gavel on the arm of his chair, and shouted for order in his makeshift court. "Everybody, quiet! The trial of Sir Stevyn Strongbow, accused of the murders of Hilda the servant and Hotard the scribe, shall now commence!"

An eerie silence fell over the hall. Heads turned and necks stretched as everyone in the room tried to get a look at the accused and his lawyer. Camilla's cheeks burned brightly beneath the scrutiny, and for a moment, her fingers played nervously among her papers, but, then, she appeared to calm herself, and when Godric asked the lawyers to make their appearances, she stood as straight as did Frederick, and said, "My name is Camilla Rosedown," in a clear, even voice.

"And I represent the accused, Sir Stevyn Strongbow," she added, to the gasps of astonishment that went up in the hall.

"So be it," intoned Godric. Waving his hand at the jury pool, he instructed Frederick to choose six.

"Any six will do," Frederick said confidently.

Camilla leaned down, and Stevyn whispered in her ear. "You might as well do the same. They are all Godric's liege men and owe their fealty to him. It does no good to question their prejudices now."

Camilla straightened. "Any six will do for the defense, as well," she said.

Godric nodded approvingly, then pointed his finger at the trestle table nearest him. "The men at the first table shall serve as jurors. That means you must pay attention to everything that is said. No getting drunk or falling asleep. And no leaving the hall to piss!"

A murmur of laughter rolled through the ranks before Godric banged his gavel again. When silence was restored, he turned to Frederick. "Bailiff, who is your first witness?"

"I call Eric, the guard, Judge Godric."

When Camilla resumed her seat, Stevyn squeezed her arm. "You are doing fine," he assured her.

She cut her round blue gaze at him. "I have not yet had a chance to make a mistake, sir. Frederick will put on a very strong case."

"All circumstantial, Camilla. Remember, I am innocent."

She offered him a slight smile, then turned her attention to Eric's story.

The guard sat in a small chair that was catty-cornered to Godric's throne, and situated between Frederick's table and the jury. Twirling his beefy thumbs, he squirmed beneath Godric's eagle-eyed gaze.

"Do you recall where you were the night of Hilda's murder?"

"I rode out to meet the advance party sent ahead by Risby, Godric's son. Then, I escorted the men back to Wickingham, and saw to it that they were made comfortable in the hall." Eric paused, apparently uncertain whether he had provided the answer Frederick was looking for. "I stood just outside the hall until the stable boys came. Once the horses were taken care of, I went inside to dinner."

"Did you see Hilda that night?"

"Yes."

"Where?" Frederick asked.

"Standing in the alleyway, between the hall and the kitchens. It was getting dark, but my eyesight is very good, and I'm certain it was Hilda. I have known her for many years now. Her daughter is my age—"

"Yes, yes," Frederick interrupted. "Just answer the question, please. So, you saw Hilda in the alley. Was she alone?"

Eric scratched his head. "No."

"Did you see who was with her?"

"Yes. Sir Stevyn Strongbow."

Whispers, head-shaking and accusatory glances in Stevyn's direction erupted among the audience and even in the jury box. But, Godric seemed not to notice. Leaning toward Eric, he listened intently, as if the boy spoke with as much authority as Moses returning from the mount with a stone tablet in his arms.

Frederick, his expression grim, slowly approached the witness. He faced the jury, giving his listeners the full effect of his sorrowful attitude. "Tell me, Eric. After you saw Hilda in the alley with Sir Stevyn, did you ever see her alive again?"

Seemingly puzzled, Eric, at length, admitted, "No."

"I have no further questions of this witness, Judge." As he walked back to his table, Frederick made eye contact with one of the soldiers and winked.

Stevyn's blood boiled, but he sat quietly, unwilling to give Godric the satisfaction of knowing how frightened he was. His fate seemed horribly clear. Frederick would offer threadbare evidence, then weave his damning case together with innuendo and insinuation. Godric would nod sagely at the trumped-up testimony elicited by Frederick, giving the prosecutor's case the illusion of substance. It would all culminate in a travesty of justice, and Stevyn would be lucky if he wasn't dancing in the wind by nightfall.

"Would you like to question this witness, *Lady* Camilla? If you are not familiar with the procedure, I will be pleased to explain it to you. Women, after all, cannot be expected to know these things."

Ignoring the giggles that arose from the jury box, Camilla rose, and as planned, replied, "I will reserve my questions for Eric until I am ready to put on my case, Judge."

Stevyn noted the sharp look exchanged between Godric and Frederick. They hadn't anticipated Camilla would be so well versed in the intricacies of trial procedure. They didn't know she'd stayed awake half the night cramming into her brain every bit of knowledge that Stevyn could feed her. And, they couldn't possibly know how intelligent she was. Even Stevyn was amazed at her quick grasp of legal concepts and her instinctive ability to argue and reason logically.

"As you wish," Godric said sourly. "Frederick, who is your next witness?"

"Igor the monk," Frederick said, waving the stoop-shouldered old cleric to the witness chair.

Once seated, Igor cast a furtive glance in Stevyn's direction. Something was odd about the man, that was for sure, but Stevyn attributed it to nervousness, or pure eccentricity.

"What's wrong with him?" Camilla whispered, leaning over.

"He hasn't swyved a woman in some sixty-odd years," replied Stevyn. "Nothing else that I know of would make a man look so jittery."

Camilla shot him an admonishing look, and folded her arms across her chest. Then she fixed her gaze on Igor and her frown deepened.

The monk's eyes blinked furiously as he testified. "When did I last see Hotard the scribe? It was on the afternoon that Lady Wynifred died in childbirth. 'Twas a tragic ending! God rest her soul!"

"Yes, yes." Frederick was disinterested in the trivial day-to-day goings-on at the sanctuary. Standing over Igor, he said, "But, did you also see the defendant, Sir Stevyn Strongbow, on that day?"

Igor said, "Yes."

"Can you tell the jury, please, what Sir Stevyn said to you that day?"

"He asked me if I knew where Hotard was. I told him Hotard had left the sanctuary, and had most likely gone home."

"What else did you tell him?"

"I told him that Hotard lives in the village, and that he follows the south road home."

"The road that borders the hunting field?"

Igor nodded.

"The field where Hotard's dead body was found a short time later."

"The next day, I believe, yes."

"And do you know who found that body, Igor?"

Shaking his head, the monk shrugged. "No."

"Would you be surprised if I told you that Sir Stevyn himself found that body?"

"Why would I be?"

But, Igor's reply was lost in the noisy upheaval that followed Frederick's question. Stevyn's chest tightened as he scanned the jury table and the rows of spectators crowded against the walls. Fingers pointed at him, narrowed eyes stared back at him and condemnation hovered in the air like a fog.

Frederick turned slowly, leveling his most accusatory gaze yet at Stevyn. "My final question to you, Igor, is this. Did Sir Stevyn tell you why he wished to see poor Hotard that evening?"

Igor hesitated. His pale face blanched even whiter and his bony fingers pulled and twisted at the wooden crucifix strung around his neck. "He—he said he had a letter for him."

When Frederick whirled and stared at Igor in disbelief, Stevyn knew something had gone terribly wrong. He nudged Camilla, but her gaze was also riveted on the scene before them.

"No further questions." Frederick's voice boomed through the hall, startling a pair of pigeons roosting in the rafters. "He is obviously *your* witness, Miss Rosedown!"

Camilla rose, and said, "I will reserve my rights to question him during my case, if it please the court."

Godric nodded. "Any more witnesses, Frederick?"

"Only the defendant, judge. I call Sir Stevyn Strongbow to the stand."

Filling his lungs, Stevyn tamped down his anxiety and stood. He touched Camilla's shoulder as he skirted her chair. "Everything will be all right," he whispered, uncertain whether his assurances were for her or for him. Walking to the witness chair, he felt the hostility and bloodthirstiness of the gaping spectators. They already believed in his guilt. They had made up their minds before they ever walked into this make-believe courtroom.

"Where were you on the night Hilda the servant was murdered?" Frederick fired off before Stevyn had even settled in his chair.

"I spoke with Hilda in the alley between the hall and the kitchens. I left her there when Risby's advance party arrived. Then, I entered the hall and went to my guest chambers. Later, I came back downstairs and spoke briefly to Godric. Afterward, I went outside and looked for my dog, Daisy. She was missing."

"Suppose I ask you this, sir. Did you slit Hilda's throat before dinner, or after?"

Stevyn's anger threatened to boil over. His hands fisted in his lap, and his muscles burned. Yet, he only allowed a tiny drop of his fury to spill into this voice. *"I did not kill Hilda,"* he bit out. He wanted the jury to understand how offended he was by Frederick's accusation, but he didn't want to give the impression he had a murderous temper.

"If you did not kill the poor old woman, sir, who did?"

"How the devil should I know?"

Frederick smiled, confident he had made his point with the jury. "And where were you when Hotard was murdered, sir?"

"How should I know? I have no idea when the man was killed."

"But, you found him, Sir Stevyn."

"Yes. I found him. But, he was already dead, and had been for quite a long time. At least twelve hours." Stevyn bit his tongue. He didn't dare mention the fact that Camilla was with him. If, as Stevyn suspected, they employed spies to keep tabs on him, Godric and Frederick already knew who was with him when he found Hotard's body. But, Stevyn had no intention of disclosing this information to the jury. The less said about Camilla, the safer she was from Godric's wrath.

"How do you know when he died, sir, if you were not present when he did?"

A ripple of muttering flowed through the jury. Frederick's logic was clearly admired and respected among Stevyn's so-called peers. Suppressing a shudder of disgust, he said, "I was not present when Hotard died, but his body was stiff with rigor mortis and the scavenger birds had pecked out his eye sockets and eaten most of the flesh off his face."

A pregnant woman leaning against the wall let out a whoop of shocked indignation, and swooned. Her neighbors supported her weight while someone held a sliver of hartshorn beneath her nostrils. As she was carried from the hall, a raucous burst of catcalls exploded.

"He's a murderer!" one old lady shouted.

"Stone him!" someone else yelled.

A young woman cupped her hands to her mouth, and shrieked, "He oughta have his ballocks chopped off and shoved in his mouth!"

Banging his gavel on the arm of his chair, Godric bellowed, "Quiet! The next one of you who disrupts this proceeding will find himself, or herself, in the stocks before sundown. Do I make myself clear? Good! Now, Frederick, proceed. And be quick about it, will you? I'm getting hungry!"

Frederick paced the floor, his hands clasped behind his back. Suddenly, he halted, his expression pensive. Then, he turned and leveled a pointed finger at Stevyn. "Isn't it true, sir, that you came here to destroy Barnabas and Godric?"

Before Stevyn could even open his mouth to answer this absurd question, Frederick shot another one at him. "And isn't it true, sir, that you did so out of greed and ambition?"

"Ambition?" Stevyn managed to insert.

"You want to be chief justice of the king's bench, do you not? You aspire to the sort of prestige and respect Sir Alfred once possessed, don't you?"

"Alfred was a good man!" one of the jurors cried.

"But, Alfred is dead!" Frederick's eyes glowed maniacally as he jabbed his finger in the air. "Alfred is dead, and you killed him, too, didn't you, Sir Stevyn?"

Stevyn could not tolerate this mockery of a trial a moment longer. Abruptly, he stood, inadvertently toppling his chair. His muscles burned with outrage; he could barely breathe and his heart felt like a dropping boulder. His fingers itched to wrap themselves around Frederick's throat, and he just barely managed to resist murdering him on the spot. After all, killing the prosecutor would hardly help his case.

"I am telling you, Frederick. And you, too," he said, facing the jury. "I did not kill Hilda. I did not kill Hotard. And I sure as hell did not kill Alfred. He was my friend, and when I find his murderer . . . well, then . . . then, you may have to hang me . . . because if I ever find out who slit Alfred's throat, I will personally kill the villainous cur."

Frederick's voice was as sultry as a cat's purr. "Well, Sir Stevyn, given that pronouncement, let me suggest to the jury that if you intend on killing someone else, they have no alternative but to convict you now and sentence you to death. To let you go free would be to condemn another man to death."

Exhausted, Stevyn stalked from the witness chair and sat beside Camilla. Pinching the bridge of his nose, he slumped beside her, painfully aware that his outburst had unnerved her. The irony of his situation assailed him. He'd frightened his own lawyer. Sir Stevyn Strongbow, one of the most distinguished lawyers in all of England, had snapped at the bait dangled before him by a two-bit country bailiff. And, in doing so, he'd earned himself a death sentence.

There was no question now that the jury believed Stevyn was a cold-blooded killer, driven by ambition and greed. The fact that Frederick's imputed motive, not to mention the bailiff's entire case, had as many holes in it as a whore's maidenhead did not signify anything to the jury. What mattered to them was that Godric believed in Stevyn's guilt.

And Godric's opinion was obvious. Frederick's shoddy showmanship, therefore, while entertaining, was superfluous. Frederick could have put no witnesses on the stand, and made his case just as effectively. Although, Stevyn noted ruefully, in light of his own recent outburst, his case would probably have benefitted had no witnesses been called at all. Not that it mattered. Either way, he was a dead man.

"Anything else, Frederick?"

"That is my case, Judge Godric." With a satisfied smirk, the bailiff resumed his seat.

"Lady Camilla, do you wish to proceed? Or are you sufficiently convinced, as is this court, that the evidence against your client is insurmountable?"

Camilla rose, squared her shoulders, and addressed the court in a quavering voice. "I should like to proceed with my case, Judge Godric."

"If he pleads guilty now, I will show mercy in my sentencing," Godric said, glaring a warning at Camilla. "A quick death is better than a slow one. Have you ever seen a man disemboweled, child? It is not a pretty sight."

Camilla's gulped audibly. "He does not wish to plead guilty, Judge, because he is innocent."

The sheriff's fingers gripped the arm of his chair. Purple veins at his temples pulsed his displeasure. His silver beard glistened with perspiration. Through gritted teeth, Godric said, "Proceed, then, Camilla. And be careful that you do not inflict more harm to your client's case. His guilt is well established. All that is left to be decided is his punishment."

"With all due respect, Godric," Camilla replied, a note of defiance in her voice, "Not only do I intend to prove my client's innocence, before this trial is over, the jury will know who really killed Hilda and Hotard."

"Call your first witness!" Godric thundered.

Camilla lifted her chin. "I call to the stand, Teresa-Marie, eldest daughter of Hilda the servant."

Chapter Fourteen

The crowd roared with boisterous speculation as Eric slowly led Teresa-Marie, the mute, from behind the screens shielding the pantry, through the center of the Great Hall, past the trestle tables and all the staring faces and straight to the witness stand, where she sat obediently. The girl looked up, smiling shyly at her escort. Eric blushed, then retreated to a spot against the wall, behind the jury table.

Godric gave his gavel a violent hammering, beating the jury and the spectators into quiet submission. The atmosphere in the hall was charged with tension and excitement. Suddenly, Stevyn's trial had gone from being frivolous entertainment to great sport. Camilla, despite her efforts to ignore the hooting and heckling of the audience, couldn't help but overhear two of the jurors wager a bet over whether Strongbow would be drawn and quartered, or simply hung.

As the gallery leaned forward, ears pricked, a silence floated through the hall. Invisible butterflies swarmed in Camilla's stomach. Now was the moment of truth. Now, all her hard work and investigative efforts would pay off. Or else, her clumsy bumbling as Stevyn's lawyer would condemn him to death.

She walked the short distance from the counsel table to the witness chair, her gaze fixed on Teresa-Marie's. The girl's face was drawn, her dark hair hanging lank around her face. Clad in rough peasant garb, anonymous in her poverty, she would ordinarily have been invisible to a man like Godric. Yet, the sheriff, leaning half out of his chair, seemed mesmerized by her, now.

"Teresa-Marie, can you understand what I am saying to you?"

The girl nodded her head.

Frederick leapt to his feet and interrupted. "Judge Godric, what sort of foolishness is this? That woman is a mute! She cannot speak! To allow her as a witness in this trial is to make a mockery of these proceedings."

"These proceedings are already a mockery," Camilla returned. "And just because she cannot speak does not mean she is dumb."

Godric chuckled. "This is most irregular, Camilla. The girl can be of no assistance to your case. She is unable to testify, for God's sake! Why don't you wave a white flag, daughter, and surrender. You have performed admirably under the circumstances, but no one expects you to seriously defend a guilty man!"

"With all due respect, Godric, you instructed Sir Stevyn to choose a legal representative, and he chose me. Now, I intend to defend his case as completely and zealously as I am able."

Frederick said, "I object to this witness, Judge!"

Stroking his beard, Godric leaned back in his chair and sighed pensively. "I am going to allow her to proceed, Frederick. It will not be said that Godric denied Sir Stevyn a fair trial. If his best witness is a mute, then that is simply more evidence of his guilt."

"And I would thank you, Judge, to cease commenting on my client's innocence or guilt." Camilla stood tall beneath Godric's suddenly stunned and stormy expression. " 'Tis most irregular that you prejudice the jury with your remarks. If you persist, I shall have no choice but to ask for a new trial, a new judge and a new jury!"

Godric's mouth smeared in an ugly sneer. "Camilla, you are treading on thin ice. Watch what you say—"

But, before the judge completed his dire warning, Camilla turned to Teresa-Marie and began her carefully thought out and rehearsed line of questioning. "Are you the daughter of Hilda, the serving maid, who worked in the kitchens here at Wickingham Castle?"

Teresa-Marie nodded.

"Was your mother murdered two nights ago?"

Nod.

"Were you entering the alleyway when the killer slit your mother's throat?"

Tears glistened in Teresa-Marie's eyes, but she nodded dutifully.

Frederick pounded his fist on the counsel table, and roared, "I object!"

The jury leaned forward, most of the soldiers perched on the edge of their benches, while the spectators behind them gasped and stared.

Godric lifted his fist in the air, and yelled, "Camilla, damme! Stop this insolent interrogation now!"

"Did you see who killed your mother?" Camilla shouted over the protests of Frederick and Godric.

Her head bobbed violently.

"Is he in this courtroom?"

Nod.

Camilla heard Godric's threats to have her taken from the room by force, but she continued as calmly as she could, grateful that her witness could not hear the tumult surrounding her. "Can you point to your mother's killer, please?"

Teresa-Marie's gaze widened, and her chin trembled. Then, slowly, while every person in the Great Hall held his breath, she raised her arm and pointed her finger at Frederick the bailiff.

Hot energy poured into Stevyn's bloodstream. Teresa-Marie's testimony was a complete surprise. Though he and Camilla had mapped out a strategy for trial, their case, as Stevyn had planned it, depended entirely on cross-examining Frederick's witnesses. Camilla must have located Teresa-Marie in the past four hours. His pride in her abilities and his gratitude toward her filled his thundering heart.

If he wasn't sentenced to death, it would be because Camilla Rosedown won his freedom.

Godric's gavel crashed repeatedly on the arm of his chair. Teresa-Marie scurried out of the hall like a frightened mouse. The crowd roared with shock and outrage. Some of the soldiers laughed riotously, while others clenched their fists in the air and hooted at Frederick. Money could be seen exchanging hands as wagers were paid, and new bets made. The trial wasn't over yet. And, now Camilla's fate was just as uncertain as Stevyn's.

"Merde!" Frederick cried. "This is pure, stinking bull manure! I object to this entire line of questioning, Godric, and move that it be struck from these proceedings, and that the jury be instructed to disregard what it has seen and heard!"

"The motion is granted!" Godric's face was as red as the slash of crimson in the flags that flew over his castle turrets. "And, Camilla, you are hereby dismissed as a participant in this trial! Furthermore, you are to be sequestered in your room for an indefinite period, until I decide on an appropriate punishment for you!"

"I will not be silenced!" she shouted back.

"Guards!" Godric's voice boomed through the hall, drowning the spectators' excited pandemonium. "Guards, come and take her above stairs. Now!"

A pair of beefy soldiers wearing chain-mail vests hustled forward, clutching the hilts of their sheathed swords. They grasped Camilla's arms, cuffing her between them. The crowd went wild, cheering and jeering while Camilla struggled helplessly against her captors' hold. At length, she gave up the fight, and looked over her shoulder. Fear flashed in her eyes as she mouthed, "I am sorry," against a background of chaotic noise.

"Take her away!" Godric yelled.

"No! Leave her be!" Stevyn stood, commanding attention. The riotous onlookers fell silent as they waited to hear what the soon to be condemned man had to say. The guards froze in their places, staring uncertainly from Godric to Stevyn.

"She is innocent of any wrongdoing, Godric, other than her misplaced desire to provide me with adequate legal counsel." Meeting her frightened gaze, Stevyn's stomach clenched. Suddenly, he wasn't afraid of dying. Disembowelment was preferable to seeing Camilla suffer. "She did what she believed was right, and just. She should not be punished, Godric. I beg of you, let her be. If you want me to plead guilty, I will. But, only in exchange for Camilla's freedom."

"In her overzealousness, Lady Camilla perpetrated a fraud upon this court," Frederick countered. "I could have asked the dumb mute if she was the virgin mother, and she would have nodded her head, yes. Hilda's wretched daughter added *nothing* to this trial; on the contrary, her presence demeaned the integrity of these proceedings. I suggest to you, Godric, that Lady Camilla should be banished from Wickingham Castle forever!"

"You agree to plead guilty?" Godric asked.

"Yes," Stevyn replied.

"No—" Camillla cried.

Stevyn summoned up all the courage in his being to quell her entreaty. "Hush!" he thundered. "I, too, have heard enough from you, Camilla. You did not follow the strategy I laid out for you, but rather pursued a meaningless course of conduct that did nothing other than to impugn an innocent man! I will not countenance such fabrications and lies, Camilla! You are no longer my lawyer! And I never want to set eyes on you again!"

Blanching, she nearly collapsed between the two guards. Strengthening their grips on her upper arms, they held her upright.

"Well, this changes everything. We have our conviction, Frederick is exonerated and Camilla is no longer a practicing lawyer." Godric leveled a thoughtful gaze at Camilla. Tilting his head, he sighed. His features softened, and a melancholy tone entered his voice. "Ah, daughter, how could you have done such a thing? I am most disappointed. But, then, you are nought but a silly woman, and you cannot be expected to display the maturity and judgment of a real lawyer."

"That's why womenfolk will never be lawyers!" someone yelled from the jury table.

Smiling wistfully, Godric said, "You will have plenty of time to consider your mistakes while you are cloistered in your room, awaiting Risby's arrival."

"You would still have me marry Risby?" Camilla yelped. "A moment ago, you were considering banishing me from the castle!"

"That was before Sir Stevyn so magnanimously admitted his guilt. Besides, as Risby's wife, you will not be causing any more trouble for Frederick," the sheriff said, eliciting more laughter from the jury. "Risby will have you with a babe in your belly before the year is out, and then, I trust, you will be spending your time in a nursery, not a courtroom."

Stevyn's nerves prickled with suspicion. Something was odd about Godric wanting to get this trial over so quickly, before Risby returned to Wickingham Castle. Something was odder still about the sheriff allowing Stevyn to choose Camilla as his legal representative. But, the fact that the man would want Camilla as his daughter-in-law, even after she'd accused Frederick the bailiff of murdering Hilda, was absurd.

Frederick sighed theatrically and shook his head. "I take no satisfaction in the outcome of this case. With heavy heart, Judge Godric, I ask this court to sentence Sir Stevyn Strongbow to death by disembowelment."

"It is so ordered," said Godric.

An ear-popping, bone-numbing fear struck Stevyn, and, had he not been determined to conceal it, his knees might have buckled more severely than Camilla's. "What about the jury?" he rasped. "The decision is theirs, Godric, not yours."

Godric dismissed that notion with a wave of his hand. "Half of them are drunk by now; the other half have wagered against you, Stevyn. Surely, you don't think there's a soldier worth his salt who would vote for your innocence if it means he'll lose a bet."

"Then, give him a new trial," Camilla said. "Based on the incompetency of his lawyer. I have heard of such things happening in the London courts."

"Denied," Godric decreed. "This is not London! Now off with you both!"

But, before the guards could spirit Camilla away, and before additional guards could be summoned to seize Sir Stevyn and dispatch him to the donjon, a great commotion sounded at the rear of the Great Hall.

The heavy double doors crashed open, and a young man wearing an elaborately embroidered jupon and richly ornamented sword belt swaggered in. His citified garments would have marked him as a foreigner to Northumbria, but his arrogant manner bespoke a filial relation to Wickingham Castle. Indeed, he entered the castle keep as if he owned the place.

Behind him sauntered a half dozen men, all tall and muscular, clad in parti-colored tunics and fine leather boots. As a group, the men were unusually well dressed and well armed. Ivory inlays, engraved silver and sparkling jewels studded their sword hilts. Some of the men wore bands of fur around their tunic sleeves and one of them sported spurs King Edward would have envied.

"It is Risby," someone at the jury table whispered, more loudly than he'd intended.

Risby. Stevyn cast a glance in Camilla's direction, and saw her sway between the guards. He ached to hold her in his arms and comfort her. He could only imagine the fear that pulsed through her body. He was frightened for her, too. When Stevyn was dead and gone, there would be no one in Wickingham Castle to protect her.

Risby slowly walked the length of the hall, his hips rolling like a panther's, his long legs graceful. Though his shoulders were not so broad as Godric's, and his thinning hair not yet shot through with silver, he was the spitting image of his father. Pausing in the center of the packed hall, he cast a challenging gaze over the sea of gawking onlookers. Many, especially the women, looked away.

He passed the ranks of the soldiers like a general inspecting his troops. In his wake, tension rippled. At length, he stood before Godric and met his father's gaze. His entourage crowded the space between the counsel tables and the witness chair. The atmosphere in the hall was rife with masculine aggression.

A feather sailing in the air could have been heard in the silence that accompanied Risby's appearance. Father and son stared at each other for a long time. Then, slowly, ceremoniously and with a flair that could only be construed as mocking, the young man bowed so low that his forehead touched the floor.

"Stand, my son." Godric waved him to his full height. "Welcome home."

Stevyn had certainly seen more joyous homecomings. Neither one of the men appeared inclined to commemorate their reunion with a handshake, much less an embrace. And, though the sheriff's eyes glistened, his expression remained stern. Occasionally, he glared at the jury table and at the spectators lining the walls as if he dared someone to challenge his son's return.

Risby drew in a deep breath, and turning, scanned the scene he'd interrupted. "What in the hell—"

"We were conducting a trial, son," replied Godric.

"How exciting. Who is the defendant, and what grievous crime has he committed?"

Godric jerked his chin in Stevyn's direction. "His name is Sir Stevyn Strongbow. He is a justice on the king's bench, sent here to investigate an allegedly illegal relic-selling enterprise run by Barnabas."

"And protected by you," Stevyn put in.

"Gutsy rascal, isn't he?" Risby remarked, strolling toward Stevyn.

Stevyn pinched the bridge of his nose.

The young man grinned crookedly.

And that's when they recognized each other.

Awareness flashed between them like lightning. The air surrounding Risby and Stevyn suddenly crackled. The men stared at each other like gladiators ready for a battle.

Stevyn, the master of his emotions, trembled. His fists clenched at his sides, and his eyes glowed like burning coals. Anger peeled off him like sheets of crumbling gold leaf. If Stevyn hadn't been so fearful of Godric killing him, and harming Camilla, he'd have strangled Risby with his bare hands right there, and been done with it. Dogs like Risby were not entitled to the protection of the judicial system.

"Do my eyes deceive me? Can it be Stevyn Strongbow?"

"*Sir,* to you," Stevyn replied through clenched teeth.

Risby gave a malicious chuckle. "I see you have come up in the world. Been knighted, eh? And appointed to the king's bench? Why, who would have thought it?"

"*Ramsey.*" Stevyn could not control the disgust and hatred in his voice. "So you are the favored offspring of Godric. How fitting. Like father, like son."

"Merde!" exploded Godric. "Get Sir Stevyn out of here! Someone take him to his chamber! Eric? Where is that loafing son of a—"

"Here I am, Godric," Eric pushed off the wall, edged the jury table and stood before Godric.

"Take your prisoner to his chamber. He will remain there until sundown, when his sentence shall be carried out in full view of the castle citizenry, in the lower bailey. I believe there is a new scaffold, which has by coincidence been constructed there."

"You are not committing him to the donjon,

Father?" said Risby, never taking his eyes off Stevyn.

"No." Godric rested one elbow on his armchair and propped his head on his fist. Sighing, he said, "Not the donjon. And, guards, take Lady Camilla to her chamber as well. Before she faints. I believe she has had more than her share of excitement for one day."

At the mention of Camilla's name, Risby whirled and faced her. "Wait!"

It was as if the planets ground to a halt. Stevyn stood as still as a statue, his muscles coiled. Under his breath, he said to Eric, "Wait. I will not leave her."

To his credit, the guard took hold of Stevyn's arm, but did not attempt to forcibly remove him from the hall.

Meanwhile, Risby shooed away the two guards flanking Camilla. Like a big cat, he circled her, raking his gaze up and down her figure, eying her with a frankly appreciative and dangerously hungry gaze. "So, this is Lady Camilla Rosedown, my bride to be."

She rubbed her arms where the guards had grabbed her. Her cheeks colored and her lashes fluttered nervously.

"I shall kill him," Stevyn whispered.

"Not yet," Eric whispered back. "You are not the hammer *yet,* my friend."

The guard's reply stunned Stevyn back to his senses. Did he have an ally in the castle? Was it possible? With herculean strength, he garnered his control. He had to. Risby's arrival at Wickingham Castle was fortuitous. Had Godric's son been one day later, Stevyn would be dead. Then, there would be no one to expose Risby, no one to avenge the death of the woman he'd killed and no one to protect Camilla.

Standing in front of Camilla, Risby said, "I am pleased, Father."

"Very well. She shall be yours. And you shall treat her fairly, do you hear me, boy?" The sheriff's fiat rattled the rafters.

Risby's cheeks pinkened. His bottom lip swelled in an attitude of juvenile resentment. "Yes, yes, Father. I shall treat her fairly." Then, something else glowed behind his pale blue gaze, something more feral, more cunning and far more lethal. He touched her cheek, then tugged at a stray hair and wrapped it around his finger. "If *she* treats *me* fairly, that is."

Camilla flinched.

His body stilled. Risby drew back his hand, and stared at Camilla through hateful, narrowed eyes. "On the other hand, if she does not treat me fairly—"

Godric's booming voice startled everyone. "Guards, get her out of here! Lock her in her room and leave her there!"

Camilla's guards quickly took hold of her, practically whisking her from the room and up the steps.

Risby watched her go, his wolfish gaze riveted to her backside. When she was out of sight, he faced Stevyn.

"After all these years, Stevyn, it is a strange twist of fate that brings us together here. By the way, who did you murder to get yourself in this sort of trouble?"

"A serving wench and a scribe. Except I didn't kill them. Someone else did."

"Ho!" Hands on his hips, Risby threw back his head in laughter. "That is rich! A worthy defense, counselor, but I see it did not succeed. Perhaps the failure of your argument lay in the weakness of your representative."

"No, *Ramsey*. Lady Camilla is as intelligent and articulate as any lawyer in London. The failure of my case lay in the bias of this tribunal. Camilla proved my innocence, but she never had a chance of earning my acquittal."

Risby clucked his tongue. "Well, it doesn't matter now. You'll be dead before sundown."

"You lying snake," Stevyn ground out. "You murderous bastard. . . . If it had not been for Sir Alfred—"

"Eric," Godric yelled, "Get that murderous villain Sir Stevyn out of here, too. Now!"

"We must go," Eric hissed, tugging at Stevyn's arm.

Reluctantly, Stevyn turned and marched out of the hall. As he passed the great double doors, still hanging open, he caught a glimpse of the afternoon sky. He had at most three hours to live. It wasn't very long, but he didn't intend to die without making a final effort to save Camilla's life and prevent her from marrying Risby.

The guards had shoved her in her room, closed the door and latched it from the outside. Having fulfilled their duty, they had laughed heartily as they stomped back down the corridor and descended the steps. Risby's arrival signaled a great feast and celebration, and they would not want to miss it. Besides, with no other means of egress from her bedchamber, the possibility of Camilla escaping was unlikely.

She sat on the edge of the bed, Bramble's golden head in her lap. Sensing her mood, the dog whined and licked her fingers. At the hound's bidding, she stroked his snout and scratched behind his ears. He stared up at her with huge, mournful eyes, seemingly as bereft as she. But, despite the comfort he gave her, Camilla knew it was Daisy he was thinking of, not her.

The scrape of the latch, followed by a brisk knock, startled her. Bramble gave a deep, throaty growl, and twisted, his body poised to lunge at the door.

Sir Stevyn slipped across the threshold while Eric hovered behind him, nervously glancing up and down the corridor.

Camilla gently pushed Bramble aside. "Go lie down, Bramble." She pointed at the dog's favorite sheepskin pelt, spread out on the floor in the corner nearest the grate.

Glancing indifferently at Stevyn, the dog shuffled across the room, curled up on his bed and laid his head on the floor.

"Do not tarry, sir," Eric cautioned. "If Godric discovers I have allowed you in here, he will kill me, too."

"Knock on the door if you hear someone coming up the steps," Stevyn said as the latch fell behind him. Then, he crossed the floor and drew Camilla to her feet and into his arms.

She lifted her face, receiving his hard, hot kiss. She couldn't stop trembling, but his presence comforted her. She couldn't satiate her need to touch him, or satisfy her lungs with his perfume; she couldn't get close enough to him. Her need for him consumed her, and she clung to him like a needy child.

They fell to the bed, their limbs intertwined, their lips pressed together. Hungrily, Camilla's tongue searched out his mouth, tasting him, possessing him. Then, driven by fear and lust, she rolled on top of him and straddled his hips.

Lying on his back, he appraised her with that strangely amused expression of his.

"Why do you look at me like that?" she asked.

"Because you are a puzzle, Camilla. And I do so love a good puzzle."

She was impatient. Reaching beneath her, she pushed up his tunic and unlaced his chausses and hosen. Then, she rucked her kirtle to her thighs, and lowered her naked body onto his.

His hardness slid inside her with ease. Shocked, as always, by that first bolt of pleasure that raced up her spine, Camilla rocked back on her heels. Then, she ground her pelvis against Stevyn's lower body and rocked forward again. The sensation deepened. The first wave of ecstasy rolled over her.

But, she was in control. And she intended to take her pleasure the way she wanted it. After all, this could be the last time Camilla ever saw Stevyn. This could be the last time she ever experienced a moment of happiness. And this could be the last opportunity she had to conceive his child.

Through the soft wool of her surcoat and her muslin tunic, he cupped the fullness of her breasts, and gently pinched her nipples. He ran his hands down the flatness of her belly, and he traced the curves of her hips. Then, he reached between her legs and, as she rocked back and forth, he massaged the most sensitive part of her body, expertly rubbing that little nub, tangling his fingers in her thatch, and stroking the slickness that her arousal produced.

She flattened her palms on his chest and leaned forward. She bit her lower lip, suppressing the moan that swelled inside her. But, her arousal was irrepressible. She moved faster and more urgently. She reached one release, and then she reached another. She gave a little hop, bouncing up and down on Stevyn's shaft. But, still he did not release his seed inside her.

"Stevyn, please," she whispered.

He knew exactly what she wanted. A rictus of pain marked his features. Hoarsely, he said, "No, sweetling. I cannot."

"Why?"

"To get you with child, and then leave you here? With no one to protect you? I cannot do it!"

"For God's sake, Stevyn, you must!" Pent-up frustration exploded within her. "I want you!"

"No, Camilla. I am to be put to death in less than three hours!"

"I shall tell your son, or your daughter, how brave you were."

"But, what shall you tell your husband?" he asked her.

Stevyn grimaced as she lifted her weight off his engorged manhood.

"Risby will believe the child is his. It is close enough to the marriage date."

His shaft was slick from the wetness of her body. With the heel of her hand, she lightly rubbed the head of his manhood. His hips moved rhythmically and involuntarily. "My son, or daughter . . . raised by Ramsey? No."

"At least I will have some part of you, Stevyn. I cannot bear to live without you—"

"I will not sire a child I cannot protect, Camilla." But, his back arched, and he winced at the torturous pleasure she inflicted upon him. He was at the brink of his release.

Hunkered over him, she made a tight little tunnel with her hands and stroked the length of his manhood. Then, she caressed his inner thighs, tickling the fine thatch of hair protecting his groin.

He gulped a desperate breath. "Camilla, what the hell are you doing?"

A sob bubbled up in her throat. "I am conceiving my future child," she replied as she deftly moved her body over his, covering his manhood, sheathing him within her.

He could not withdraw; her weight straddled his groin. And it was too late for him to resist his release. With a violent shudder, he thrust upward, shooting his semen deep within her. His back bowed like that of a woman giving birth. He clenched his teeth, and growled, "God help me!"

Camilla leaned forward, clasping his shoulders, pulling him as tightly into the core of her body as she could.

Then, at length, as Stevyn lay flat on the bed, his body damp with perspiration, his chest heaving, he looked up at her, and said softly, "Dear God, Camilla. I do love you so."

Chapter Fifteen

"Dear God, Camilla, what if you become pregnant?"

She rolled off him, smoothing down her tunic. Stretching beside him, she propped her head on her hand. Though they had but a few remaining hours before the execution, she felt a strange sense of completeness. "I hope I am pregnant, Stevyn. I would like nothing better than to raise your child."

"But, you will have no one to assist you, woman. I will not be here. And Ramsey—"

"Who is Ramsey?"

"Godric's son." Stevyn's expression settled into grim lines.

Her pulse skittered. "Do you mean there is another son?"

"No." He pinched the bridge of his nose. Then, he sat up, and drew her up, too, so that they sat side by side on the edge of the mattress. "Listen, carefully, Camilla, for there isn't much time. You cannot marry Risby. In a few hours, I will be dead and gone, but you must not marry Godric's son."

"I have given my solemn promise that I will," she said, heat suffusing her face.

He turned his black gaze on her, and for once, there was not the slightest hint of amusement in his expression. "How long have you lived in Wickingham Castle?"

"Five years now."

"And no one has told you anything about Godric's son in that time?"

Camilla shook her head. She hadn't many friends among the castle women. They seemed to avoid her. "Not a thing. All I know is that the womenfolk in the kitchen were in a twitter when they learned he was returning home. I took it to mean he was a handsome lad, perhaps something of a rogue. But, then Godric told me he had changed his ways, and that he was very much looking forward to taking a wife."

"He is very much more than a rogue, Camilla."

Alarm streaked through her. "How do you know so much about him?"

Stevyn sighed. " 'Tis a long story, and we haven't much time. Before I was appointed to the king's bench, I was a paid champion. The best in London, it was widely said; perhaps, the best in all of England."

"You told me. What has that to do with Risby?"

"It was the last case I accepted. A duel with swords, and Alfred of Kent was my opponent."

"Sir Alfred? The circuit judge who presided over assize court in this shire before you?"

"He was not a knight, then. Nor was I. We

were just two gladiators, paid to fight our clients' battles for them. Alfred was a worthy opponent, and the fight was long and brutal. We both suffered cuts, and our faces were bloodied, our bodies near collapse. But, we kept on fighting."

Camilla touched Stevyn's arm, frightened by the bleak look that hooded his eyes. "Who won?"

He swallowed hard, and closed his eyes. "Alfred fell. I put sword to his neck, nicking his throat. I had only to press my weight on my hilt, and he would have been a dead man."

"But, you did not kill him."

"No. He begged for mercy, and so I withdrew my sword."

Camilla released a breath she hadn't known she was holding. "What has this to do with Risby, Stevyn?"

"The man you know as Risby was Alfred's client. His name was Ramsey, then. I suspect he changed it because of the notoriety associated with his crime."

"His crime?"

"He raped a nun, Camilla. 'Twas widely known in London. Risby was one of the most despised men in London. He left for France soon after the trial by combat, and I suppose that is when he changed his name. But, now he is home, and the people of Wickingham Castle are to call him Risby and act as if nothing ever happened. Good God, he must have been the scourge of this county even before he turned up in London!"

Fingers of ice clutched at the back of Camilla's neck, and her chest ached. Risby, Godric's son, the man she intended to marry, the man who would raise the son she'd just conceived with Stevyn, had raped a nun?

A wave of nausea replaced her chill. God, but what was she going to do now? How could she honor her promise to marry a beast? How could she share his bed? How could she force herself to look at him without spitting in his face?

"You see," Stevyn continued, "when I allowed Alfred to go free, then his client was granted a pardon as well. Those were the rules we agreed upon, and so it was the law of that case."

"But, why didn't Alfred tell me this awful truth? I thought Alfred cared for me. Why would he sit by quietly while Godric conspired to marry me off to the little weasel?"

"I believe that Alfred did care for you." Stevyn snapped his fingers. "It makes sense. Yes, the puzzle fits! Perhaps Alfred finally had enough of Godric's lying and cheating. My guess is that when Alfred heard of Godric's plan to marry you off to Risby, he objected vehemently. Up till then, he went along with Godric's criminal schemes. He turned his cheek to the illegal relic-selling enterprise. Perhaps, he even took a small percentage for the protection he provided Godric and Barnabas."

"But when he said he wouldn't lie for Ramsey, he was murdered in his bed." Camilla felt sick.

"His throat was slit," Stevyn said. "Hardly a coincidence, do you think?"

"So Risby, or rather Ramsey, walked away from his crime without an ounce of punishment."

"That is not the worst part, Camilla." Stevyn's voice cracked. "Within a fortnight, he raped again."

"Oh, God, Stevyn! Is he a monster?"

"No more a monster than I," Stevyn said through locked jaws. "I am the fool who allowed him to escape justice! I showed his champion mercy, and in so doing, I liberated a rapist. I might as well have raped the poor wretched woman myself! I am responsible for her fate, Camilla! That is why . . . that is why I became a lawyer, and why I have driven myself so relentlessly in the pursuit of justice! But, I have only deluded myself. For, there is no justice. I am about to be put to death for two murders I did not commit. While Ramsey remains at large, free to rape again, free to take you as his bride."

Camilla's heart nearly burst. Wrapping a protective arm around Stevyn's shoulder, she said, "No, no. I will not let this happen. I must do something!"

"No, Camilla. Make an enemy of Ramsey and you will wind up dead, too. You must not breathe a word of this to anyone."

"But, I cannot marry him."

"Then, don't! Run away. But, for God's sake, do not challenge Godric and his son. They are too powerful for the likes of you, sweetling. They will squash you as they would a bug."

"Run away?" she repeated softly. "But, there is nowhere to run, Stevyn." She fell silent. A queasy dread passed through her as she realized the hopelessness of her situation. "And I will not have my child—*your child*—delivered in some dirty hovel, attended by a midwife with grimy fingernails. No, Stevyn, I want my child to be delivered in Barnabas's Sanctuary!"

Turning his head, he murmured, "I do, too."

"Perhaps I did not conceive." The possibility was almost as heartbreaking as the grief she'd felt when her first pregnancy ended in a stillbirth. "I should not have attempted to steal your seed. Oh, God! What have I done, Stevyn?"

He hugged her close to him. For a long moment, the two sat quietly, Camilla resting her cheek on Stevyn's shoulder, her tears dampening his tunic.

The trial had happened so quickly, and the results had been so unreal, Camilla felt she was in a nightmare. Surely, she would awaken soon, and everything would be as before. Sir Stevyn Strongbow would be a name she'd never heard of, and the arrival of Risby would be greeted with joy.

But, deep within, she realized the shock of Stevyn's sentencing had not yet registered with her. She preferred to think of other things, such as the warmth of Stevyn's skin and the way he made love to her. She had to marshal her emotions, and force herself to confront the reality of her future . . . and Stevyn's.

After a while, Stevyn took her hand in his, and held it to her cheek. "So many puzzles as yet unsolved, Camilla." A sad, nostalgic smile curled at his lips. "So, tell me, how did you know that Frederick murdered Hilda and Hotard?"

"Do you not wish to talk of other things? Do you have any messages that you wish for me to transmit? Or, any family that you wish for me to inform—"

"I have no family," he said without sentimentality. "I would fain discuss your legal expertise, Camilla. I was sorely impressed. Too bad women cannot be lawyers. You would make a fortune as a barrister in London."

His blandishment brought a weepy smile to her lips. "Well, then, I shall tell you how I approached the case. After I left you, I remembered something about the night of the feasting, when Risby's advance party arrived. I recalled that when I went below stairs to dine with Godric, Frederick was not at his usual place."

Stevyn nodded. "You are a very observant woman."

"Then, Eric the guard helped me fill in the missing pieces. He is Teresa-Marie's lover, in case you didn't know."

Stevyn gave a knowing chuckle. "I should have. Dear Lord, I am losing my touch!"

Camilla nuzzled the side of his neck, and kissed his cheek. "No, dear, you have not lost your touch. You have been too absorbed in trying to expose Barnabas's relic-selling operation to focus on the goings-on in the castle. Eric saw you talking to Teresa-Marie on the road, just before you were arrested. But, he knew you would not be able to communicate with her because of her inability to speak. She is, however, adept at a crude form of sign language that it seems only she and Eric can understand. Anyway, he took me to her, and, with his help, she was able to tell me that she saw her mother's killer."

"Frederick must have known Teresa-Marie saw him at the scene of the murder," Stevyn pointed out.

"He did not care, really. He thought she was a dumb mute who couldn't speak."

"And, as it turned out, her testimony meant nothing." A note of bitterness seeped into Stevyn's voice.

"Perhaps not," Camilla conceded. "But, at least, the truth was told."

Stevyn shrugged. "If the truth is told, Camilla, and no one believes it, then what does it matter? Frederick killed Hotard and Hilda because he did not want them talking to me. And I still do not know what they would have said. No one knows, I suppose, except Frederick."

"Stevyn, can't we do something, to delay the carrying out of your sentence?"

Stevyn scoffed. "No, Camilla. Godric wishes to silence me, and so this thing will be done. I am resigned to my fate." He reached inside the pocket attached to his belt. "Before it is too late, though, I wish for you to have this."

The small silver locket he placed in the palm of her hand was slightly tarnished and dented.

"Open it," he said softly.

Inside the locket was a lock of brown hair, too pale to be Stevyn's, too dark to be her own. "Whose is it?" she asked.

"That is a lock of Christ's hair." He snorted with derision. "At least that is what Sir Alfred believed. He showed it to me many times before he died, bragging that he had purchased an authentic relic that would accord him special consideration at the gates of heaven. I hope it was so."

Closing the locket, Camilla turned it over in her hands. She had seen another one identical to this one, but she could not quite remember where. Perhaps, Teresa-Marie had worn one. . . . But, before Camilla's mind could grasp the memory she searched for, Stevyn cradled her face in his hands, and lowered his head to hers.

His kiss was sweet and deep and long. Camilla clutched at the front of his tunic, desperate to keep him near her. Blinding need swelled inside her, threatening to consume her. The feel of Stevyn's lips against hers, the sensation of his tongue moving inside her mouth, robbed her of her ability to think clearly. She thought she couldn't live without Stevyn. She thought that if he left her, she would cease to exist.

"I don't want to live without you," she managed, gasping for breath. "If they kill you, then I cannot survive."

The sound that came from his throat sounded as if it had been wrenched from his soul. Shaking his head, he said, "No, no, Camilla. You can survive without me. You must."

It seemed impossible. "How is it that so much could have changed in my life these past few days?"

"I wish I had never come to Wickingham Castle. I have only succeeded in ruining your life."

A shaky breath rattled Camilla's shoulders. Through her tears, she managed to whisper, "You rode into Wickinghamshire on a day when I thought my life was ending. It was as if God answered not only my prayers, but also my deepest, most private desires. I never dreamed any man could make me feel the way you do. Oh, Stevyn, I thank God you came here!"

"Even though I have destroyed your future happiness?"

"I would not have been happy with Risby. Ever. I know that now."

"Can you give me one more piece of the puzzle, Camilla, before I have to leave you? Can you tell me why you agreed to marry Godric's son?"

A gentle scrabbling at the door interrupted. A sob caught in Camilla's throat, but she swallowed her sadness. If Stevyn had to leave her now, she wanted him to leave knowing that she loved him. She never wanted him to know the devil's bargain she made with Godric; it seemed so obscene compared to the noble character he had demonstrated since she'd known him.

"It's not important," she said.

He kissed her again, and she felt the wetness

of his tears against her face. The door opened, and Eric hissed, "Hurry! The dinner feast is getting under way. Soon, the sheriff will be sending for Camilla!"

They stood, and Stevyn held her in his arms for a brief instant, whispering against her ear, "I love you, I love you."

And then he was gone, and Camilla was left with a gaping wound in her chest and a cry of anguish on her lips. Collapsing to the floor, she released her tears. Her body shuddered with grief as Stevyn's footsteps sounded on the steps. At last, she heard the door of his guest chamber close below stairs. She felt as if her life, which had just begun anew when Stevyn entered it, was over.

A cold wetness pressed against her cheek. Opening her eyes, Camilla looked into Bramble's sad gaze and wrapped her arms around his furry neck. Her faithful hound had always been there for her. Burying her face in his thick coat, Camilla cried until she had no more tears left to cry.

Stevyn's mind turned like a rickety wheel tearing up the road beneath it. He had no intention of submitting to Godric's punishment, not without an uproar worthy of Zeus. But, Camilla would not be privy to his plans. If Godric ever discovered her involvement in a conspiracy to free Stevyn, she would suffer a fate more heinous than disembowelment.

And Stevyn would rather die than see a hair on Camilla's head harmed.

At the door of his guest chamber, he turned to Eric. "You were willing to help me and Camilla. Why?"

The guard's rough complexion darkened. "On account of Teresa-Marie. And what that scoundrel Risby did to her."

Stevyn's skin tingled. "He's been gone from here for more than five years. What could Risby possibly have done to her?"

Eric stepped inside the room, and drew the door shut behind him. Shifting his weight from foot to foot, he threw an uncharacteristically skittish glance around the room. For a man who weighed close to ten stone, he suddenly looked extremely vulnerable. "She was just a girl when he done it to her."

"What did he do?" Stevyn's hand rested on the top of Daisy's head.

"He forced himself on her. From what I've been told, he did it to others, too, like as if they was his to trifle with." The young man's voice was strained, the cords of muscle in his neck pulled taut.

Moving to his desk, Daisy pinned to his side, Stevyn fell quiet. Another piece of the puzzle had materialized, bringing the larger picture closer to focus. Seated, Stevyn slowly opened his journal and ran his fingers across the lines he had written. In his mind's eye, bits of evidence sparkled like stained glass; he groped for meaning in the detail of the mosaic. Eric's pacing jolted him back to the present.

"Did he get her with child?" Stevyn asked softly.

Eric halted. "Yes, sir."

"Was her babe delivered in Barnabas's Sanctuary?"

"Yes."

"And did the abbot attempt to sell Teresa-Marie a dispensation of any sort? Or a relic that might have had special healing powers?"

Eric crossed the floor and stood before Sir Stevyn's worktable. "Barnabas offered to sell her a virgin cloth, a square of muslin cut from the shroud of Mary, mother of Christ. The abbot told her that if she sewed this cloth into the hem of her tunic for thirty days, her maidenhead would be restored, and she would once again be a virgin."

"Did Teresa-Marie believe this?" Stevyn asked incredulously.

"She was desperate," Eric replied. "Risby threatened her. If she ever told anyone he'd forced himself on her, he would deny it. He would kill her. He told her that Godric would discharge her mother, and the two of them would be cast out of the castle. He would spread the rumor that they were diseased, and no one would associate with them. They would die penniless and lonely."

"And so she paid for the virgin cloth?"

"No. Hilda found out about the abbot's offer, and interceded. She told the abbot she did not believe in his chicanery, and that she did not have the money to squander on such worthless trifles."

"Good for Hilda. But, she is dead . . . murdered by Godric's henchman, Frederick, so that she would not repeat that story to me. Damme!" Stevyn's fist banged on the tabletop. Daisy whimpered, and reminded of her presence, Stevyn stroked her ears. "Despicable rogue! What happened to the babe?"

"The babe died shortly after birth. Teresa-Marie still cannot speak of the ordeal without crying, but, perhaps it was for the best. . . ." Eric's voice trailed.

"She is young, Eric. You can give her another babe."

"Not if I am a dead man, sir."

Stevyn's head shot up. "What are you talking about?"

Thrusting back his shoulders, Eric straightened. "Teresa-Marie didn't tell me of this ordeal until today when Risby returned. She came here while you were with your lady, sir. I told Teresa-Marie that I saw the look of terror on her face when Risby entered the hall. I squeezed the truth out of her. And, now that I know, I cannot call myself a man if I do not call that villian out, and challenge him to a duel . . . *to the death*."

Stevyn stood, his heart pumping ferociously. In Eric's unwavering stare, he saw a glimmer of hope. The guard and the king's judge shook hands, pledging themselves to avenge their women and wreak justice upon the head of Risby, the sheriff's son. Daisy looked on, wagged her tail, then quickly lost interest and slid to the floor in a yawning heap.

As the two men crouched around the worktable, the afternoon sunlight waned. Daisy, in answer to the call of nature, scratched at the door. Eric opened the door and released her, quickly locking it behind her. Beneath them, the sounds of a great celebration boomed. Two hours passed, and their plan was not yet finely tuned, not to Stevyn's satisfaction. But, a sudden shout from the Great Hall ended their plotting. Godric's war cry was a bloodthirsty, heart-pounding sound that rattled the rafters of the old stone keep. Laughter and tankard clanging signaled the end of the meal, and the beginning of the evening's entertainment.

"He is deep in his cups tonight," Eric muttered, rubbing his palms together. "Godric enjoys a good execution like some men love a bearbaiting."

Stevyn winked at the younger man. "Tonight, however, he will know what it feels like to be the bear."

Soldiers' boots pounded up the steps. Then, before Eric crossed the room, the door crashed open and half a dozen of Godric's most loyal liege men charged in. Two of them took hold of Stevyn and dragged him from the room.

As he was taken, Stevyn looked over his shoulder and met Eric's gaze. He could only hope that the lad had the courage and daring to carry through their scheme. Otherwise, he'd have to hope the pantler's knives were sharp.

Camilla's throat closed. Clutching her serviette to her lips, she watched as Godric's soldiers hustled Stevyn through the Great Hall. Seated between Godric and Barnabas, her hand trembled as she drew her mazer to her lips. The feasting celebration that Godric had ordered to fête the arrival of his son had turned into a vulgar spectacle. Risby, seated on his father's left, had fondled the buttocks of at least three serving wenches. And the soldiers lining the trestle tables were rowdier and drunker than she'd ever seen them.

She hadn't descended to the Great Hall because she wanted to. When Bertha had arrived with a jug of hot water and a cup of warmed wine to help prepare Camilla's toilette, Camilla had still been in a heap on the floor, sobbing her eyes out. But, the maid had sternly insisted she bathe and dress for dinner. Godric had summoned her, Bertha explained. And his invitation was one that could not be refused.

Camilla's formal introduction, performed beneath the scrutiny of a platoon of liege men, and a roomful of curious servants and revelers, was painfully awkward.

"Well, daughter," Godric had drawled from his seat of honor, "What do you think of my son? Handsome, isn't he?"

Camilla gave a tight little nod and averted her eyes.

Risby stood behind the table and made a little bow. "Come, Camilla. There is a place for you on the other side of my father. I understand that you have already made a place for yourself in the castle. I am glad of that. For someday this castle will be mine, and I will fill it with children." He turned to his father, eyes gleaming. "And some of them, dear girl, may even be yours!"

Now, Camilla sat stiffly, her limbs numb with fear, her heart pounding. Beneath the table stretched Bramble, his weight half resting on her feet. Sir Stevyn, surrounded by guards, stood before the sheriff.

Her gaze met Stevyn's, but flickered away. She couldn't look at him without betraying her feeling and revealing the depth of her emotion. And she was afraid of what would happen when Godric learned she had fallen in love with the sworn enemy. Feeling traitorous and weak and frightened, she bit her lower lip and sipped her wine.

Godric seemed oblivious to her unease. Lifting his cup, he bellowed, "A salute to Sir Stevyn, who came to Wickinghamshire with the intent of destroying me and Barnabas, but who leaves here . . . as offal for the curs who scavenge the castle grounds!"

A roar of approval went up from the soldiers in the hall.

Risby laughed a high-pitched laugh and banged his tankard of ale on the table. "I drink to you, too, Stevyn. You have made my homecoming far more enjoyable than I had anticipated. 'Tis a rare day, indeed, when a man gets to celebrate his upcoming nuptials and witness a disembowelment at the same time!"

Stevyn smiled sardonically. "I am pleased I was able to provide you some entertainment, Ramsey. I am only sorry that I showed you mercy five years ago—"

"Enough!" thundered Godric, pounding his fist on the table. "Guards, take him away! Prepare him for his execution. The party shall be at the execution site, anon!"

The guards roughly grabbed Stevyn's arms. But, before he was removed, he looked at Camilla. His eyes held hers and everybody else faded to the background. Camilla's blood ran hot and her cheeks burned. The urge to leap across the table and throw herself on Stevyn's body was strong. She half rose from her seat, but he shook his head. *No*.

A chill flashed over her. She pushed back in her chair, defeated. Her shoulders sagged. Stevyn walked from the Great Hall without hesitation, his proud carriage devoid of fear or submission. Loathing herself for failing to rescue him, she stifled a sob and poured more wine down her throat. Desperation surged through her veins. If she could not save Stevyn from his fate, then living at Wickingham Castle was impossible. If Stevyn died, then she had no reason to live . . . save the babe she hoped would grow in her stomach.

Tucking her toes beneath Bramble's warm body, she dared a glance at Risby and Godric. They had drunk heavily, and while the sheriff still possessed his senses, Risby was nearly incoherent. He giggled and swayed in his chair, ogling wenches and grabbing for every serving girl that passed. So, that was what she had to look forward to in the marriage bed. A shudder racked Camilla's shoulders. *No*.

A glimpse of movement at the far end of the hall caught her eye. Looking up, she saw Eric the guard descend the steps, pass the screens and slip out the front door. It wasn't odd that he would be heading outside. The men with manners routinely went in and out of the hall during dinner to relieve themselves. The ones without manners simply used the corner.

What was odd about Eric's movement was the studied way in which he avoided the trestle tables, and the worried look of concentration on his face—not to mention the quiver of arrows slung across his back and the two bows he carried.

A frisson of hope awakened Camilla's nerves. Perhaps Eric had a plan.

She drew in a deep breath, mindful of the dimming sunlight.

When Godric leaned close to her, she smelled the beer on his breath and, on his beard, the precious clove spices that had accented his food.

"Why are you not celebrating, daughter?" the sheriff asked her.

Barnabas leaned in from the other side. "You should be happy. Today, the man who would have destroyed our refuge for unwed mothers is dead. Our sanctuary will continue to thrive. God's work will continue."

"Yes, Father." Camilla forced a tiny smile to her lips. "I am pleased about that. Though, I admit, I take no joy in the execution of any man, be he our enemy or no."

Strangely, Barnabas appeared not to share this sentiment, the most basic of Christian precepts. "God punishes those who sin against him, Camilla. Sir Stevyn is getting what he deserves."

"Perhaps," she replied. "Who am I to judge?"

Godric and Barnabas exchanged looks as well as shrugs of exasperation. Nevertheless, the sheriff patted Camilla's hand and said, "There, there. You are overset with the excitement of the day. I am to blame. 'Twas a mistake to allow you to participate in the trial, Camilla. 'Twas also a mistake to allow you to befriend Sir Stevyn. I had thought you could learn the identity of the spy who nestles in our midst. But, you didn't. Instead, the enemy aroused your . . . sympathies."

"There is no spy, Godric." She didn't tell him it was Alfred who'd exposed the relic-selling enterprise to the king. But, she knew in her heart it was true. The kindly old judge must have been appalled when he learned that Godric intended to marry her off to Risby. Alfred knew the sheriff's son was a rapist and a murderer. He must have threatened to reveal the sheriff's corruption to the authorities if Godric didn't call off the wedding. In response, he had been killed.

"Did Risby do it himself?" Camilla suddenly blurted.

Godric's smile remained frozen, but his pale blue eyes narrowed. Though his teeth, he said,

"*Pardonez-moi,* daughter. I do not understand what it is you are asking."

"I said, did he do it himself?" she repeated. "Did he kill Sir Alfred in his bed? Or did someone else do it for him?"

"Watch your tongue," the old sheriff growled.

She drew back, awed by the powerful menace in his voice. Tweaking the giant's nose, now, just minutes before Stevyn's execution was scheduled would do no good. Batting her lashes, she murmured, "Forgive me, Godric."

He stroked his beard pensively, staring at her. But, before he could respond, a noisy commotion sounded in the rear of the hall. From behind the screens suddenly emerged a phalanx of cooks and bakers and servers, all carrying elaborate dishes on silver platters.

A parade of delicacies, heralded by trumpet and set against a backdrop of lute and cymbal, roused the diners to fever pitch. Plates of roasted peacock, swan, heron and wild boar were carried into the room. Tiny quail impaled on skewers came from the rotisserie. A costumed acrobat turned flips around the hall as the main course was presented to Godric.

Dipping his fingers in a tiny gold bowl scented with rosemary, Godric smiled at the presentation. His pantler made a production of sharpening knives, while the ewerer and butler ceremoniously tasted the wine.

Then, the kitchen's chief cooks came forward, their knees sagging beneath the weight of the huge round platters they held. On one plate was a rare beast called a cockentrice, actually a capon and pig cut in half, stuffed and sewn together. On the other plate was an oversized pie in which live blackbirds had been baked. When the pie was cut open, the birds would fly out. It was not a dish Camilla favored eating, but the spectacle of serving it never failed to delight her.

At her feet, Bramble whined and fidgeted. Reaching beneath the table, Camilla took hold of his collar. When the birds were released, he would be sorely tempted to give chase.

A bud of a scheme unfolded in her mind.

Touching Godric's sleeve, she said, "Father, might I ask a favor of you?"

Chariness gleamed in his gaze. Then he scanned her shoulders and fixed his stare on her bosom. At length, a hungry smile twisted at his lips. "Ask me anything, Camilla. We are family now."

"The blackbird pie. . . .'Tis my favorite."

"I knew you would enjoy it."

"But, the birds will fly up in the rafters and be caught there, scattering their droppings on us for the rest of the week."

He chuckled. "I shall have someone come with a bow and arrow and shoot them, then."

"Why not release the birds out of doors, just before the execution? Or perhaps afterward, to celebrate. I should like to see the birds take flight, I think. Please, Godric, indulge me."

He patted her hand again, but this time he held it a bit longer than a future father-in-law should. His calloused thumb stroked the back of her hand, drawing gooseflesh to her nape. "All right, Camilla. If it will make you happy."

A wave of revulsion washed up her throat. But, Camilla smiled fluidly as a newfound bravery coursed through her veins. "Thank you," she whispered, lowering her head to kiss Godric's ring.

It was only then that she remembered where

she had seen another silver locket identical to the one Sir Alfred had owned. Lifting her head, she met Godric's gaze. He nodded, then turned his attention to the food.

Lady Wynifred wore the locket to her grave.

Rotating in her seat, Camilla faced Barnabas. The abbot smiled calmly around a mouthful of savory rabbit stew. His eyes glowed from the effects of his wine, and his bald pate sparkled beneath the candlelight.

How could she have trusted this man so? Barnabas had sold enough of Jesus' hair to weave a tapestry. 'Twas ludicrous! How could she have been so taken in by his smooth talk and paternal concern? How could she have been so blind to his ignominy?

Camilla's fingers twisted in her lap. She had been betrayed! Betrayed by the men who called themselves her protectors! And she had foolishly trusted them over Sir Stevyn, the only good man she'd ever known.

She had a mind to reach out and scrape her fingernails down the side of Barnabas's face. She had a thirst for his blood. A desire to see the abbot and the sheriff suffer suffused her blood.

But, she suppressed her hateful thoughts. *Justice sought truth,* Stevyn would have said, *not revenge*. Still, the little scheme incubating in her brain grew exponentially.

She had to get out of the hall.

Lurching forward, she cried, "Oh, my stars! My stomach! I am going to be sick!"

Barnabas's chair scraped the floor as he stood. "Come, dear, I will help you up the stairs and to your chamber."

"There is not time, Father, and I do not want anyone to see me. . . .'Twill spoil your dinner."

Godric barely looked at her, so mesmerized was he by the juggler in the long pointed cap who leaped around the room tossing leather balls in the air. When she brushed against his shoulder, he asked, "Are you all right?"

"I will be fine." She forced a wobbly chuckle. "I am looking forward to the blackbird pie, Father," she said, rubbing her belly and making a moue of discomfort. "I am afraid the pickled frog's legs did not agree."

"Ah." The sheriff dismissed her with a wave of his hand.

And with that, she grabbed Bramble by the collar and jerked him from beneath the table. The startled dog yelped, but trotted loyally alongside her as she raced for the great double doors. In the courtyard, she paused, her heart racing. She had little time in which to put her plan into motion.

Running toward the aviary, she realized the irony of her situation. A few days ago, she'd been determined to prevent Sir Stevyn Strongbow from destroying everything that was important in her life. Now he was everything to her, and she was more determined than ever to prevent Godric and Barnabas from destroying him.

Chapter Sixteen

As dusk deepened, torchlights illuminated the lower bailey. The Great Hall disgorged its diners, dancers and drunken soldiers into the courtyard, where they milled about excitedly. A buzz of anticipation rose as Godric and his entourage marched through the crowd, parting it like the Red Sea. Behind them waddled the baker, struggling with a blackbird pie, easily the size of a wagon wheel.

Onlookers pointed and snickered at the spectacle of the sheriff approaching the condemned man. Children rode on their fathers' shoulders and women stood on tiptoe, straining to see the drama unfold.

Bracketed by guards, Sir Stevyn Strongbow stood beside the scaffold with a noose round his neck. A rough trestle table had been erected beside the hanging platform, and on it lay the executioner's tools, a metal meat hook and a collection of gruesome knives. Camilla and Bramble snaked around the periphery of the crowd. Daisy had gone missing again, but Camilla couldn't waste the time to hunt her down. Sooner or later, the dog would return in search of Stephen. Camilla could only hope Daisy's master would still be alive when that time came.

Surveying the grisly tableau, her stomach truly lurched. This time when she clutched at her middle, the pains were real. Nervousness shot through her arm and transferred to Atalanta, who gripped Camilla's gauntlet with her strong talons and anxiously flapped her wings.

Even with a falcon on her arm, and a dog at her side, she slipped through the crowd like a wraith. All eyes were trained on Godric and Stevyn. Camilla thought she could have stripped naked and not been able to draw a drop of attention to herself.

She positioned herself at the edge of the crowd, far enough from Godric so that he wouldn't catch sight of her, near enough so that she could hear his speech to Stevyn.

"I hereby sentence you, Sir Stevyn Strongbow, to death by disembowelment and hanging, for the murders of Hilda the maid and Hotard the scribe."

In addition to his posse of henchmen, the sheriff was surrounded by Barnabas, Frederick and Risby. Risby, his face split in a grin, looked as if he might tip over. A drunken glaze filmed his eyes, and in his hand sloshed a brimming tankard of ale.

Barnabas folded his hands piously over his stomach. "Would you care to confess, sir? Perhaps the Good Lord will have mercy on your soul—"

"No, thank you," Stevyn spat back. Bare to the waist, his face bludgeoned and bruised, he stood tall.

Camilla drew a deep breath. The soldiers had clearly beaten Stevyn to within an inch of his life on the short journey from the hall to the lower bailey. Judging by the looks of Stevyn's wounds, he had put up a worthy fight. As the crowd's thirst for blood roared to a crescendo, his muscles flexed defiantly, and his black gaze snapped. But, the fight was over. Even Hercules could not withstand the cutting blade of an executioner's knife.

Noting the placement of the blackbird pie, Camilla patted Bramble's head. When the pie was cut, a dozen or so birds would be flung into the sky. After that, Camilla could only pray that her animals would follow her instructions. She made the sign of the cross over her bosom. Her own instincts told her she was finally doing the right thing. *Finally*.

Camilla's sole regret was that she had wasted five years of her life in bondage to fear and intimidation. She should have left Wickingham Castle the moment she was strong enough to walk away. Punishment as a poacher would have benefitted her soul more than the five years she'd spent lying to herself about Risby, her intended husband.

A hush fell over the crowd. The executioner, his identity concealed behind a black hood, picked up a long butcher's knife. The guards next to Stevyn pushed him toward the table. Resisting their authority, Stevyn struggled, spat and cursed loudly. Vastly outnumbered and overpowered, however, he was soon pummeled into submission and tossed on the table.

Camilla's heart threatened to explode. Swallowing hard, she wended her way through the crowd, edging closer to Godric.

On his back, Stevyn continued to struggle against his captors, but to no avail. His hands were tied to the table and his legs thrust apart and hobbled. The executioner stood over him, testing the sharpness of his blade with his beefy fingers.

Then, slowly, the executioner poised the tip of his knife on Stevyn's chest, nicking his sternum, flicking at his tender skin like a fishwife boning a fillet.

Suddenly, at the rear of the congregation, a commotion stirred. A wave of murmurs fanned through the mob, then heads turned and the sea parted once again. Camilla turned, watching in slack-jawed fascination as Eric the guard, with Teresa-Marie at his side, strode through the populace.

They stopped before Godric. Eric made a deferential leg, then straightened, staring boldly at the sheriff.

"What is the meaning of this interruption?" Godric demanded.

Eric gently pushed Teresa-Marie to arm's length. Then, jerking his chin in Risby's direction, he said, "I wish to call out your son, Ramsey, and to challenge him to a contest of bows and arrows in order to defend the honor of my bride, Teresa-Marie."

Ramsey's eyes widened, and the silly grin on his face wavered. Godric's complexion darkened and his nostrils flared like an angry bull's. Camilla, stunned, moved a step closer to the front of the crowd. *So, Eric had his own axe to grind,* she thought. Risby certainly did not make many friends during his tenure at Wickingham Castle, did he?

If there was any doubt in her mind as to why Godric had been desperate to marry his son to a pregnant penniless poacher, Eric's accusation settled that account. The young man had clearly been banished by his father for a reason, which explained the restrained welcome Risby had received from his father when he arrived at the castle. Godric's own feelings toward his son were unquestionably conflicted.

Glancing at Risby, Camilla shuddered. The boy's conduct had apparently been so heinous that Godric couldn't marry him to a decent girl from a well-to-do family. Only a girl desperate for food and shelter would have overlooked Risby's checkered past and voluntarily married him. Only a woman willing to sacrifice her integrity and principles would allow the man to touch her.

Godric's booming voice ruffled Atalanta's nerves. "You mean to do what? Are you a fool, daring to accuse my son of offending a . . . a . . . dumb mute, and a wench, to boot?"

Eric drew himself up, his chest swelling. "Teresa-Marie is not dumb, as evidenced by her testimony at trial today. She witnessed Frederick the bailiff murder her mother, yet justice was not served. Therefore, I have no faith in the justice system, sir. I wish to make my accusation public, and challenge Ramsey to defend himself against my greater strength. He has committed a wrong against Teresa-Marie, and I intend to make it right."

"What do you accuse me of?" Ramsey inserted, despite the hand Godric threw up to silence him.

"I accuse you of the rape of Teresa-Marie."

A collective gasp went up. As the tension around him thickened, Eric swallowed hard, and turned to Barnabas. "And I accuse you, Barnabas, of attempting to deceive Teresa-Marie by offering to sell her a fraudulent virgin cloth, and by refusing to render her infant child adequate care. The child died because Barnabas couldn't be bothered with tending to a poor woman's child. It seems that at Barnabas's Sanctuary, medical care is rendered at a high price."

The babble that followed Eric's accusation was deafening. Godric, his face a mask of anger, bellowed like a hurricane. "Damn you, man! Are you the veriest fool in all the kingdom? You accuse my son of raping a cow and my abbot of neglecting her stupid offspring? Are you insane? Do you wish to die?"

A brace of guards huddled around Godric, their armor clacking. Swords were drawn from sheathes and knives glinted at the ready. Eric had done more than tweak a giant's nose; he had stomped on his toe and spit in his face, as well. He'd riled the big man so violently, he would be lucky if he escaped with his own entrails intact. But, shoulders square, he held his ground, not retreating an inch, not retracting one word of his indictment.

Camilla's gaze flew to Stevyn. He writhed and moaned against his restraints. His bloodied face sent a chill up her spine. One of his eyes was nearly swollen shut and his lip was split. Dear God, but the sight of him in pain impaled her like a burning pikestaff through the heart. Her love for him would last an eternity, regardless of whether he lived the day. Garnering her inner strength, she sent him a silent message of hope.

He didn't even know she was there, but in her heart, she felt he could hear her whispered prayer.

His head turned, and his gaze scanned the crowd. His eyes lit on her. A streak of awareness passed between them. He was prepared to die; the stubborn resignation was written on his face. Yet, his lips twisted in a crooked smile, as if something amused him. Camilla clutched at Bramble's fur, desperate to run to Stevyn. But, she didn't dare. If she meant to save him, she must stick to her plan.

But, her plan was quickly going awry. She had not anticipated this turn of events, and she fretted at the effect Eric's challenge might have on Stevyn's fate. Fearing the sheriff would order Stevyn's death to be carried out immediately, she cupped Bramble's head and whispered soothing words in Atalanta's ear. Her body was coiled to spring, too. The next few moments would decide the fates of everyone.

Stevyn's body ached in places he didn't know existed. Between the hall and the lower bailey, his captors had seen fit to knock him about like a quintain, battering him for sport and abusing him for twisted pleasure. By the time he was delivered to the execution spot, he could barely stand.

He thought a couple of ribs were cracked. A tooth was loose and his lip was split and bleeding. Black spots danced before his eyes, and his head throbbed. But, still he refused to confess to Barnabas or bow down to Godric. If he had to die, he would do so without a whimper, without an apology and surely without a show of fear.

His bravery was short-lived. The sight of Camilla hovering at the edge of the crowd threatened to undo him. The expression on her face was so forlorn, so hopeless, it drove him to a mindless frenzy. Stevyn gulped for air, drawing nothing but piercing pains into his lungs.

Increasing his struggles, he fought vainly against his restraints. The guttural sounds of his own growling unnerved him. For a moment, he stilled. He would not become an animal, nor would he make the spectacle of his death any more gruesome than it had to be. Camilla would see his insides removed from his body; she did not have to see his dignity excised, as well.

Her smile flickered. On her arm, her prized peregrine sat elegantly. At her side, her faithful dog awaited her commandments. Despite his pain, a wave of warm serenity moved through Stevyn's body. He had loved Camilla like no other woman he'd ever lain with. She had captured his heart and touched his soul. His most grievous regret in leaving this earth now was knowing that he would not be around to protect her from Risby's cruelty. In that endeavor, he had failed.

Unless Eric's challenge succeeded. . . .

"This is absurd," Godric yelled. "Guards, shackle this man!"

But, the guards hesitated to seize one of their own, and in that split second, Eric found his advantage. "Risby may choose a second, if he so desires," he said, thrusting his chin forward. "If he does not wish to fight me, I will fight a representative of his choice."

At that, Godric burst out laughing. "You fool! You really do have a death wish! Well, then, that changes everything! Risby, choose your champion, boy. And be smart about it! Choose the biggest, meanest soldier in my command."

Risby blurted, "I choose Frederick."

Stevyn's hopes sprung to life. Frederick might be cruel and canny, but he was no battle-hardened warrior.

"Now, son . . . ," Godric started. But, the choice had been made, and the crowd, hearing it, cheered in approval. Godric had no choice but to turn to his bailiff, and say, "Well, then, you are to represent Risby in his contest. Are you certain you are up to it?"

Frederick eyed Eric from head to toe, and grinned. "Yes, sir."

Eric grinned back. "And as my representative, I choose Sir Stevyn Strongbow."

The news that Eric had chosen Strongbow as his champion flew through the throng. Huzzahs turned to near hysteria. The bloodthirsty crowd loved this twist of plot. Caps were thrown in the air, and men stomped their feet in loud approval. Women clapped their hands and laughed from the gut.

Stevyn met Camilla's gaze and winked.

Godric's face was purple with rage. For the first time since she'd known him, Camilla heard him stammer.

"This is unheard of! This cannot be allowed. The man is condemned to death!"

Risby practically bounced at his father's side. "But, the people love it, Father! I do not believe we have any choice."

"You fool," Godric snarled. "As long as your hide is not in danger, you don't give a damn for the consequences of your actions! Don't you understand—"

The momentum of the drama squelched any further discussion. The executioner who had been slicing Stevyn's chest hairs retreated while the guards untied his restraints. Stiffly, Stevyn rolled from the execution table, landing on his feet with a grimace and a groan. His body bent like an old man's, and one arm was tucked to his side. A lesser man would not have been able to move, much less rouse himself to fight.

"Name your weapons," Godric demanded.

Eric shot Frederick a questioning look. "Bow and arrow?"

The bailiff nodded. Camilla thought he was relieved that the younger soldier did not suggest swords or jousting or, God forbid, bare-knuckle fighting. Although in Stevyn's current state Camilla could not imagine Stevyn posed much of a threat in that arena.

Stevyn, ragged and beaten, stood before Godric.

"You are an unusually lucky man, Stevyn," Godric said.

"Lucky?" Stevyn snorted his derision. "Am I to thank you for granting me ten more minutes of life?"

"If you wind up with an arrow through your heart, sir, you will be spared the pain and suffering of disembowelment. And Eric shall be forced to pay my son a sum of money sufficient to compensate for Frederick's services."

"But, if Frederick is struck with my arrow, sheriff, then what?"

Godric frowned in the silence that awaited his answer. The curious audience leaned forward. What sort of punishment would be meted out to Risby, the wayward son, in the event his champion failed him?

"If Frederick loses, then Ramsey will be punished accordingly," he said gruffly.

Camilla held her breath, hardly believing what she'd heard. But, the sad, grudging look on Godric's face lent his promise the ring of truth. After all, it was the sheriff's honor at stake, now. Everyone in Wickinghamshire knew the young man was evil to the core. He'd terrorized the castle women during his randy youth, and he would doubtless continue to do so in his maturity. If Godric refused to adhere to the code of honor that trial by combat dictated, then his authority as a lawmaker would be sorely diminished.

"The punishment for raping a woman, Godric, is castration."

Risby gulped. "Father!"

"Shut up! You created this debacle, Ramsey. Now you shall have to reap the consequences of your recklessness."

"Ho!" Stevyn laughed heartily. " 'Tis my lucky day! Well, then, shall we commence this contest?"

With amazing order, the crowd quickly backed up and formed a ring, allowing the center of the bailey to serve as an open arena for the contest. Frederick passed his quivers to Godric, who inspected them, then chose four arrows, dispensing two each to the chosen champions.

Camilla sidled up to the baker and his pie, her arm crooked as a perch for Atalanta, her heart pounding. From the pocket attached to her belt, she withdrew a small hunting knife and slid it into the savory crust of the pie. Beneath the surface, a live bird struggled for release. As soon as she split the pastry open, a flurry of wings would erupt in the night sky.

The men stood back-to-back. Then, at Godric's signal, they walked thirty paces in opposite directions. At the count of thirty, they stopped and whirled. Frederick quickly nocked an arrow and sent it flying. Stevyn, grimacing in pain, moved more slowly. His arrow was launched a split second later.

Camilla's fingers trembled, but somehow she managed to loose the jesses that tethered Atalanta to her wrist.

Frederick's arrow planted itself in Stevyn's shoulder; he fell to his knees.

Stevyn's arrow glanced Frederick's neck, drawing a trace of blood, but landing with a plunk in the hard earth behind the bailiff.

Had they been witnessing a cockfight, the onlookers could not have been more barbaric. Spectators jostled one another, yelling and screaming their encouragement to the contestants. Camilla whispered a silent prayer, her stomach clenched in a knot. Stevyn's pain was palpable; his hands shook as he reached for his second arrow. His shoulders hunched as he positioned the red-stained balsam shaft in the sights of his weapon.

Frederick replaced his arrow, lifted his bow, aimed and pulled taut the catgut string.

Camilla watched in horror as Stevyn's head dipped, and his body sagged. *The arrow snapped*. Pinching the bridge of his nose, he stared in amazement at the broken pieces in his fingers. He'd been sabotaged. Godric gave him a defective arrow.

Sensing the sheriff's stare, Camilla turned. Godric met her gaze and chuckled. Red-hot lava flowed through her body, filling her with courage and determination. Glancing down, she plunged her knife in the pie, slicing violently from top to bottom. The pastry split open, releasing a savory aroma and a dozen living blackbirds.

Then, without a second's hesitation, Camilla lunged to the center of the arena, and jerked the hood off Atalanta's head. Swinging her arm, she thrust the falcon toward Frederick. The hawk flew like a fireball, hurtling through the air. Frederick, shocked and distracted, twisted his body and inadvertently released his arrow in the wrong direction.

Blackbirds filled the sky, their bodies invisible against the darkened canvas, their wings flapping wildly. Then, Bramble, a furry disc of teeth and paws, entered the fray. Camilla pointed at Frederick and yelled, "Attack!" The dog leaped like a deer, his mouth gaping, his tail flung straight behind him. He knocked Frederick to the ground and, teeth bared, stood over him like a lion protecting the carcass he had hunted down and killed.

Frederick's arrow went wild, landing with a thwack in Risby's quilted tunic. The young man's mouth fell open and his eyes bulged. He looked down at the widening stain of blood on his tunic. For a moment, he seemed to think it very funny that he'd been pierced in the heart with an arrow loosed by his own champion. Turning to his father, he struggled to speak. But, only a gurgled and pitiful keening sound escaped his throat. Slowly, he crumpled to the dusty ground, dead.

Godric threw back his head and roared.

Frederick, realizing what he'd done, tossed Bramble aside and raced to Risby's body. Kneeling at the boy's shoulders, he jerked out the arrow, releasing a wide, arcing spurt of blood. "Breathe, Risby, for God's sake!"

But, the bailiff's efforts at reviving the boy were for nought. Blood trickled from Risby's mouth, and his glazed eyes stared fixedly at the starless sky.

"You idiot!" Godric pulled out his short dagger and plunged it between Frederick's shoulder blades. The bailiff fell over in a heap.

Then, face crumpling and back bowed, the sheriff bent over his son. He lowered his forehead to the boy's bloody chest and clutched his only child's lifeless fingers. Sobbing, Godric remained beside his prodigal son's body as the spectators, their appetites for blood sated, their spirits dampened, slowly and quietly dispersed.

Camilla ran to Stevyn and wrapped her arms about his shoulders. She pressed his face to her breast and kissed the top of his head. He was badly wounded, but not mortally so. He would survive. The worst of his ordeal was over.

As the torchlights snapped and crackled, the night spun into morning. And when the first light of day drew life into the lower bailey, the castle denizens found Godric's stiff body, still frozen like a statue at his son's side, a dagger thrust in his own heart, his fingers wrapped around the hilt.

Epilogue

London, nine months later

Camilla lay nestled in her bed, her infant son nursing at her breast. Bramble crowded her feet at the foot of the bed, but his body was warm and his presence comforting. On Stevyn's side of the bed lay Daisy, a big bejeweled cross dangling from her collar. While Bramble had been chasing blackbirds, Daisy was digging among Barnabas's collection of counterfeit artifacts. Since she'd loped into the bailey the morning after Godric's death, the purloined relic clamped between her teeth, Stevyn and Camilla had decided she should wear it in perpetuity.

After all, it was the dogs who'd first located the relic storehouse in the abbot's rose garden. Stevyn had only figured out where the abbot's hiding place was after Camilla told him about her confrontation with Igor.

It all made sense to her now. The dogs had apparently wandered into the greenhouse, and gotten themselves locked in. Igor, fearing Camilla would stumble onto the cache, tried to shoo her away. When she refused to leave, another monk must have released the dogs, pushing them into the garden and slamming the door behind them.

A happy sigh escaped Camilla's lips. Life in Town, with the whirlwind society of Court, and Stevyn's busy schedule as Chief Justice of the King's Bench, had been an adjustment for her. But, the dogs provided constancy and companionship. And their rowdy puppies were a delightful source of entertainment.

Closing her eyes, she looked back on all that had happened in her life. It was hard for her to believe that five years earlier, she'd been destitute and desperate enough to accept Godric's Faustian bargain. As her baby's tiny fingers closed around hers, she breathed a sigh of relief. Those hard years were over. Life with Sir Stevyn Strongbow was more rewarding, indeed more challenging, than any life she could ever have imagined.

He was a serious man, meticulous and detail oriented. He worked too hard, and often came to bed exhausted. He pushed himself to his limits, physically and intellectually. He obsessed over the tiniest of his failings, and demanded near perfection of himself. He worried about things over which he had no control, such as hunger, famine, the plague and injustice.

Yet, he was the most sensitive man she'd ever met. He was honest, caring and would give the tunic off his back to a stranger who needed it. He was a loving father. He never cheated or stole or tried to take advantage of his position as Chief Justice of the King's Bench. His sense of humor had returned since the ordeal at Wickingham Castle. He was gentle and funny and, at long last, entirely at peace with himself.

He was also, Camilla thought with a tiny surge of pleasure, great in bed.

"They are all tethered to various chair legs and stair posts below stairs," Stevyn said, entering the bedchamber in his woolen robe and cap.

He handed his wife a cup of warm wine, then crawled in bed beside her. "Now if the little buggers will just calm down. That yapping all night is going to drive me to drink. How are you feeling, sweetling?"

Opening her eyes, Camilla sipped the spicy aromatic drink. "Much better, thank you. And this will put the babe to rest, as well."

Stevyn leaned over, his cheek on Camilla's shoulder. Staring at the infant they'd named Eric, he cupped the baby's head, softly caressing the soft spot on the child's skull, testing the fineness of his hair. With a sigh of contentment, he looked up, meeting Camilla's cornflower-blue gaze.

She amazed him, with her warmth and kindness. Since they'd been in London, she had petitioned King Edward for permission to open a sanctuary for unwed mothers. The ardors of a difficult childbirth had caused a slight delay in its opening. But, as soon as she was up and on her feet again, the refuge would be opened.

Barnabas had been duly arrested and sentenced to a life's imprisonment in the Tower, where he penned his memoirs and wrote long, vitriolic letters to the pope about his ill treatment and the unfairness of the king's laws.

Stevyn silently marveled at the twists and turns his life had taken. He'd never dreamed he could be so happy. He would never have known he could love so deeply had Camilla not entered his life.

"What are you smiling at?" Camilla asked him, as she so often did.

He lifted one shoulder in a shrug. It was hard to say. He smiled because Camilla Rosedown was a puzzle he would never figure out. But, he would spend his life fitting the pieces together. And, at the end, when the big picture came clearly into view, he would spend eternity with her, safe and sound, and happy in the knowledge that she loved him.

The Sword and the Flame

Patricia Phillips

The fire that rages in Adele St. Clare is unquenchable. The feisty redhead burns with anger when King John decrees she marry against her will. Then her bridal escort arrives—Rafe De Montford—and the handsome swordsman ignites something hotter. But Rafe has been ordered to deliver her unto a betrothed she cannot even respect—let alone love. But Rafe's smoldering glances capture her heart, and with one of his fiery kisses, Adele knows that from these sparks of desire will leap the flame of a love everlasting.

Lair of the Wolf

Also includes the seventh installment of *Lair of the Wolf*, a serialized romance set in medieval Wales. Be sure to look for future chapters of this exciting story featured in Leisure books and written by the industry's top authors.

__4726-8 $4.99 US/$5.99 CAN

Dorchester Publishing Co., Inc.
P.O. Box 6640
Wayne, PA 19087-8640

Please add $1.75 for shipping and handling for the first book and $.50 for each book thereafter. NY, NYC, and PA residents, please add appropriate sales tax. No cash, stamps, or C.O.D.s. All orders shipped within 6 weeks via postal service book rate.
Canadian orders require $2.00 extra postage and must be paid in U.S. dollars through a U.S. banking facility.

Name____
Address____
City_______________________State________Zip___________
I have enclosed $ _________ in payment for the checked book(s).
Payment must accompany all orders. ☐ Please send a free catalog.